TIDE OF SILVER

PRAISE FOR BOOKS
BY DIPAK BASU

TIDE OF SILVER

"The prince's character arc is emblematic of the novel's central theme: that good people will rationalize profoundly immoral behavior for wealth and power"

"Providing enough action to make this a page-turner. Basu's prose offers evocative images"

Kirkus Reviews

MISSION TO TEACH

"Brave and beautifully crafted"

John Moir

"A moving, inspiring book"

Chitra Divakaruni

A FLIGHT OF GREEN PARROTS

"With echoes of Forster's *A Passage to India*"

"Beautiful prose with poetry-like rhythm"

Ellen Taylor Marsh

ALSO BY DIPAK BASU

A Flight of Green Parrots

Mission to Teach

TIDE OF SILVER

DIPAK BASU

JBF Books

Copyright © 2020 Dipak Basu

Library of Congress Catalog Number: 2013930379

ISBN: 978-0-9888385-1-2

JBF Books
14435C Big Basin Way #256
Saratoga, California 95070, USA

FOR RADHA

always

"If the English servants of the East India Company had carried out the orders of its Court of Directors, honestly and scrupulously, there would have been no British Empire"

From "How the British Occupied India"
Asia Publications, New York, 1963

AUTHOR'S NOTE

This book uses place names as they existed at the time the events occurred.

Canton is named Guangzhou today, Peking is Beijing, Calcutta is Kolkata, Siam is Thailand, Annam is Vietnam, etc.

PRINCIPAL CHARACTERS

in order of appearance

Vikram Sena - Prince of Rajmahal

Paul Miller - Governor of Canton

Jerome Winkley - A naval officer

Joy Morley - Trade Councilor of Calcutta

Charles Cornwallis - Governor-General of India

Jagat Seth - Banker of Bengal

Margaret Andrews - A passenger on *Albatross*

Mickey Fenwick - First Mate of *Albatross*

John Newbond - Midshipman of *Albatross*

Tau-pei - A sailor

Joaquim Fernandes - Captain of *Gulab*

Wu Cha-tan - Pirate Chief

Angry Feng - A pirate

Irving Macardle - Selectman of Canton

Juan Menezes - An interpreter

Howqua - Merchant of Canton

Lian - A *sing-song* girl

Michael Holbrook - Captain of *Prince Rupert*

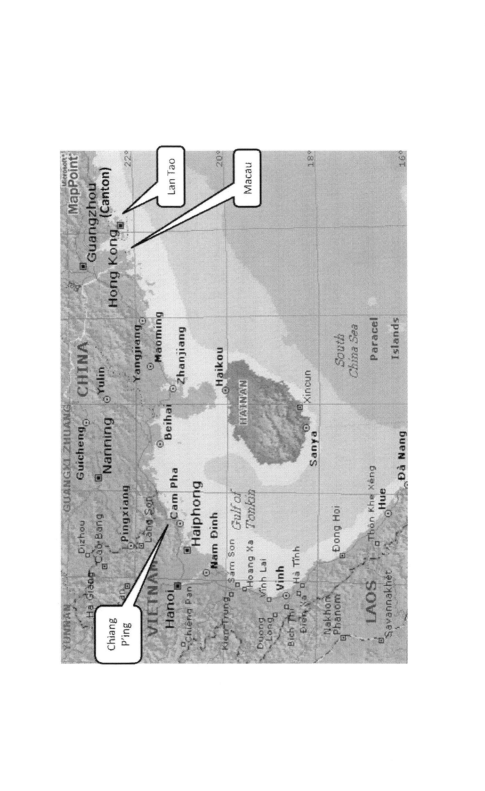

BOOK ONE

THE LITTLE YELLOW FLOWER

1

The hidden watcher, silent and motionless, looked out from dense foliage as the setting sun cloaked the riverside in deep shadow.

Her unblinking eyes studied the large boat with its furled sail as its prow grounded on a sandbank and a noisy traveling party came ashore. She watched while a camp was set up, cooking fires lit, and a meal distributed on the spit of land by the water's edge. People ate. Their excited voices called to one another. Cheery laughter rang out frequently, excited sounds of people on a happy journey.

Through the tumult the watcher remained intensely alert and completely still, surveying the scene with infinite patience.

It grew dark with tropical suddenness and the travelers made preparations for the night. One by one they lay down on the warm sand under the open sky, shrouding themselves in sheets against mosquitoes. Following preliminary grunts and yawns, they lapsed into corpselike immobility of sleep and soon the only sounds were rhythmic lapping of wavelets and occasional cry of a night bird.

When all activity ceased and the last torch had flickered to extinction, attention of the observer became centered on two figures that slept close to each other and apart from the rest. Unlike their companions who were wrapped from head to foot in sheets, these two were partially covered with thin blankets. The half-moon was clearing the trees when, ever so slowly, the watcher emerged from thickets of the sandbank. Behind her the jungle became deathly silent as if its denizens held their collective breath in anticipation of tragedy. Though ravenously hungry, the carnivore had waited with consummate hunting skill until she was absolutely certain her intended victim would not escape. Creeping low on her belly, the tigress moved forward soundlessly with extreme caution. Not a leaf rustled, not a twig snapped on the littered ground, as the huge striped form approached the blanketed figures, step by wary step.

From fifteen feet away, she charged.

"Haaaa-loom!"

The short roar shattered the stillness of the night like a thunderclap and a grey blur launched itself on the smaller of the two sleepers. The intruder sank its fangs in her victim's throat and, as people were jerked awake by the explosion of sound, she lifted it like a rag doll and leaped back into the bushes.

Before Prince Vikram Sena, who had been lying close to her, could sit up or even make a sound, his sister Monideepa, on the way to her wedding, vanished in the jaws of the marauder.

2

A few months before the tragic death of Princess Monideepa in the tropical jungles of India, on a frigid afternoon in 1786 a large congregation of grandly dressed men and women spoke in hushed tones. They were inside the cavernous Throne Room of London's St James Court, waiting for King George III to appear.

'Farmer George' was third in a line of four Hanoverian kings of England, all of whom were named George. He was called farmer because of his plain and thrifty manners and his passionate love of agriculture. Unlike his father, the second George, whose sobriquet was "The Grocer King," and who had ruled mightily, Farmer George's 26-year reign had been marked by severe ups and downs. Following the Peace Treaty of Paris which ended the Seven Year War and Britain emerged as the world's greatest colonial power, George III's merciless taxation of the American colonies precipitated their declaration of independence. England's subsequent loss against America cost king and country dearly. George's sanity was rumored to be stretched to breaking point and some said he took arsenic with his medication. Fortunately, his failing efforts to rule a fractious country had received fresh strength three years ago when the brilliant William Pitt became England's youngest prime minister at the age of 24.

Amid the country's many travails, today's was to be a happy occasion, a British monarch's birthday honors.

A weak wintry sun shone through high windows of St. James, making little impression on the vast chamber. The Throne Room was lit by hundreds of torches in wall sconces and in massive iron chandeliers that hung on long chains. The sharp fragrance of burning whale oil mixed with natural mustiness of old stone created the unique aromatic ambiance of the hallowed palace. Velvet pennants on lofty arches swayed gently while strains of Handel's *Water Music* wafted from the minstrel's gallery.

At the front of the crowd, Lord Benjamin Morley, fifth Earl of Ashford, was deep in conversation with Paul Miller.

Lord Morley was a senior member of the Court of Directors of England's renowned trading firm, the British East India Company. Miller was chief of the Company's Canton station in China. They were both in their late fifties and longtime friends. During their eventful careers at headquarters and foreign outposts, the two had seen a huge growth of revenue and power of the Company and had watched its reach extend from Arabia and India to Malaya and China and Japan.

Lord Morley, bewigged and stooped, was speaking with an errant sunbeam reflected from powerful gold-rimmed spectacles.

"Your opinion, Miller? Will His Majesty do something about the tea trade or won't he?"

The answer was unexpected.

"Hanoverians! *Hah!*"

Miller's disgusted invective made the earl wish he had not asked the sensitive question. The Governor of Canton did not actually stamp his foot, but his friend was quite sure he would have in more private surroundings.

"His Majesty's Teutonic obtuseness," fumed Miller, "is matched only by his Teutonic obduracy! The entire future of the tea trade depends on the Prime Minister's powers of conviction. Can young Pitt sway the King? At the royal supper last night, Pitt could not say enough about the unchecked flight of capital to China." Miller's lanky frame shook with emotion as he waded into his favorite topic. "Morley, do you know what Pitt said? He said 'When trade is at stake, one must defend or perish.' Fighting words, but a sheer waste on our Farmer. His Majesty completely missed the point. *'Nein!'* he said, *'Die Kanal und die Mittlemeer!'* Good God! China's bleeding us dry and he wants to protect the damned English Channel and the Mediterranean. And, my dear friend, do you know what's worse?"

Lord Morley waited, not sure if he wanted to know.

"Our Germanic monarch does not care for tea. As a consequence, he has no grasp of the magnitude of the problem."

Standing beside her bowed husband, Lady Pauline Morley, a

golden-haired woman who carried her forty-six years with elegance, wondered as always how the two free-spirited friends could be such a study in contrast. Lord Morley, dressed as befits a peer in velvet and gold braid, had a bent back, a pronounced limp, and a glass eye, relics of incarceration decades ago in the infamous Black Hole of Calcutta[1]. Miller, on the other hand, was very tall, very angular, and very patrician. He wore a simple cotton shirt, black breeches and a severe frock-coat under purple ceremonial robes.

Miller continued to breathe fire.

"Look here, Morley. Our effort of decades will be undone by our country's infatuation with tea. And by George's vacillation. After supper I took Pitt aside and convinced him that the situation in China was desperate and that he *had* to get some action." He took a deep breath and tried to relax. "I hear that King and Prime Minister argued all night."

Lord Morley sighed and wished again he had not opened so controversial a subject on a day that was momentous for his dear friend. He was saved by the appearance of two young men in naval uniform.

"Aunt Pauline! Uncle Benjamin!" Reginald Morley whooped. "Oh, and Mr. Miller too! How are you, sir?" Reggie turned to his uncle. "Look whom I've found. Old Winkley. Don't you recognize him? We were at school together and in the Navy."

Everyone shook hands and Reggie explained to Miller.

"Jerome Winkley here was skipper of our warship *Steadfast*

---

[1] Story in this author's earlier book, *A Flight of Green Parrots.*

until recently." His eyes glowed in excitement. "Sir, you should have seen him lead action against the Americans!"

Lord Morley had to make an effort to look up and survey his nephew's tall friend. The Winkleys had once lived in Ashford and the two young men were childhood friends. The well-built and handsomely dressed naval officer before him bore little resemblance to the shy and colorless boy that Lord Morley remembered, a boy dominated by an overbearing mother. He saw that young Jerry had matured into a handsome man in his early thirties with lean frame, craggy face, and clear blue eyes making him stand out among the pampered lords and powdered ladies.

"Why 'recently', Captain?" Miller wanted to know. "Has the ocean ceased to attract you?"

"On the contrary, sir," Jerome's voice was deep and authoritative. "The sea and ships are my life. However, the chill of the north Atlantic has not been conducive to my health. Consequently, I have accepted honorable discharge."

"I see. How unfortunate. And how are you presently occupied?"

Jerome hesitated.

"It is too soon, sir," he said at last.

Paul Miller studied the imposing officer quizzically. The man looked quite fit and robust. Then a movement on the steps down which the royal procession would come attracted his attention. The heralds were getting ready with their trumpets. The King would arrive in a moment. He turned back to Jerome.

"Have you considered commercial shipping, Captain?"

"Can't say I have, sir. But as I said, it's too soon."

"Would you like to go to China?"

Jerome stared at Miller in astonishment.

"China, sir? Why, that's at the other end of the earth!"

"Not any more, young man, not any more," remonstrated Lord Morley, listening with interest. "I will remind you that my son, Joy, is stationed at Fort William in India."

A loud fanfare rang out.

"Can't talk now, Captain," Miller said hurriedly. "Come and see me at the Company offices on Leadenhall Street. We may do business."

ᦥ

The robed and bejeweled King of England held his sword high as Miller knelt before him and the Lord High Chamberlain sonorously read out the proclamation.

"Paul Miller...Founder and President of the Select Committee of the China Office of His Majesty's British East India Company at Canton...Forty years of distinguished service to King and Country...Founder of the Company's Macau Station...Founder of the Company's trade in the Orient that has made silk, tea, and nutmeg commonplace in the Realm...Architect of the East Indiaman Clipper expeditions that have opened the seas to England...Founder of the Company's Japan Station at Yokohama..."

The accolades rolled on.

Even at the moment of supreme honor, his eyes focused on Farmer George's high sable boots, Miller felt terribly unhappy at the irony of the circumstances. He was about to be rewarded for unleashing a monster, tea, on the mother country. His tense body flinched as the King's sword come to rest on his left shoulder.

And then a strange thing happened.

Instead of immediately moving to his other shoulder, the sword stayed where it was for a full minute. The blade's coldness penetrated through Miller's robes. Had the Farmer forgotten the ritual? Finally, just as Miller was about to break tradition and look up, the sword lifted and descended on his right shoulder. Simultaneously, George's booming voice, fruity and profligate, rolled out across the massive hall.

"Arise! Arise, Sir Paul!"

Miller tried to get on his feet, but the heavy sword still rested on his shoulder and he settled back on his knees in awkward discomfiture. He was about to try to rise again when George spoke, this time in a curious mixture of English and German, interspersed with wheezes. Miller knew Cantonese, but did not have the aristocratic upbringing to know German, the King's hereditary tongue.

"Silberstrom!" Miller heard the word repeated twice over. And then *"Cathay!"*

What was going on?

Unable to resist, he looked up at the blue bulbous eyes and sagging jowls of the King and realized Farmer George was in the grip of a strong emotion. As their eyes met, the monarch admonished the newest knight once again with the word *silberstrom* and nodded meaningfully. Miller, thoroughly confused now, was certain that his knees would give way and he would collapse in a heap on the steps.

At last the King finally lifted his rapier with a grunt. Sir Paul Miller struggled to his feet and swayed for moment as he looked around bemusedly. There was total silence in the chamber. Everyone was looking at him expectantly as if he was required to deliver a speech. Then Lord Morley, his second for the knighting, hastily limped forward and broke the spell. He took his friend's arm and led him away from the dais, his face wreathed in smiles. His words finally dispelled the new knight's agony.

"It's quite all right, my dear fellow," Morley said excitedly. *"Pitt came through!* God bless the PM." He saw Sir Paul staring at him blankly. "Eh, what? You didn't understand the King?"

When Sir Paul shook his head, Lord Morley stopped walking, turned, and told him theatrically, *"Silberstrom,* my dear fellow. The Tide of Silver. Listen carefully. His Majesty has just charged you thus: 'It is thy sacred duty to turn the tide of silver that flows in a stream to Cathay.'"

3

Thousands of miles away from London, a tropical sunset was painting a spectacular canvas over a dense jungle.

Joy Morley, perched high on a tree limb, watched colors in the sky dramatically ebb and flow. Around him, diurnal forest birds united their voices in farewell to the passing day. A symphony of calls, ranging from the pulsating shriek of jungle fowl and deafening chirp of massed mynahs to the ascending *coo-ooo* of the cuckoo, rose to a climax.

Joy shook himself and looked carefully down the sights of his musket at the cadaver that was fast disappearing into the evening gloom. He was sitting on a camouflaged platform of branches that villagers had built on a tree overlooking the body of the tiger's victim. It had been an unusually hot and humid day so that when a breeze arose from the valley below, Joy welcomed it ardently. It cooled his face, dried his sweat-stained clothes, and reduced the stench of death that pervaded the clearing. The sun sank behind a range of hills and night birds took up evening stations. The shrill wailing *mia-ow* of a peacock, an iconic sound of India, resounded as the large regally plumed birds scratched for insects in the gathering darkness.

Thirty-year-old Joy was Lord and Lady Morley's only child, born while his father was stationed in India. He was sent back to the family estate at Ashford in the West of England for his education. When he was eighteen he rejoined his parents at Fort William in Calcutta as a junior employee of the Company. Now a broad-shouldered and adventurous young man who avidly embraced India, Joy enjoyed his role in growing the Company's trade. In addition to mercantile prowess, his reputation as a big-game hunter had spread across Bengal and was why he was sitting on a tree limb in a hot Indian wilderness.

The tigress would soon be on the move.

As darkness fell Joy cocked both firearms, kept one musket comfortably in the crook of his elbow and the other within easy reach. He took a drink of water from an earthenware jar that his servant, Murali, had left behind. Wiping his face on a sleeve, he measured the narrow ditch up which the man-eater would most likely approach.

Joy knew that tigers, largest and loveliest of jungle cats, lived in harmony with rural folk. Bullock-carts plying between villages encountered the majestic creatures on forest roads, singly or with gamboling cubs. If it was the right time of the year, a traveler might hear the earth shaken by deep-throated roars of a tiger calling its mate.

But there was one exception to the peaceful co-existence of

man and animal. A scourge that periodically tyrannized the countryside: a man-eating tiger, an aberration of nature created by wounds or by old age. Then the jungle creature, abandoning its diet of deer and wild pig, became a fearsome engine of destruction. A huge striped face with glaring malevolent eyes would rise magically from behind a bush or around a bend in a forest path. A short roar would follow, and one more defenseless cowherd or village girl would be carried away with a broken neck.

But the victim below Joy tonight was neither a simple cowherd nor a village girl. The day before, this man-eating tigress had stalked a traveling marriage party as it camped on the banks of the Hooghly River. In the darkest hour of the night, when fires burned low, the tigress had carried away the fifteen-year-old bride-to-be and sister of Joy's dear friend, Prince Vikram Sena of Rajmahal.

As he waited, Joy's mind wandered in the absolute darkness before moonrise. If the tigress came now there was nothing he could do to kill her. But, he surmised, the animal had eaten well off her prey and had lain sleeping in the shade for most of the hot day. He had ascertained there was enough on the corpse to entice her back. From her pugmarks in soft sand of the creek bed, he had determined the animal was female. Yes, she would wait for the night to cool, go to the river to drink, and only then revisit her kill.

A long interval followed during which Joy remained absolutely still. He knew a tiger would notice the minutest movement in the pitch blackness, while he could not see the branch in front of his face. This was *her* element. And what if she saw him? Would she melt away as a normal tiger would? Or being a man-eater, would she attack? And would then his fifteen feet of elevation prevent her from getting a second victim? Would his musket fire true in the dark? Would there be time to aim and fire a second musket?

Joy pushed away the bout of uncertainty and thought back to the events of the day. Guided to the village by Price Vikram's servants, he found his friend, normally a proud and commanding figure, slumped in the sand. With tears in his eyes, the prince beseeched him to recover his poor sister's remains, however pitiful they may be. No good Hindu soul could leave this world without cremation of her earthly body. The Senas, one-time rulers of Bengal, had been closely allied with the Morleys for three decades and Joy willingly acquiesced. Then, upon hearing that Morley-sahib, the great hunter, had come, the residents of the village entreated him to rid them of the slayer.

It grew cold and the wind stilled. Stars twinkled in the sky and a brilliant moon rose and ascended the heavens, lighting up the jungle.

A sharp crack sounded like a pistol shot in the still night.

Joy looked down and there, beside the victim's body just forty feet away, by magic, was the tigress. Not a leaf had rustled, nor had any movement drawn Joy's attention to her coming. But there she was, her russet coat appearing bluish-white in the moonlight.

The slight motion of Joy's head immediately drew the tigress's attention. And her response was instantaneous. The hind legs, already bunched, launched her across the inert form, and in two leaps and a thunderous roar she was at the base of Joy's tree.

Joy hurriedly raised the heavy musket with fingers numb with cold. A gruesome mask loomed at his feet as the tigress leaped up the tree trunk. There was a scrabbling sound and a pair of fiery green eyes, balefully reflecting the moonlight, grew larger, came closer.

Joy leaned over the edge of the platform, aimed between the eyes, and pulled the trigger. The flash and bang of the musket merged with another blood-curdling roar. For a moment the claws of the animal fought for purchase. Then she fell back and vanished.

Joy shakily lowered his weapon. His hands were trembling violently and nausea welled up his throat. The viciousness and instinctive hatred of this animal surpassed anything he had seen in years of hunting. Another second and she would have got him. His head pounded from the roars and the explosion and from the sight of the ghastly face that leered at him in the musket flash.

There was nothing further that he could do tonight. He had no idea whether he had hit or missed. He was certain that the animal had received a bad fright and would not return. To walk through the jungle in darkness now, with a wounded man-eater at large, was the surest form of suicide. So he sat back, drank some water, and waited for his jangling nerves to subside.

The morning sun was brilliant when several men walked along a heavily wooded game path bordered by crystallized dewdrops.

Prince Vikram Sena, carrying an old flintlock, led the group. He was a dark man of medium height, normally intense and businesslike, respected for fair treatment of subjects that worked his vast lands.

During the night he had heard the roaring of the tiger and the bang of the musket and hoped his friend had ended up the hunter not the hunted. They reached the tree and found Joy asleep on his perch. While Vikram helped him down, Murali cast around and found big splashes of blood and a piece of bone near the tree-trunk. When he came to give this information he was appalled by his master's tiredness and hurried to find his kettle.

"Here, sahib, drink tea. It is still hot. Thanks to Lord Shiva, the brute did not get you."

Murali spoke in Bengali. In reality he was much more than a servant to Joy, a constant and garrulous companion from the time Joy arrived in India. Murali had taught him to speak the local language and introduced him to local customs. Now, while his master gratefully drank the steaming mud–colored brew of tea leaves, mashed ginger, ground cardamom seeds, cane sugar and milk, Murali prattled on.

"Shall we take Princess's body to the boat? The tiger must be dead by now. Don't worry, Sahib. Today is the very first day of the spring festival. Only good things can happen today. Oh, Sahib! Sahib! Look at all the blood!"

Refreshed, Joy got to his feet and readied himself to follow the blood trail, taking with him Murali and a villager. Normally his first companion would be the prince, but he decided against this in view of Vikram's emotional state. For their safety he ordered the remaining men to stay in a tight bunch in the middle of the clearing, protected by Vikram's weapon. Joy knew he *had* to kill the tiger. To leave the beast in a wounded state would not only allow her to get away but, if she healed even partially, would thrust an even greater scourge on the countryside. He looked back and saw Vikram staring unseeingly at the forest while his people wrapped his sister's remains in banana fronds.

The copious blood trail led in the direction of the river. It became quickly apparent the tigress was badly wounded and the trail weaved erratically. Joy knew, nonetheless, that ahead of them was the most dangerous animal in the world, a wounded Royal Bengal tiger. Any rock or bush could well be the site of an ambush and a last-ditch stand. They advanced slowly, giving clumps of undergrowth and large boulders a wide berth and intense scrutiny. Joy in front, the villager in the middle, Murali last, armed with the second musket against a very possible rear attack. Soon they heard the gurgle of the river and the rank odor of muddy vegetation grew strong. They rounded a bend and Joy, parting the last fern, saw the tigress which must have died in the act of drinking, lying half in and half out of the water. Their arrival caused a flurry in the mud. A massive scaly crocodile backed away from the carcass, turned, and glared at them with yellow eyes and big black pupils. The overhang of trees had kept keen-eyed vultures at bay, but several crows, intent on a quick breakfast, flapped noisily away. The river sparkled in the morning sunshine.

An hour later, as the group trudged tiredly into the village with the tiger hanging from a pole by its legs, the white-haired headman hurried over to Joy.

"Sahib!" the headman announced. "A fast runner has arrived from Calcutta. The *Laat-sahib* has sent urgent summons. You are to return to Fort William at once. Someone has come from China."

4

The *Laat-sahib,* Charles Cornwallis, Governor-General of India, made the introductions.

"Sir Paul Miller, Governor of Canton, recently arrived from England on *HMS Albatross,* may I present William Joy Morley, Trade Councilor at Fort William, only son of Lord Benjamin Morley, Earl of Ashford, Senior Director of our Company, and Lady Pauline."

With the sound of rain falling in the background, Joy regarded the tall, spare, middle-aged man standing beside the gaudily arrayed Governor. *Is this why Corny hauled me back?* he asked himself. *Chappie here looks a starchy sort but harmless enough. Why did Corny want me so urgently?*

Meanwhile, Sir Paul was returning the scrutiny.

He saw before him a blond and muscular young man, browned

by the tropical sun. During the three days he had spent so far at Fort William *en route* to Canton, Sir Paul, remembering Lord Morley's glowing praises of his son, had asked members of the Executive Council about Joy. To his surprise he found that the younger Morley had not risen up the Company ranks as rapidly as his father's reputation would suggest. As he dug into reasons for the anomaly, his interest in the man quickened. He discovered that Joy was known for being adventurous with a penchant for getting into scrapes while he tried one harebrained, danger-prone scheme after another to increase British trade. The Council Members of Fort William, risk-averse and process-driven, as a body disapproved of Joy's exploits. A recent example, he learned, was conversion of rice fields to profitable (for England) indigo plantations, a scheme which members initially considered juvenile, but which had driven up Company revenue and profit. Sir Paul discovered that Joy was well-traveled in the vast country that was India and said to have an inexhaustible store of local knowledge. Unlike almost every other Company officer in the Orient, he learned that Joy took a genuine interest in his adopted country and conducted his work solely with interests of Company and King at heart. Based on his findings Sir Paul had asked Cornwallis for a meeting with Joy before he left for China.

During the mutual examination, Lord Cornwallis, himself a lofty figure of British politics, formerly supreme commander of the American colonies, described Sir Paul's accomplishments. Joy learned Sir Paul was author of journals about the East, material he had studied during his apprenticeship in London. He learned that Sir Paul had founded the Company's operations in China, but unlike most successful merchants, even after his recent knighthood, he had not returned to the Home Office. Joy wondered why.

Dinner at the Governor-General's Residence was just over. It had stopped raining. A cool breeze from the Hooghly blew over the fort and dispelled the oppressive humidity. With crystal goblets of port in their hands, Joy and Sir Paul passed through a tall doorway onto a balcony that looked out over the wide ramparts of the fort. Sir Paul lit his pipe and for a few minutes they stood gazing at sheets of accumulated rain water in the parklands and at the twinkling lights of the town in the distance. The breeze rippled the moonlit water and a sonata of frogs offered up a pleasing ambiance.

"Well, Morley, what do you think?"

Joy jumped at the unexpectedness of the question. He turned to find Sir Paul looking at him steadily. Not being sure as to what the older man was referring, he did not answer.

"Morley, you run the business end of things here," the older man went on. "And I gather you have a reputation for knowing the ropes in this part of the world."

Sir Paul paused while Joy nodded, feeling a flush of pride. The next question came just as unexpectedly.

"How much do you know of the China trade?"

Taken aback and again not certain of what he was expected to say, Joy considered his words carefully.

"Well, sir, I have not been to China but I've read a great deal about the country. I have spoken with visiting merchants and naval officers about China's commerce and society. I know our primary trade revolves around ships arriving in Canton with cotton and bullion and returning laden with cargoes of teas, silks, spices, pottery..."

"Yes, yes!" Sir Paul broke in with sudden vehemence. "It's an adverse trade, my boy, an adverse trade! Our cotton is a sorry trading article, as are the few tinpot metals we bring. We pay for our purchases chiefly in coin. Our ships to China carry chests of silver bullion and bales of cotton in a ratio of a hundred to one in value. Britain craves tea. Everyone craves tea. And China has good tea. England has known tea for merely seventy years and yet, last year our country consumed twelve million pounds of it. Twelve million pounds! The Chinese thrive on our addiction. They possess all commodities that we can possibly offer in counter-trade, which forces us to pay with silver. Silver, d'ye hear? Spanish silver earned from the accursed slave trade! D'ye know how much is the drain on our country's capital to pay for our craving?"

There was a pause. At first Joy thought the last was a rhetorical question. Then he realized Sir Paul was actually expecting an answer. He hurriedly did the mental calculations for he knew the market price of tea - and the resulting figure jolted him.

"Two million sterling, sir? For just tea? Sweet Jesus! That's more than the total Indian outlay for the Company for a whole year."

"*It is!* And mostly in bullion. Morley, d'ye see what I'm driving at? We urgently, desperately, need a commodity, not silver, not gold, to trade in return for tea. We have none."

Joy looked out at the sodden fields sparkling in the light of the waxing moon. A woman was singing in the dance hall behind them.

From far in the distance, a wolf howled mournfully. The enormity of the problem began to sink in. If the balance of trade with China continued this negatively, England would be forced to reduce its tea imports for want of capital. This in turn would lead to inflation and speculation back home, and a decline in the Company's and ultimately the country's fortunes, setting back Britain's hard-won prosperity.

"Sir, what options have been found? What *will* the Chinese buy in quantity?"

"Nothing, Morley, nothing. Nothing from Britain or Europe interests them. The Chinese are a self-sufficient and complacent lot. They have much to sell and little to buy. They have no need for material goods – they have it all – and an insatiable appetite for silver and gold. They've managed to steer us 'foreign devils' into a pretty corner. And to top it all, this year China's Imperial Government has closed all ports except Canton to foreign traders."

Sir Paul stopped and breathed heavily. Joy's mind raced. He was certain Sir Paul had not sought out his company simply to lecture him on adverse trade with China. What *did* he want?

After a long silence Sir Paul began to speak.

"When King George placed his sword on my shoulder, he said, 'It is thy sacred duty to turn the tide of silver.' That word *silberstrom*, which means 'tide of silver' in German, will ring in my ears to my dying day. And to my eternal shame that I have found no avenue to carry out my King's command. It is also to my eternal shame that our glorious Company is riddled with scalawags that think nothing of lining their pockets at the Company's expense, never thinking of ways to help the

King. When the Company calls for help, they're too busy building their own fortunes. Too busy to devote time to so unremunerative a pursuit as serving the Company, let alone saving it. Morley, I have just spent seven months in England trying to find a solution to this problem. I have spoken to parliamentarians, to the Court of Directors, to the Chief Factors, and to senior merchants, present and past, from stations around the world. Without exception none can identify an article that can reverse the balance of trade." He stopped and added, "In fact, I brought it to your very own Chief Councilor McPherson's notice today. Do you know what his response was?"

Joy carefully considered his answer.

"Uh...should I be told, sir?"

"Oh, that's right, Morley. I was forgetting he is your lord and master, isn't he? John McPherson, the bloody...!" Sir Paul caught himself. "Y'see, young man, I'm already treating you differently. Your father thinks the world of you. And at risk of swelling your vanity I am convinced you are one of the few, very few, merchants that puts Company before self."

This time Joy's breast *did* swell with pride. Here was high praise indeed.

"I do my best, sir. The Company has been in our blood since its founding by Good Queen Bess almost two hundred years ago. So I probably treat it differently than do most Company servants."

"I gather you have had run-ins with McPherson?"

"He is my superior, sir." Joy would not be drawn.

"Oh, all right, let it go, let it go! Let us not clutter the paramount with the petty. Now listen carefully. I hereby enlist you in the King's call to arms against mercantile China. What can you do?"

Joy blinked and his voice came in a squeak.

"Me?"

Sir Paul nodded.

Joy stared at him blankly. He tried to think but his mind would not focus. It was too much. His shoulders felt suddenly burdened with a huge weight. What did *he* know of trade between England and Europe and China that his superiors did not? In the end he asked Sir Paul that question.

"Morley, if I were calling on experience, I would look elsewhere. I am appealing to your commitment to the Company, to your manifest intelligence, your superior education, and, shall we say, your originality. To your ability to listen and to your awareness of Eastern customs. Did you know that few Company merchants listen? No matter. I want you to advise me if you think of anything, be it however strange, difficult or unconventional."

The two men talked more and then stood lost in their own thoughts, watching the bright moonlight ripple in the pond.

Suddenly Sir Paul slapped Joy's shoulder.

"Enough of business, my young friend. Let's return to the dinner guests. Corny must have the guards out looking for us. And, good gracious, I've kept you from the ladies!"

5

Joy returned to Writer's Row in a vile mood. The novelty of tête-à-tête with the great Sir Paul Miller had worn off. It was replaced by a strange pressure that brought an unfamiliar feeling of inadequacy to the usually in-charge merchant.

"Honorable William Joy Morley, savior of England! *Forsooth!*" he announced as Murali opened the door to his apartment. His man-servant took a startled step back.

"Sahib?"

"Oh nothing, nothing." Joy threw off his dress coat. "Only trying to save the world."

"Yes, Sahib." Murali was used to his master raging about things he did not understand.

It was well past midnight by the time Joy composed himself, loosened his collar, took off his boots, and settled into his favorite chair with a flagon of Scottish whisky. He began to analyze the problem in the structured manner for which he was known.

On the face it's really quite simple, Joy told himself. *England must find something, anything, to sell to China. Something that China wants badly. But it must be something China does not have. It has to be in bulk. That's the knotty part. Should I assume exalted minds have researched all sources in Europe and concluded such merchandise is unobtainable? I probably should not. Otherwise why should Sir Paul ask little me for ideas?*

He settled himself for a long vigil.

What did England have that China did not?

His mind went back to the years of apprenticeship in the Company's business at its home office and tried to recall everything commercial he had learned. He began the laborious process of checking into each item of trade that he had ever heard of or read about, analyzing its relevance to the problem at hand.

Cloth? Joy asked himself.

Finished garments?

Ships?

Iron?

Guns?

Sugar?

Paper products?

Crockery?

One by one he rejected them all. China made the best silks on earth for her aristocracy. She had all the world's known metals and

the best metalwork for shaping copper and iron and brass. China had
no interest in travel across oceans and believed the world came to its
door to pay homage. Chinese paper and porcelain were exquisite. And
being at peace with the world she had no need for armaments.

Wheat?

Coffee?

Corn?

Fur?

China possessed the best food in the world: rice; the best drink:
tea; the best materials: cotton, silk and animal skins from its frozen
north. Impatiently Joy finished his whisky, grunted, poured another
and put the jug down with a bang. This was getting him nowhere. He
rose and began to pace the room distractedly. Suddenly he stopped,
turned up the lamp, opened a large sea-chest that stood at the foot of
his bed, and spread his collection of reference books on exploration
and commerce on the table. Ever since his earliest years, Joy had been
an avid reader and book collector. He had saved and brought to India
every book that he ever owned. Every arriving ship carried more sent
by his father. Joy began to delve into commercial aspects of all possible
commodities. Before long books overflowed off the bed to the floor.

The list was endless.

Liquor?

Leather?

Timber?

Livestock?

Coal?

Medicines?

Paints?

Dyes?

Nuts?

He rejected them all. China had them or did not want them.

Someone was calling him.

"Sahib!"

Joy woke with a start and found he had been sleeping slumped on the bed with his back to the wall.

"What do you want?" he asked irritably.

Murali handed him a piece of paper.

Joy yawned mightily and unfolded the note from McPherson. *Morley,* it said. *Why are you not at your desk? Are you unwell?*

Startled, Joy pushed aside books that lay on him, stood up and discovered he was stiff in all his joints. He groaned, stretched and threw open the shutters. Bright sunlight streamed in. He tried half-heartedly to remove traces of the sleepless night and hurried to attend to his duties. The visit of Sir Paul had upset the easy-going routine of Fort William and there was much to do. Soon it was midnight again and he was staggering back to his rooms, too tired to renew his investigation. He collapsed into an exhausted sleep.

It was the next afternoon before he returned to his books and continued the painstaking examination of tradeable commodities. Outside the open window the sun was slanting over verdant rice fields and sending shafts of golden light into the room. Murali dozed on his woodframe-and-rope *charpoy* by the door.

Curios?

Joy sat up straight. He was deep in the reference book, *An Embassy to China,* written by a historian named Cranmer-Byng, when he discovered that China had a proven partiality for exotic keepsakes.

Cranmer-Byng informed him that the K'ang-hsi Emperor, most illustrious of the Manchu dynasty and grandfather of the present monarch, had been a great admirer of imported clocks. The historian wrote that in1694 the Emperor had given the Portuguese missionary, Father Thomas Pereira, a special fan made of ivory and gold. On one side, a clock was painted. On the opposite side, the Emperor had himself composed a poem about a *clepsydra,* a Chinese water clock, and brushed it onto the fan in beautiful characters. Joy found Cranmer-Byng's translation of the Emperor's verse fascinating:

Ceaselessly revolving
Day and Night;
Old clepsydra dropping
Out of sight.
Beautiful to look at,
And pleasant to listen,
Telling time a work
That would never slacken.
Through lunar and solar
Amity ever last;
And from places afar
It has come for past
Two hundred years.

Joy discovered that Chinese high-ups had a weakness for novelties. The advent of modern Europe had introduced into China a host of new curiosities, elegantly called 'automata' but better known as 'sing-songs' that combined jewelry with machinery. His Imperial Majesty, the present Ch'ien-lung Emperor, possessed many sing-songs. Of these, what did Chinese like most?

Clocks?

Watches?

Jewelry?

Toys?

With his hopes rising, Joy read that taste for exotic among Chinese nobility and bureaucracy was not limited to just things mechanical and precious. For example, English traders had successfully appealed to the aristocratic Chinese palate with strange and foreign edibles including soups made from bizarre things like sea-swifts' nests and fins of sharks.

Was *that* the answer?

Could exotica become a commodity and stand the test of long-term bulk import?

Joy switched from book to book, turning his room into a surging sea of paper. Clock- and toy-makers were plentiful in England. Sharks, sea-swifts, turtles and God alone knew what other creatures Chinese liked to ingest, were plentiful in tropical seas of the Orient. The English could even employ native fishermen to catch them. He began getting into details. Exotica could be collected at a central place such as Malacca on the Malay coast and shipped to China.

Joy sat up with a jerk.

Great heavens! What am I thinking?

Something exploded in his head and he sat staring into space while thoughts tumbled through his brain.

Sharks! Swifts! Tropics! I'm not thinking of England anymore! Nor of Europe. Oh dear God! Has no one made the connection yet?

If the Company's supply is not limited to Europe, the whole world's wealth came up for consideration, the Americas, Africa, Arabia, even India and the Far East. The East India Company could very well exchange Guinean slaves for Chinese tea if there was demand. Joy detested the slave trade with a passion and would oppose the idea tooth and nail but, on principle, it could be done.

What are the major commodities of Asia and America? Does China like figs from Aden or copra from the Pacific? Does China desire whale oil from New England? Alpaca wool from Peru? What about maple sugar from the Canadian provinces? What about...?

Joy settled into another long analysis, this time of things from around the world. The hours passed inexorably. Slowly his initial excitement waned and frustration grew. *Nothing!* Nothing made sense. Other than those "sing-songs" whose volume import was questionable, China wanted of nothing. Joy was exhausted and dripping with perspiration by the time he finished his fruitless survey of India, Indo-china, Africa, Arabia, the Levant, and Northern America. Close to despair, he began a desultory review of the last geography, Southern America. There was, of course, something in Southern America the Chinese liked. A lot. Inca gold and Spanish silver! With a hollow laugh he shrugged and went on to examine produce from the high Andes. After rejecting wool from the alpaca in favor of Chinese goose feather, he came across coca leaves. Coca leaves were habitually chewed by Andeans to provide energy in their cold, high-altitude world. He was about to move on to Bolivian ornaments when a faint bell rang at the back of his mind and he returned to coca leaves. But try as he might, he could not make the connection. China, at least most of China, was neither cold nor high. So what was the relevance to Andean coca? He studied some more and discovered that coca leaves were used to produce cocaine. And cocaine was an addiction much favored by European poets.

European poets and Chinese imports?

Joy groaned disgustedly. This was crazy. There could be no connection. But his mind would not leave the subject. It was as though he had run aground on a reef of coca leaves. The bell in his brain rang a little louder. An old memory stirred and began to assume ethereal form, but adamantly would not gel. Still his mind refused to give up and harried the idea like a dog would a rat.

Where, oh where was an addictive connected to China? What else were coca leaves used for? What other addictives were out there?

Cannabis? Hemp?

And then the connection closed with an almost physical jolt.

Opium!

Joy breathed in slowly, afraid to lose the thought. He said the word again softly, in wonder. Opium! No doubt about it. Opium was the answer. He knew it. Several long moments passed as he felt physically weak. He took another deep breath and tried to regain his analytical mindset.

The maddening exploration began once more. Opium was an addictive. *All right, so what?* The elation passed leaving behind a cold vacuum. *What had opium to do with China?* Where had he heard of opium in connection to China? It *was* there. Just behind the agonizing bend in the trail back into his memory. *I must find it. I must find it.*

"Murali!"

The elderly Indian woke with a start and sat blinking his eyes. He had been sleeping bare-chested because of the heat, wearing a *dhoti* wrapped around his loins. Joy jumped up, scattering his books. Forgetting protocol, he grabbed Murali by the shoulders and shook him. Murali, groggy and certain he was about to be murdered, tried to fend off his lunatic master. Just as suddenly, Joy forgot about him and began to pace the room, walking around the bed, skipping between littered books and papers. He began to vocalize his thoughts as he was wont to in times of stress.

"Where is it? Which is it?"

Joy turned and found Murali staring at him open-mouthed.

"Murali! Tea!"

Murali scuttled away.

With great difficulty Joy composed himself and began to think systematically and aloud, speaking in short stuttering phrases.

"Where have I read of opium? And China? Yes. It is opium that I read of. And China. Ah! Opium was taken to China. By someone. Who took opium to China?" A long pause. "Oh God, I can't remember. Wait,

let's see. *What* took opium to China. Ah! I know that. A ship." Joy
jumped to his feet. "Yes! A ship. No. Wait! Not a ship. Not a *real* ship.
Then what? A fictional ship? *Yes!* And by a fictional character? *Yes!* A
fictional character sold opium from a ship. To China. *Yes!* Now then,
who was it?"

Joy swept reference books aside and ran back to his sea-chest
and sat on the ground before it. Murali entered, gingerly moved aside
books, and set a cup of tea down on the bedside table. Prudently, he
had roused the cook and washerman and had made them wait outside
the door in case his master had another fit and needed containment.
Or in case he, Murali, needed rescue. Joy, indifferent to the
consternation he was causing his domestic staff, ignored the tea.

"Fiction!" he told Murali. "D'ye hear, my man? Fiction! Whose
fiction?" Then he forgot Murali and ran through the pantheon of
English writers.

*Swift? No. Johnson? No. Pepys? Yes. Lots about ships and sea-
stories by Pepys, but nothing about China.*

But he was sure it was something he had read in England. In
Ashford. At Ashford Castle. In his school room.

*What was it, then? Something for children? A poem? Something
from Dryden? Milton? A play by Shakespeare? No. A story. Not a play.
Not a poem.* Of that he was now sure. *A fictional story.* Joy began to
pull his oldest books out of the chests. Soon they piled up and fell over.
Titles swam and merged before his eyes.

Among the volumes Joy had picked up and tossed aside was
Moll Flanders. Struck by a thought, he picked it up again. *Defoe!* Was

this it? Daniel Defoe had written *Moll Flanders.* His excitement mounted, and then ebbed. *Moll Flanders* was about an English woman of leisure. Had Moll Flanders gone to China? Ridiculous! *Moll Flanders* was not the book he wanted. But it was Defoe. He was now sure of it. What else had Daniel Defoe written? *Robinson Crusoe!* His heart jumped. Crusoe had ventured from England by sea. *But wait.* Crusoe had been marooned in the Brazils, an island chain in the middle of the Atlantic. With his Man Friday. Crusoe had never gone to China. And yet it *was* Robinson Crusoe. Joy was sure it was so.

"Oh, God!" Joy cried out loud. "I'm close. I'm close. I'm almost there. I've got to get it. Murali! Tea! Whisky!"

Joy dived into his chest, rummaged like a dog digging up earth and came up triumphantly with a leather-bound tome titled *The Adventures of Robinson Crusoe.* He scanned the book, flipping the yellowing pages frantically, every sense alert. After half an hour, he closed and put down the heavy volume with a thud and a groan.

Nothing!

The book ended exactly as he remembered it. Crusoe, rescued with Man Friday after twenty-eight years on an island off the coast of Africa, lived happily ever after in a Spanish castle. Robinson Crusoe had never gone to China. He never had anything to do with China.

Exhausted and discouraged, Joy was close to tears.

What was it then? Where had he read about opium in China and why was he so sure that Crusoe was involved? He tried to recall all the books he had read as he grew up as a child in Ashford Castle. Had someone misled him? Had someone made up a story for him in his childhood? If that were true it would be heartbreaking. Listlessly Joy went on with research into other commodities. He downed shots of whisky and delved into more books. After a while a book slipped out of his grasp and he sat on the floor in a trance, propped against the wall staring into space.

Opium, China, Defoe, Crusoe, continued to tantalize him but he simply could not make the association.

"Sahib!" Murali called. *"Ki holo?"* What happened?

Joy opened his eyes and looked up stupidly. He had again fallen asleep propped against the wall, surrounded by books. The old man was staring down at him anxiously. Joy stretched and all his joints creaked. It was probably quite late. He had a splitting headache from the whisky but his thought processes continued as though sleep had not interrupted them.

"Help. I need help," he told himself aloud. "I need more books! Who has books?"

The answer came unexpectedly.

"Book, Sahib?" Murali recognized the English word. "Judge-sahib has book."

Joy jumped to his feet with a screech, terrifying his man.

"Fleetwood! Oh my God!"

Magistrate Fleetwood's library was famous. Why hadn't he thought of it? He almost got to Murali to shake him by the hand but the man fled in terror. Joy pulled on his boots and headed for the door.

"Sahib?" Murali called from a distance. But Joy was gone.

The grandmotherly Mary Fleetwood, paisley shawl thrown hastily over her nightgown, opened her front door to frenzied knocking, and staggered back in fright.

Joy Morley stood unsteadily on the mat. But this was a Joy she did not know. His eyes were bloodshot. His clothes were rumpled and stained. He reeked of alcohol. And he was trembling as though cold in the summer heat.

"Joy, lad, what's with ye? Jeremy!" She called over her shoulder. "Come quickly!"

Joy pushed past her into the living room. Mary's husband hurriedly put aside the *hookah* he was smoking and got to his feet.

Joy did not waste a moment.

"Mr. Fleetwood, sir! Have you read *Robinson Crusoe?*"

Mary backed away from him and stood beside her husband. The elderly couple stared blankly at their deranged visitor. Then pressure got the better of Joy.

"Have you?" he shouted.

Husband and wife recoiled as though struck and gaped at him dumbly. After a silence during which Joy glared at them through red-rimmed eyes, the magistrate said, "Morley, look here, you're raving! Sit down and have some tea."

The next thing Fleetwood knew Joy had rushed across the room and grabbed him by the lapels of his robe and was shaking him, breathing whisky fumes in his face.

"Have you read *Robinson Crusoe,* sir? Have you? Have you?"

"Joy!" screamed Mary. "God save us all! Let him go."

She pulled him from her husband. Joy, his strength suddenly gone, collapsed into a chair. His voice took on a pleading tone.

"Please, sir. Tell me. It is of vital importance. I can explain everything later."

Fleetwood studied the young man's bowed head and decided to humor him.

"Yes, I have read the book, Morley. Everyone has. Now will you please tell us what this madness is about?"

"Have you read a reference to China in *Crusoe?*"

"Yes, Morley."

"What?" Joy leaped to his feet with a roar, knocking his chair over with a crash.

"There's China in *Crusoe?*"

"Yes, damn you. In Part Two."

"Part Two?"

Joy took a step forward. Fleetwood retreated and stumbled over a low table.

"Great Jupiter! You're out of your mind, Morley."

"Part Two! How many parts are there?"

"Just two, you absurd idiot. Defoe wrote *Robinson Crusoe* in two parts. Didn't you know?"

"By glory, I did not bloody well know! Crusoe was marooned on an island."

"He was. Off the Brazils. That was in Part One. He went to Bengal and Java and China in the second part when he was sixty-one. *Here! Steady!* What's the matter? *Keep off, you lunatic!"*

Joy had rushed over and swung the old magistrate in an impromptu waltz while Mary looked on with popping eyes.

A half hour later Joy walked back to his rooms, whistling. He had left the Fleetwoods mystified. No matter. Time for explanations would come. Under his arm, guarded as a king's treasure, was Daniel Defoe's *The Farther Adventures of Robinson Crusoe*.

The rest was easy.

After turning two hundred and fifteen pages of the book, Joy established that Crusoe, with his partner, a merchant of the English East India Company in Bengal, *"made this voyage to Acheen, in the island of Sumatra, and thence to Siam, where we exchanged some of our wares for opium...a commodity which bears a great price among the Chinese and which, at that time, was very much wanted there..."* Their enterprise had been so profitable, that under his partner's persuasion Crusoe *"...spent from first to last, six years in the country of Bengal, trading from port to port, backward and forward, and with very good success..."* And, on his final voyage to China, at a place Crusoe took to be Quinchang, a Japanese merchant *"...bought all our opium, and gave us a very good price for it, paying us in gold by weight, some in small pieces of our own coin, and some in small wedges of about ten or eleven ounces each..."*

Robinson Crusoe thereafter went on to Peking where he had more adventures before moving northward to Naun on the frontier of the land of the Mongol Tartars.

But Joy had absolutely no interest in Naun or the frontier land of the Tartars. He locked the book away making a mental note that

Crusoe's expeditions between Bengal and China were between 1700 and 1705, eighty years ago. Sing-songs, exotic soups, opium. He now had three *bona fide* suggestions for Sir Paul Miller.

6

Prudence prevented Joy from bursting into Sir Paul's rooms as he had with the Fleetwoods. Ironically in this case, restraint worked against him. Relief and tiredness had made Joy sleep soundly and wake late so that by the time he arrived at the Governor's office, Sir Paul had made an early start to inspect the new ship-building docks at Garden Reach, seven miles downriver. Deciding that following Sir Paul to Garden Reach would be a useless exercise, Joy waited at Fort William and fretted.

It was late afternoon when he finally faced Sir Paul in the Governor's office. To Joy's chagrin, Cornwallis insisted on being present. Joy wished he could have had Sir Paul to himself for this important interview, but he obviously could not order the great man out of his own office.

"Well, Morley?" opened Sir Paul warmly. "You don't look as if you've had much sleep. Mind working overtime?"

"No sir. I mean, y...yes sir."

Joy was sure he had washed and shaved and attended to his attire well enough to conceal the trauma of two tempestuous nights, but Sir Paul had been perceptive enough to notice. Joy had a moment of panic as he imagined the two most powerful Englishmen in the Orient laughing uproariously over his 'brilliant' research based on a fairy tale. But the die was cast. The peer and the knight were waiting expectantly. Joy took the plunge.

"Yes sir. I have indeed been busy. And I have reached some interesting conclusions." He paused. "In addressing the issue of adverse balance of trade between England and China, it is my opinion we put in operation a three-way trade involving an intermediate country, rather than a bilateral England-China deal."

"Morley, what?" Cornwallis interposed.

"Please, m'Lord," Sir Paul said quietly. "Let us hear him out. He's on to something."

"Thank you, sir," said Joy. "If we carry out tripartite trade we may be able to export commodities from our colonies to China, or even trans-trade articles we procure from the Spanish or the Dutch."

He stopped to catch his breath. Sir Paul was staring at him intently and Joy concluded he was on the right track, at least for the moment. Even Cornwallis, the career military man, showed interest.

"Sir, m'Lord, to cut a very long story short I have two suggestions for easing our adverse balance of trade."

He paused again and thought carefully. *Better to give them the scholarly work first.*

"The first suggestion encompasses an expansion of traditional Europe-China trade. I have read that Chinese like exotic curios."

"Oh, good man!" Sir Paul applauded heartily. "An excellent idea. But it's been tried before. You are correct in that the Emperor and his nobility are infatuated with sing-songs, but the volume of their import pales to insignificance when compared to China's export of tea."

"Yes sir, but could not we extend their craving for the exotic?"

"Meaning what?"

"The Chinese like exotic smells, tastes, experiences. If we go down this path, we could experiment with foods, drugs, aphrodisiacs and the like. I know this area has met success with items like soups made of nests of birds and fins of sharks."

Cornwallis began to breathe heavily, his usual prelude to a scathing remark. But he was forestalled.

"We can give it a try, Morley." Sir Paul's words lacked conviction. "I'll have Macardle and the chaps in Canton talk to the *hong* merchant. But do go on, dear fellow. What is your other suggestion?"

"Opium."

Sir Paul's eyebrows shot up.

"What?"

"Opium, sir. An addictive drug."

"For God's sake, man, I know what opium is."

"Yes sir. And I have determined that there is demand for opium in China."

"Bless my soul! Morley, you can bet your Sunday boots there

is demand for opium in China. But the Turks handle that one."

"Begging your pardon, sir, the Turks?"

"Morley, you most definitely are talking about the one commodity the Chinese want but don't have. I should have mentioned it to you the other night. I know a great deal about it. Opium does indeed rival tea in England in its demand in China." Sir Paul became professorial. "Opium has been used medicinally in China since the seventh century. But only after tobacco was introduced in Formosa in the early 1600s did the Chinese begin to *smoke* the thing. And from that time its consumption has exploded."

"May I ask a question, Sir Paul?" Cornwallis interjected. "Why is there an opium shortage in China in the first place?"

"Why a shortage, m'Lord? Opium is made from juice of the poppy and it appears that the requisite level of quality of the little yellow flower is not attainable in China. Please don't ask me why. To complicate matters, the Emperor of China is very strict about enforcing a ban on its harvest. The best opium today is found in the land of the Ottomans, in Turkey, with a flourishing market in Constantinople. Small quantities are smuggled to China by Turks overland along Marco Polo's Silk Route. It's a hazardous trail, beset by bandits. As a result, good quality opium is more precious in China than gold."

Joy was ecstatic.

"But that's wonderful news, sir. In the light of my suggestion of doing a three-way trade, couldn't we buy opium from the Turks and sell to the Chinese? Our ships could get to China faster and safer than the land route over mountains and deserts."

Sir Paul did not speak for a while. When he did, it was to Cornwallis.

"Mark my words, m'Lord, you *do* have a good man here." He turned back to Joy. "Nevertheless, my dear fellow, I hate to pour cold water on your astute deductions, but what you suggest has been tried by our old Levant Company. The Turks are aware of the price that opium commands in China and are unwilling to sell it to us at a cost at which we can make a profit."

Joy was taken aback. So it was known that opium was a possible commodity and trade in it had already been attempted. Well, so much for his dramatic 'discovery' through *Robinson Crusoe.* Luckily, he had not revealed the source of his 'research' to the governors.

Seeing his crestfallen face, Sir Paul said, "Please understand, young Morley, I'm not trying to be difficult. I'll listen to anything, try anything, that can corner the opium trade. And if anything can break the stranglehold the Chinese have us in, it is that. But there are some real obstacles. By Imperial edict in 1729, China has banned import of opium. It can only be smuggled in as the Turks do."

Joy recalled something out of Defoe.

"But, sir, isn't opium grown in Siam?"

"You really have studied this, my friend! Yes, the poppy is indeed grown in Siam and, yes, we *are* coming closer to China now. The difficulty remains the same however. Not enough quantity and too high a price. And the Siamese quality is similar to the locally grown Chinese variety and is thus inferior to the Turkish product. Even if we overcome these obstacles, the imperial edict would still be in our way.

We, the English, are not allowed to carry opium in on our ships. And as a further complication, foreign imports are allowed only through Canton and our ships are subject to extensive scrutiny at berthing."

Joy's enthusiasm dropped in stages as Sir Paul enumerated the impediments. The day was nearing its end. Behind the two famous men was a large open window. In silence Joy watched waves of large bats called flying foxes silhouetted in the dying sun as they winged south to feed. His prospect of contributing something meaningful to the Company and the country was ebbing.

Close to giving up, he tried one last time.

"Couldn't we control the price, sir? Couldn't we dictate terms to the supplier? Perhaps in exchange for other concessions? And we could – maybe, just maybe – find a way around the imperial edict. Oh God, we are entering the realm of multiple maybe's."

Joy's voice faded and he stared dismally at the floor. The silence lengthened. Through all this, Cornwallis had been looking from face to face, appreciating the magnitude of the conversation, trying to keep up. He suddenly frowned and said, "Morley, weren't we talking about something we might buy from your prince last month?"

"My prince, m'Lord?" Joy replied impatiently. "Prince Sena of Rajmahal? But that was about cotton and..."

He stopped dead and stared at Cornwallis, his eyes wide. It was Sir Paul who now looked from one to the other, not following the sudden turn in dialogue.

"M'Lord!" Joy almost shouted, looking around wildly. "Here? Could it be possible?"

"*Now* what, Morley?" said Cornwallis irritably. "*Must* you always be so confoundedly dramatic?"

But Joy wasn't listening.

"Oh my God! *That* could be the exact solution!"

He stared out of the window, eyes glazed, mind whirling.

"Explain yourself, man!"

This came from Sir Paul. But Joy did not reply, lost in another world. While Joy concentrated, Cornwallis quietly briefed Sir Paul about Prince Vikram Sena and his kingdom of Rajmahal, northward up the Hooghly River. He described the Executive Council's efforts to generate new exports from Bengal for reduction in duties imposed by Mughal rulers. Then they quietly watched the younger man and waited for him to come out of his trance.

"M'Lord," Joy spoke softly. "Does opium grow in India?"

Sir Paul's eyes narrowed.

"Here?" said Cornwallis. "Damned if I know, Morley. Never dealt with that substance myself nor, I think, has anyone at the fort. I've heard tales of opium being smoked in the royal Mughal courts. There's been talk of it growing near Patna. The natives probably know."

Patna!

Joy's mind jumped again. The graying general of American wars was on to something. Joy itched to get moving. He *must* get local help to crack this at once. Then his mind jumped again, this time painfully. *Vikram!* The Sena lands were in Rajmahal. Rajmahal was near Patna. He might have an ideal go-between right here! He felt faint with excitement. Cornwallis had said opium may be growing near

Patna, just five days' upriver. Then a deflating thought. How was its quality? Adrenalin rushed back through his veins again as the urge to know took over. He wanted to run to Vikram at once and start investigating.

Sir Paul, watching the chimeric play of emotions flitting across Joy's face, compressed his lips in a tight line. When he spoke his voice was iron-hard.

"M'Lord! I implore you to recognize we have a supreme maritime opportunity at hand. Kindly relieve Morley of all his duties, every one of them, for the days before I sail for China."

Cornwallis nodded assent and Sir Paul turned to Joy.

"Young Morley, now you listen to me carefully. Find out all you can about opium growth, production, procurement, and export from India. Report everything to me before my departure. Even your wildest theories. That's an order."

With his heart beating madly Joy stumbled out of the Governor-General's office. Sir Paul looked after him. Then he turned to the bemused peer and said thoughtfully, "It's no wonder Old Morley in Ashford can't stop talking about this son of his. That fellow will become a mercantile Francis Drake if he pulls this off."

7

Ten days later, four men, all remarkably different from one another, stood together on a lofty stone balcony in Fort William. It was quite late in the evening. The thick wall of the garrison and an impressive colonnade rose directly behind the men, while in front of them the river shimmered in the moonlight.

The men were Joy, Vikram, Captain Jerome Winkley, and a rotund distinguished-looking Indian known as the Jagat Seth.

Captain Winkley was master of *HMS Albatross,* the ship that had brought the Governor of Canton to India. Soon after his meeting with Sir Paul at the King's birthday honors in London, Jerome had presented himself to the Company offices at Leadenhall Street. A survey of his naval record provided evidence of excellent leadership qualities to the Company's Nominating Committee. The Committee also found a curious propensity of the captain to attract thugs and muggers at ports of call. The record indicated Jerome had survived three knife attacks in European back alleys and had been involved in two duels of honor. However, when the Committee submitted their findings to the Court of Directors, Jerome's naval accomplishments outweighed this dark attribute. With maritime trade exploding and senior officers in short supply, the Directors quickly offered Jerome command of *Albatross.* The ship was of a new class of merchant gunboats called East Indiamen that were being pressed into long-haul service. Jerome accepted and was told his ship had been assigned double duty as cargo carrier and convoy escort in the Orient and was responsible for keeping India-China shipping lanes safe. For the latter role she was outfitted with twelve nine-pounder cannon. On her maiden voyage, with Sir Paul Miller aboard, *Albatross* was to provision in Calcutta on the way to Canton.

Prince Vikram Sena, in his mid-twenties, was attired in off-white loose-fitting silk garments. Following his sister's death, Vikram had returned to Rajmahal for her funeral and responded to his friend's urgent appeal after conclusion of the 13-day mourning period. Vikram's family owned extensive landholdings around the ancient city in the northeastern part of the Province of Bengal. He was a descendant of a proud dynasty that once ruled the huge province and was defeated by the Mughals in the fourteenth century. More recently, following the Battle of Plassey in 1757, where Robert Clive defeated Mughal king, Shiraj Doula through intrigue, and assumed control of Bengal, the East India Company rewarded the Company's key allies, including the Senas, with land and power. Joy's father, Benjamin, and

Prince Ajoy Sena, Vikram's uncle, were close friends.

Vikram was a capable businessman and administrator, ever on the lookout to increase his wealth and his sway over the land. Joy and Vikram became close and continued the family ties.

'Jagat Seth' was a title, not a name. Translated literally from Bengali, it meant 'banker of the world.' The dynastic Jagat Seths, fabulously rich, were mercantile immigrants to Bengal from Rajputana in western India. The first Jagat Seth, Manik Chand, had provided cash for battles that led to Mughal ascension to the throne of Bengal in the seventeenth century. Since then the Jagat Seths had dictated and financed commerce, war and politics of Eastern India.

The present banker of the world, whose name was Kushal Chand, was an elderly, plump and mustachioed personage. His was a formidable presence in starched white kaftan and *dhoti,* liberally sprinkled with rose water. In addition to his wealth, he had the shrewd political mind of his forebears. While the two Englishmen and Vikram sipped *madeiras,* the Jagat Seth, who never touched alcohol, watched carefully, trying to assess the importance and intent of the meeting.

Captain Winkley was describing his orders.

Joy had called the men together after his audience with the governors. He tried to control his eagerness for the venture knowing that launching into the subject of opium at once would be a mistake. Indians took their time getting to important matters. It was vital he approach the delicate topic with care and obtain everyone's support.

Jerome's precise Kentish accent was pleasant to the ear. Joy listened as the captain described naval action in America at a place called Chesapeake Bay. He explained how Sir Paul's recommendations had allowed the East India Company to obtain approval from Parliament to step up 'country trade' between Calcutta and Canton. This, the Company hoped according to Jerome, would alleviate the adverse trade balance between England and China.

Oh well, Joy mused ruefully, *three-way trade isn't my brainchild either!*

Jerome revealed that the eastern seas were infested with privateers operating from hideouts along the Arakan coast of Burma and western Siam. Shipping required armed escort if country trade was to succeed. *Albatross's* territory was the expanse of ocean between the Ganges delta, from which ships from Calcutta emerged into the Bay of Bengal, and the Pearl River Estuary, which led from the South China Sea into Canton. Joy waited patiently for him to finish. Jerome impressed them all with his seafaring acumen and Joy felt his confidence growing. Captain Winkley would be a key participant in the operation that was forming in his mind.

Joy turned his attention to the two Indians. Both were competent men of honor. Prince Vikram, though young, was a solid administrator and a hard man to ruffle. He was an independent thinker and had a large and loyal following in his principality. The Jagat Seth was kingpin of every business venture in Bengal. Joy reminded himself that the prince and the banker were not malleable British vassals and would need to be carefully recruited into his mission. He had his nucleus. Now he had to play his cards well.

Jerome obligingly gave him the opening.

"...and now, Morley," he asked. "What cargoes beside textiles and saltpeter will China-bound ships carry from India?"

Joy responded with his own question.

"What do you think, gentlemen? Captain Winkley has assured us safe passage and a large market. We must rise to the challenge. What should we transport?"

The Jagat Seth looked at him speculatively. The fact that the Company's Chief Councilor, Donald Macpherson, was absent for this apparently important conference was not lost on him. His experienced nose smelt a plot.

"Do the Chinese have good dyes, Sahib?" he ventured, testing the water. "Bengal indigo is famous the world over."

Prince Vikram raised a hand.

"Seth-*ji*, may I speak?" He turned to Joy. "It is almost midnight, Morley-sahib. The owl has already screeched twice. It is a bad omen to hear it even once. Why have you summoned us here?"

Joy took a deep breath and a sip of *madeira*. He said a silent prayer. It was now or never.

"Thank you, Prince Vikram," he said pacing the balcony, speaking from deep within himself. "We have before us a great challenge. And an even greater opportunity. Seth-*ji*, do you remember our conversation of a month ago? The one where the Chief Councilor demanded concessions for cotton? The one where Prince Vikram advised us that instead of taking a hard line we should offer something in return to cotton buyers? It was then that something stirred in my mind. I tried to discover if there was another article in which middlemen wished to trade. Something against which they would agree to reduce the price of cotton. Something they would buy in quantity."

Joy paused.

"Is there such an article?" he asked.

To his surprise, Jerome replied matter-of-factly, "Yes, there is!"

"There is?" repeated the startled Joy. "What?"

"Damned if I know, Morley! But there *is* one and you obviously know what it is. Else why the wine? And the cloak-and-dagger act? Get on, man, it's late. Spill the beans! What's the confounded article?"

The references to cloaks, daggers and beans mystified the Indians. Joy broke the suspense.

"The article is opium."

Everyone gasped. Joy took a step back to watch the reactions.

The banker and the prince stared at him in puzzlement. Jerome's expression was completely blank. The hiatus grew. He saw that Vikram was interested but baffled. The Jagat Seth, trying to match credit and debit columns, was not succeeding.

The banker broke the silence as he mused aloud.

"The English? The English want to trade opium in bulk? This is strange. There has not been any interest in the past."

The man knows something, Joy told himself. *I must get him to talk. Careful though. He's a clever rogue. Can't ask him outright.*

"How do you know, Seth-*ji*?" he asked.

"How do I know what, Sahib?"

"How do you know that there has been no interest from the English in the past? Has there been interest from others?"

Joy held his breath. The tubby banker chewed his whiskers and deliberated. Suddenly he blew out his moustache like a flag.

"In opium? There has been interest, Morley-sahib. But are you sure your country wishes to trade in opium out of all things? It is a dreadful thing, this opium. It reduces humans to living corpses. To import opium into England is a vastly different matter from clothes for English bodies and spices for English food."

Joy let his breath out slowly and, as the Jagat Seth expounded on the ills of opium, a slow anger built up. He was furious with himself. In his heady plunge into solving the Crown's problem he had not thought about the article itself. He now realized how little he knew about the adverse consequences of opium. *Am I premature in holding this meeting?* he asked himself and the answer was clear. He *had* heard of the debilitating effects of opium. He should have found out more before showing his hand. He felt like kicking himself.

"Is it really *that* bad, Seth-*ji?*" Joy feigned ignorance. "Do you know much about opium?"

The elderly Indian raised his eyebrows.

"Should I, Sahib? My vices run to snuff and *supari* nuts. As do those of my intimates. Opium is a dangerous business. Now take indigo dyes, Sahib, they..."

"No, Seth-*ji*. I am serious and would like to know more about opium. I must decide whether it is a tradeable commodity."

There was a silence. Jerome made to say something but Joy quieted him with a look. The Jagat Seth turned to Vikram.

"Prince Vikram Sena rules from Rajmahal, which is but a few

miles from Patna, the opium center of Bengal. Perhaps the prince can tell us more?"

Joy was ecstatic. *An opium center! There was an opium center in India! And one only a few hundred miles away.* Then he caught himself. The banker's excessive formality was bothering him. Was it a subtle put-down? *Watch the man,* he reminded himself.

Vikram, who had said little so far, launched into the subject with his dramatic and accented English.

"Opium, Sahib? A dirty business! An object not spoken of in polite society. Recourse for the defeated. The hopeless. The poorest of the poor. Liquor intoxicates and numbs the mind. Opium seizes it, fills it with visions, with dread, destroys it. *Destroys it,* Sahib! It is far from honorable to introduce this poison to your country in the northern seas. Better, much better, to suffer loss in cotton." Agitated now, Vikram's voice rose with emotion. "Opium? Have I before me the same idealist from England my family so admires? Is this the..."

Jerome Winkley broke in.

"Belay there, Mr...uh...Sena, if ye don't mind. We're losing the point of this discussion. Morley here wants to know if there's a history of opium production in India. We were getting into that before the digression into moralistic claptrap. Mr. Seth, you appear to know more than you have said."

"Captain-sahib!" The Jagat Seth turned on Jerome angrily. "Consider your words! Your Councilor appears to know more than what *he* has said, and he has already assumed our support. I shall not associate myself with this business unless I know what the stakes are.

If at all I do!"

The big captain's chin went up and his eyes blazed. A muscle twitched above his left temple. No fat native spoke to him this way.

"Sir! I will have you know..."

Joy laid a restraining hand on his arm. Did Jerome *have* to compound his own gaffe?

"Gentlemen! Gentlemen! The fault is entirely mine." He backed out and away from the trap into which he had fallen. "It was wrong of me to have invited you to a venture without adequate preparation. I wish only to find out more before I commit myself, yourselves, and the Company to a course of action."

Joy paused. Jerome grunted. Vikram smoldered. The Jagat Seth looked at Joy with new respect and made peace.

"Councilor-sahib, I shall tell you all I know."

There's much about diplomacy I can learn from this man, Joy thought. *He's bailing me out. But then, he has a vested interest.*

The tension lessened and the Jagat Seth began his story.

"Morley-sahib, long before the English came to this country, even before my own ancestors arrived from the west, even before Sultan Shah Jahan built the Taj Mahal in Agra, the province of Bengal had thriving commerce and attracted traders from far and near. Bengal exported rice, salt, silk, fruits, and ivory on her own ships to Java, to Sumatra, to Ceylon, to the Moluccas, even as far as Japan. Then foreign merchants arrived in their ships and trade was extended west to Arabia and Europe and east to China. But such ships did not carry opium. Opium was a minor item of trade. The smoking of opium in

India is popular – if that is the correct word for a poison – only among the very rich or the very poor."

"Why is that, Seth-*ji?*" Joy asked.

"Smoking opium is a dangerous pastime. The stakes are high. One gambles in opium only if one has everything or nothing to lose."

Jerome, still smarting under the banker's reprimand, petulantly interjected, "That doesn't make sense!"

The Jagat Seth sighed.

"Let me put it this way for you, Captain-sahib. If you have been so fortunate that life has given all you desire, you will develop a restlessness. Ordinary life will lose its challenge. The temptation will arise to flirt with that which can take it all away. To the truly rich and powerful, Mughal emperors and Maharajas, opium is the ultimate seduction. Conversely, to the utterly destitute, a pipe of opium is release from the blackness that is life. Thus an opium addict will exchange his kingdom or steal without compunction to support his habit. *Shiva! Shiva!* What a terrible thing. What a terrible thing."

The banker shook his bald head and looked sadly at his feet.

Vikram took up the story.

"Morley-sahib, Patna and Varanasi, two ancient cities on the Ganges River, have been centers of opium trade during centuries of Mughal rule. Poppies grow in the Bihar highlands, on the south bank of the river. They are processed and brought to these two riverside towns for onward transportation to other countries."

"By whom?" asked Jerome.

"The Portuguese mostly. Although there are a few Indian

merchant ships that carry opium cargo."

"To which countries?"

"I do not know. Do you, Seth-*ji?*"

"No, I do not. But it can be determined."

Croaking frogs filled the long silence that followed. A nightjar chuckled in the darkness. Then a hunting owl screeched harshly from very near, startling the men. The superstitious Vikram fidgeted but said nothing.

A maelstrom swirled in Joy's brain. What should he do? Who could he ask for help? He *had* to solve Sir Paul's problem. The King's problem. The country's problem. England would be in disarray unless the trade imbalance with China was righted. *Was* opium the correct answer? Could he, *should he,* unleash a demon on that antediluvian country? He had to know more. He had to see more. He had to do this before he took a step whose short term profit might lead to a long term calamity. And he had to do it before Sir Paul left India.

"Cap'n, when does *Albatross* sail?"

"In two weeks I expect. Sir Paul and the other passengers would like her to sail immediately I wager. But we have to belay for inbound *Beowulf* that's bringing powder for *Albatross's* guns."

Joy did some mental calculations. He had a great deal to accomplish in two weeks and thought rapidly. Then he studied Vikram for a long moment. *Will he do it,* he asked himself. *Does he want it badly enough?*

"My friend," he said to the prince. "I have a problem. Will you help me?"

The prince stared back at him wordlessly. He sensed the importance of the moment and waited.

Joy took a deep breath.

"Prince Vikram, two hundred and fifty years ago in our country, there lived a poet and writer." The others looked at him in surprise at the sudden change of subject. "His name was William Shakespeare. Most famous of his immortal characters was a Roman emperor named Julius Caesar. Fifteen hundred years ago, Rome had an empire that spanned the known world."

"Morley, what the devil...?"

Ignoring Jerome, Joy continued.

"Julius Caesar was Rome's greatest emperor. Much of his success was due to luminous advisors."

Jerome again tried to interrupt.

"Hold on Cap'n, this is crucial. Prince Vikram, please listen. In Shakespeare's story an advisor, Brutus, who later became an enemy, gave his master, Caesar, an abiding piece of advice: 'There comes a time in the tides of all men, which taken at the full, leads to fortune.'"

"Sahib," Vikram frowned in perplexity. "I do not understand. Tides of men?"

Joy explained Shakespeare simply and saw that Vikram understood the point. Joy's own excitement grew. His assessment of the Indian prince's intelligence had been accurate. At the same time, he realized that Jerome's impatience was diverting everyone's concentration. He had to get rid of the naval officer.

"Captain Winkley," he said. "We shall need your services in this venture later. This conversation makes you weary. It will not displease us if you leave." When Jerome hesitated, Joy put a hand on the captain's arm and gently pushed him toward the exit. "I will explain all after we have talked, the prince and I." Under his breath he added *"Go for God's sake! Now!"*

While the captain rumbled rebelliously, Joy led him into an inner room, summoned Murali, and had him shown out. When he returned, the two Indians listened somberly to his speech.

"My friends, I was talking about tides of men. Yes, a tide has come to the lives of men. Our lives. A tide of silver. If we take it at the full, it could mean fortune. Fortune for us. Power for us. Power for India. Power for Britain. Caesar built an empire that spanned the world while Rome rode its tide. Later, galleons of Spain and Portugal rode their own tides to world sovereignty. Can the clippers of Britain do as much? Can a tide of silver build a British Empire with Bengal as its foundation? Do you understand what I am saying?"

The Jagat Seth nodded, deeply engrossed. Vikram's countenance reflected his interest. Joy returned to the present.

"Opium! You call it a dirty business, Prince Vikram. And so it is. But only at first glance."

"Sahib," interrupted the banker. "What is this tide of silver?"

Joy recounted the crushing effect of tea on Britain's economy and the countervailing potential of opium. He talked rapidly and the Indians absorbed each word.

"The supplier of that trade commodity will become intensely rich and powerful. And if Bengal becomes the source of that trade, she too will become rich. Bengal will hold the key to British success in the entire world. Key to the British Empire. Calcutta will become the second city on earth after London. When that happens Britain shall do all in her power to ensure that supportive monarchs rule Bengal."

Joy and Vikram's eyes locked. The moment had come.

Joy asked very slowly, "Is the *Nawab,* Mubarak Doula, a supportive monarch?"

The immensity of what the young Englishmen was saying dawned on Vikram. In stages his face exhibited incredulity, elation, uncertainty, and confidence. From being bowed by grief for his sister, he grew straight in front of their eyes. His hands clenched and unclenched. He took a deep breath and steadied himself. When he spoke his voice had a controlled ring.

"You ask, Sahib, 'Is the *nawab* supportive?' I say it is of no consequence. Prince Vikram Sena shall be supportive. Infinitely more supportive. The Senas shall rise and sweep away the Mughals. At last. And Rajmahal, Calcutta and Bengal shall be the base of your empire."

"The British Empire!" The friends spontaneously clasped arms.

Through the exchange of rhetoric, the Jagat Seth said not a word. He watched vignettes of interplay of character being performed before him. He understood this was a defining moment. His highly trained nose scented money. A lot of money. He prepared himself to wait. In the end they all came to him. *Nawab* and Emperor, Indian and Afghan, Arab and Portuguese, English and French. They all came to the banker of the world. And, sphinx-like, the émigré from Rajputana, gently and impartially, extracted his pound of flesh from all.

8

On an oppressive misty night three scruffy men came out from a side alley of Calcutta's infamous Black Town. They wore dirty turbans and ragged cotton clothing and had dusty sandals on their feet. They were at once swallowed up by the multitude that was always present in the crowded streets.

The White and Black Towns of Calcutta adjoined each other but were worlds apart. White Town included Fort William and homes of senior Company officials like Jeremy Fleetwood as well as well-to-do Indians like the Jagat Seth. Riotous tops of flame-of-the-forest trees lined the streets of White Town, each tree adorned with masses of yellow-bordered crimson flowers. Behind the trees stood two-and three-story high-ceilinged brick houses set in gated low-walled gardens, balconies brilliant with multi-hued bougainvillea.

Teeming with people from all over India, Black Town was also the temporary home of many foreign traders, craftsmen, confidence tricksters and travelers. Arabs walked up the river path from dhows with bundles of olives and dates which concealed gold ornaments. Afghan moneylenders, whose stands of Turkmen pistachio and dried apricot were deceptive fronts, offered loans at usurious rates. Armenians held court in pawnshops. Pigtailed Chinese winked and displayed bad teeth, and accosted sex-starved seamen with aphrodisiacs. Off European clippers came big dangerous sailors, easy to anger and handy with knives, men looking for liquor and for women and for a boisterous night on the town. Drinking dens, brothels, and inns of doubtful repute lined the waterfront of Black Town and spread into verminous back alleys. Smoke from coal-fired cooking grates hung eerily in unlighted lanes and formed swirling eddies in lamplight streaming from open doorways. To the east of Black Town were notorious malarial marshes that stretched for a hundred miles along the vast mangrove-choked Ganges delta. Here roamed monstrous crocodile, wild boar, scorpions of many colors, enormous king cobra, and the Royal Bengal tiger. The only humans who ventured into this marshy jungle were derelicts and footpads.

Paradoxically, Calcutta was the richest and fastest-growing city in the East. From a central core of the rich and powerful, where the English Governor-General and the Jagat Seth formed the apex, Calcutta expanded in concentric social circles of humanity that scrambled for tenuous foothold at the edges.

At this time of night, the residents of Black Town slept on cane mats in small thatch-roofed, mud-walled houses, with their windows barred and doors bolted. They had blown conch-shells at dusk, intoned prayers, and finished evening meals before darkness fell. Now the narrow malodorous lanes were ruled by the criminal, the depraved, the avaricious.

The three scruffy men walked along in silence. Nobody noticed them. They did not carry anything to sell. Nor did they appear rich enough to be badgered into buying something or mugged. They were simply three scruffy men going somewhere. Two were short and dark, one of whom led the way. The other was tall and fair. They hurried along, occasionally stopping to ask the way, or to watch an especially lurid spectacle. There were many such. Two big-headed dwarves executed a tumbling act at a street corner. A prostitute bared her breasts from an open doorway. A group of transvestites with hard faces and dressed as women, performed a lascivious street-corner song and dance, their voices deep baritone. After fifteen minutes of walking, the leading man stopped in front of a tumbledown house in a dirty neighborhood. There was a hurried conversation after which Gopal, Vikram's attendant, went into the house, leaving Joy and the prince in the street.

Vikram's face was taut with loathing. His enthusiasm for the venture had reduced considerably since they set out. The disguised Joy looked around glassily, overwhelmed by the sights. Even though he had come to Calcutta long ago, he had not dared to enter Black Town at night. He was thinking of the tambourines and lewd gestures of the transvestites when Gopal came back.

"Sahib, you have to pay two *annas* each for two hours. And

Sahib," Gopal looked at Joy, *"you* must say nothing. If it becomes known that you are *feringhi* there will be difficulties. And it would be better if you left me your valuables."

"*Must* we go through with this?" Vikram asked.

"Let's go in and find out," Joy replied brusquely. "We have brought no valuables."

He walked purposefully towards the door. Gopal scurried to get ahead and lead the way in. Vikram trailed behind. As they approached the house they became aware of a sickly sweet odor. Joy pushed aside a ragged curtain, entered the house and found himself in a small room, dimly lit by a smoky lantern in a barred window. He saw a corpulent, unshaven man wearing a torn singlet and sarong, sitting cross-legged on a frayed reed mat. On the other side of the room, a small boy squatted on the floor.

As he entered, Vikram flinched as a furry animal scuttled over his feet. Gopal and the fat proprietor held a hurried conversation. The man looked at them doubtfully and scratched his crotch. He was about to speak when Gopal handed over some coins. At this he appeared satisfied and peered through the gloom at the boy.

"*Ei,* Selim!"

Selim got to his feet. He was pitifully thin and wore a short sarong. Shivering, he stumbled toward another curtained doorway on the far side of the room. The proprietor motioned them in the same direction. Gopal went back to the street.

Joy followed the boy and gingerly pushed aside the drape through which he had disappeared and came to an abrupt stop at the threshold unable to see anything. Even though the room they had just left was lit by a single sooty lantern, he still had to wait before his eyes adjusted to the murk of the interior.

And then, as his eyes adjusted, from the shadows appeared figures. Vikram pushed up against him. The two men stood transfixed at the entrance for a long time. Lying on the beaten earth floor or propped against walls were skeletons. Skeletons on which they would have stepped had they not waited at the entrance. The addicts' most characteristic feature was unfocussed open eyes that reflected the faint orange light of an oil lamp hung on a rafter. They could be cadavers except for those glistening eyes. Suddenly one moved. As they watched him in fascination, with great effort the man lifted the stem of a pipe from his side to his lips and inhaled deeply. The charcoal glowed in the bowl. Another addict did the same. Then they put the pipes down with agonizing slowness.

The hellish scene gradually resolved itself.

Spittle drooled down smokers' chins. A low muttering came in a continuous undertone. Glutinous smoke clouded the room. Vikram and Joy had to peer through the haze to decide which way to proceed. The floor and the smokers lying on it were encrusted with filth. Joy realized that mixed with the sickly odor of burning opium was the ammonia reek of human urine. He shivered uncontrollably. *What vermin must there be in this hell-hole!* He made out a brazier of coals glowing dully in a far corner of the room. The ceiling lamp flickered through the pall like a faint sun in a dense fog.

The boy Selim hopped over the prostrate forms and went

through a dark opening on the opposite wall.

Suddenly an addict screamed in falsetto at their feet and Vikram and Joy reflexively shrank back. Joy's resolve had almost caved when Selim reappeared. He carried a pipe in each hand and made his way towards the brazier. Joy shook off his revulsion and carefully stepped over the addicts to the boy. Vikram hesitated, then gingerly followed. At the brazier Selim tried to use a pair of tongs to put a glowing coal into the bowls of the two pipes but found it impossible. Joy saw that he was pitiably thin, some nine or ten years old, possibly more, uncoordinated, or simply stupid, and in imminent danger of setting fire to his sarong. Joy went to help. He noticed the boy's eyes were bloodshot and watery. His hands shook as he tried to pick up a coal with the tongs while holding a pipe in the same hand and the two clattered together. Joy took the tongs from him. His wrist touched the boy's arm. It was fiery hot.

"You have a fever," he told Selim in Bengali.

Vikram's pressure on his shoulder reminded him of Gopal's warning. But the boy did not notice the accent and abruptly sat down as close to the brazier as he could.

"Yes, *janab,*" he said. "I have had malaria for two days and I am going to die."

"Then what are doing you here?" Vikram asked unimpressed, adopting the dialect the boy spoke.

"If I do not work, master will sell my mother away." Saying this Selim got up. "Take your coal now so that I can go to the front room. Your place is there."

The boy pointed towards a part of the room which did not seem any less congested than the others. Joy took his pipe, put a coal in it and walked carefully to the spot indicated. He really did not want to fathom the boy's statement about his mother, nor did he have much sympathy. He hoped Selim, and thousands of destitute children like him in India, would survive their awful world. But contrary to what he had just said, Selim did not go away. He swayed for a moment where he stood, then roughly pushed aside two elderly smokers, picked up a rag, dusted off a spot, and indicated that they should sit. Then he swayed again and would have fallen had not Joy caught him. He laid the boy on the ground and sat down beside him. Selim began to shiver violently. The thin sarong he wore was pitifully inadequate for his fever and the clammy environment. Vikram came across. Joy explained the situation in a few words and Vikram distastefully undid his turban and folded the long material over the upper half of the boy's body. It was not much of a cover and Selim continued to shiver in starts. Vikram shook his head as Joy put his hand to his own turban. The Englishman's blond hair would be a dead giveaway. Joy looked at the pipe in his hand, wiped the mouthpiece on his sleeve and grimaced.

Should I smoke this vile thing? he wondered.

Joy looked around the room.

From a blurred collection of emaciated derelicts, the addicts began to take on individuality. And while there appeared initially to be a large mass of people, he now realized there were only about fifteen smokers in the room. And they were not all old and decrepit either. Some were quite young. Thirty was considered old in this country, and the natives rarely lived beyond forty. All the addicts were gaunt and wasted with vacant expressions. Many exhibited smallpox scabs or disfigurement of leprosy or discoloration of leukoderma. Joy shuddered and distractedly puffed at his pipe, then recoiled as he realized the enormity of what he had done. An immediate warm and heady sensation filled his body and he sat back in surprise. Looking round guiltily he saw Vikram frowning in his direction. *The devil take him!* he thought. *So this is what it's like, this cursed drug.* He was considering another drag when Selim sat up. Vikram found an earthenware pitcher and poured water for the boy to drink from a cup made with his little palms. Drops spattered onto the ground.

When the boy finished drinking, Joy nodded meaningfully at Vikram. The prince looked around sulkily, then shrugged and asked the boy his name.

"Selim Haider, *janab.*"

"Selim, do you want money to help your mother?"

"Yes, *janab.* I want it very much. With a little money we can go back home to Khulna district."

He arranged the turban around himself, looking stronger.

"Well, Selim, let's see what can be done. How long have you worked for this master?"

"Three years, *janab,* since father went away and did not come back. Master keeps mother and sister as long as I work for him. He is always very angry. He will sell them if any of us do anything wrong. During the day I carry his messages."

"But you have malaria."

"Yes *janab*. But I could *die* and I would still have to work! You do not know Master."

"I see," said Vikram. "Now look here. My friend and I are new to opium. We want to know what it will do to us."

"This is the first time?"

Vikram nodded and Selim stared at them.

"Yes *janab,* I see now. You are both healthy and strong. Why do you want to smoke opium?"

"That is none of your business."

Vikram glared at the sick child. He desperately wanted to get the experience over with. He yearned for a bath and clean clothes.

Selim chattered in his piping voice.

"Look around you, *janab.* You will see what happens to smokers. Over there is Afzal Masood who pulls dead animals out of the river and sells their skin to tanners in the swamp. This pays for his habit. Kalidas there, lives in the mangroves and robs travelers to maintain his habit. Others have the same story. Oh, and there is Gani Mia. He confides in me. Gani Mia had a cloth shop in Chittagong. Last year the Arakans raided his village. They looted his shop and killed his family. Gani Mia escaped but they should have killed him too. He had borrowed heavily from the moneylender and could not pay back. He was hounded out of Chittagong. He could have begun again in Calcutta but somewhere between Chittagong and Calcutta he tasted opium."

They looked across at Gani Mia.

"Call him here," Vikram ordered.

Selim went and spoke softly to the man. Gani Mia got up in

slow motion and Selim took him by the hand and led him to them. The man's cheeks were hollow, with an unkempt beard. Like the others he wore a filthy sarong and smelt vile.

Selim seemed to think his job was done and held out his hand.

"You shall be given a rupee when we leave," Vikram told him.

It was a month's wages for the boy and Selim went away satisfied. Then they turned their attention to Gani Mia.

An hour later, Gopal was sitting propped against the outside wall of the den, trying to keep warm and not fall asleep, hoping he would not be robbed. He started up as he saw his master and the boy Selim emerge from the opium den supporting the English sahib. The sahib seemed totally overcome by the effects of opium. It was incomprehensible to Gopal why his master, the Prince, and the English sahib would stoop to such depravity. When he reached them he discovered the English sahib had not only lost the power of his limbs but also had tears running down his cheeks. Gopal was appalled. He silently promised Lord Vishnu that even if his life was at stake he would not touch opium.

"Gopal! Give the boy a rupee," Vikram spoke harshly.

They staggered back to White Town. It was late and there were very few people about. Drunks lay by the roadside.

Joy was overcome by a rush of sentiment, or maybe the opium he had sampled was having its effect. He held Vikram's arm tightly.

"Never!" he said brokenly. "Never! Never can we do this to the Chinese. All those poor wretches. Gani Mia. Kalidas. They'll all die. In days. Weeks. Nothing can stop it. Oh my God. What have I done?"

9

The next day was very hot, the hottest of the year. When Joy entered, the wooden shutters of the Governor-General's office were closed to keep out the searing heat. A coir mat hanging at the entrance was sprayed with water to generate a token coolness. But the room remained uncomfortable. A long heavy cloth strip called a *punkha,* pulled by someone with a rope outside, swayed from a horizontal pole overhead, but it only managed to recirculate the stifling air. Every door and window was tightly shut, yet the glare of the summer sun penetrated sufficiently for business to be conducted without lamps.

Joy did not look forward to this meeting. His mood was black and his face was pale as he stood before the tall figure. Lord Cornwallis was at his afternoon siesta and the two men were alone this time. Sir Paul stood beside the Governor-General's desk and regarded the young man quizzically. Joy, wasted after the experience of the previous night at the opium den, rocked on his feet as the moment he was dreading finally arrived.

"Well?" Sir Paul asked as the silence lengthened into minutes. "Something on your mind, young man?"

"Yes sir. And it's not pleasant."

There was another silence before Sir Paul said "We are adults, Morley. I've had my knocks. Man to man now. Let's not waste time."

Joy took a deep breath and began "I'm not sure where to begin, sir..." and paused uncertainly. Sir Paul sat down on the Governor's plush chair and waited. Joy took another deep breath and his words came out in a rush.

"I think it's best to summarize, sir. I earnestly recommend we abandon the idea of opium as a trade commodity for China."

Sir Paul's eyes narrowed. His nostrils flared. When he said nothing Joy plowed on desperately.

"Opium is a devilish business."

"Devilish, Morley?" Sir Paul grunted in disgust. "A moralistic observation. Might I point out we are gentlemen of commerce?"

"So we are, sir. But that does not give us authority to dabble with the psyche of the poor."

"*Poppycock!*" burst out the patriarch, jumping angrily to his feet. "Psyche of the poor' indeed! What drivel! There are enough didacticians in this world to weep for the downtrodden. Neither you nor I are of their ilk. Great heavens! I finally find a man capable of original economic thought and within days he is preaching altruism. Come Morley, you can do better."

Joy looked unhappily at the gray and rangy old man who held the weight of British commerce on his shoulders.

"Sorry sir. That didn't come out right. What I meant was opium has an extremely debilitating effect on the nervous system, thereby leading to total destruction of the addict."

"I know that, Morley. But before we debate the demerits of the drug, might I remind you that your mandate was to look into the possibility of procuring good quality opium from India for export to China at a profit. Did you do as I asked?"

Joy looked down at his feet.

"Did you?"

Sir Paul was furious. An ashen-faced Joy realized he should have made his report before voicing his subjective opinion. Would he *ever* learn? He tried to undo the damage.

"Yes, sir, I did. That makes my recommendation so difficult."

Sir Paul calmed down.

"Perhaps it would be better for both of us if you began there."

Both men took their seats. Joy brought his mind to order and began the explanation.

"Yes sir. Here is the story I have pieced together from Magistrate Fleetwood, our Indian banker, Prince Vikram Sena, the chief Portuguese trader in Calcutta, *and* from a personal visit to an opium den." Heartened by renewed interest in Sir Paul's expression, he went on. "Opium, good quality opium, is indeed grown in India. And by tremendous coincidence, here in Bengal itself. It is called Patna Opium and is primarily consumed by the court of the Mughal *sultan* in Delhi, and by the *nawabs* and *rajas* who rule the *sultan's* domain. Some of it is exported by the Portuguese to China and to Arabia and Europe. The Portuguese in India have failed to capitalize on the immense Chinese opportunity for opium for two reasons. First, because their presence in Bengal is minor, and second, because their powerful Jesuits in the field frown on the drug trade.

"However, I believe their disadvantage is only temporary. The Portuguese have a stronger presence than ours on the west coast of India. At Bombay. Also at Surat and Goa and Cochin. From western India, another variety called Malwa Opium, is showing distinct signs of growing into an exportable commodity. The Malwa region is under hegemony of the Marathas who are in opposition to both Mughal and English, and are potential allies of Portugal. So Malwa Opium may soon enter into Portuguese hands. However, we have a temporary strategic advantage because the Portuguese do not realize the immensity of the opportunity for a very simple reason."

"And what is that?"

"They do not drink tea."

Sir Paul, deeply fascinated, muttered *"Touché!"*

"The source of opium," Joy continued, "is the poppy, a little yellow flower grown by tribal villagers on the highlands of Bihar in the northeastern reaches of Bengal province. Poppies are harvested by tribals and processed by middlemen for the opium market at Patna. The entire purchase is controlled by the Nawab of Bengal under suzerainty of the Sultan in Delhi."

"Hmmm," intoned Sir Paul. "Intriguing. Are you suggesting that we wrest the opium export trade from the Nabob and the Portuguese? Very good, very good. Now then, how do we do that?"

Joy said nothing.

"Well?"

Joy still said nothing. Sir Paul scowled.

"Well?"

Joy gritted his teeth.

"We do not, sir."

Sir Paul's lips tightened into a thin white line, but before he could say anything Joy went on, his words tumbling out in a torrent.

"Sir, I have personally seen the effect of opium on smokers. I have even smoked it myself and experienced hallucinations. I have talked to addicts who are reduced to derelicts by the intoxicant. It is terrible. Believe me sir, it is reprehensible. Inevitably every addict's tale is of slow disintegration of first the body and then the mind. They are helpless in the drug's grip. In India the quantity of the narcotic that filters down to the wretched is minimal because the Mughals control its production carefully. Much like the Chinese Emperor who controls its import into China."

"So?" The monosyllable was a rumble in Sir Paul's throat.

"So sir, I am convinced we shall unleash a deadly scourge on China if we succeed in exporting opium on the scale of the tea trade."

"You are convinced, are you?"

Sir Paul's attitude became threatening, but the demoniac images of the night had taken hold of Joy. He *had* to finish.

"Yes sir, I *am* convinced." He looked the older man full in the eyes. "I am really very sorry, sir, that I have to say this. I wish no further part in this venture."

He dropped his eyes and leaned back heavily.

There was dead silence.

Joy's mind began to wander. It was over. The two governors would throw him to the wolves. He would be sent home in disgrace. Chief Councilor Macpherson, his rival, would be delighted. When he returned to Ashford humiliated, he hoped his parents would understand that he had stood by his principles.

Sir Paul stared down at the slumped figure. He rose and began to pace the area behind Cornwallis' desk like an impatient, white-maned lion. When he spoke his voice was unexpectedly gentle.

"Morley, I came down on you rather hard then, didn't I? Let us talk about this a little differently."

Joy sat up warily, confused by the change in tone. He had expected the Governor to tear him from limb to limb. Sir Paul stopped pacing. His eyes, boring into Joy, had an almost fanatical intensity. He spoke with a resonant timbre as if addressing an assembly.

"Right, Morley, you've had your say. Now listen carefully to what *I* have to say."

He paused, collecting his thoughts.

"The human race marches on," Sir Paul began. "Civilizations rise and civilizations fall. Greece, Rome, Byzantine, Mongolia, Spain, Portugal, China, India, have all had their shining hours. Their ascent was crafted by visionaries, strong men driven to transform the unknown into grandeur. Ashoka, Alexander, Caeser, Constantine,

Hammurabi, Genghis, Prince Henry, Lao-Tze, Akbar. Men who built enduring empires and great cultures. The decay of these empires was precipitated by subsequent corrupt rulers in positions of power.

"Now then! Can Britain wrest the maritime lead established by the intrepid Columbus and the resolute Vasco?" When Joy nodded, Sir Paul asked, "How?" but without waiting for an answer he went on. "I'll tell you how. Look back to see how we've come so far. Through the valor in the ocean of our grand sea-dogs Francis Drake and Walter Raleigh, and of James Lancaster who commanded the first Company voyage and set up our first factories in Java and the Moluccas."

Sir Paul reached down and shook Joy's shoulder. "Now Morley, look up, look forward. You are one of the very few who have the capacity to do so. Tell me, who is the future of England?"

Sir Paul stopped, breathing heavily. Joy sat frozen, hypnotized, acutely aware that something so momentous was happening that it was beyond his capacity to understand.

The Governor of Canton continued in a softer voice.

"Difficult question isn't it, m'boy? So hold tightly to your chair handles and *hear this!* The future of the selfsame England of Drake, Cromwell, Newton and Shakespeare rests with *us!* You and me. Morley and Miller. Unknown, unheralded Morley and Miller. In our pairs of unpretentious hands lies the future of Britain." Joy could not breathe while the older man went on inexorably. "History awaits, Morley. Are you strong? Do you have vision? Do you have integrity? Are you durable? Can you carry the impossible, unreasonable, but necessary burden? Or are you fearful of change? There is no middle ground.

"William Pitt told me in London, '*Empire is never for the faint-hearted.*' He was right. It isn't."

Sir Paul rapidly paced the room, unmindful of the heat. Joy watched him, bewitched. What Sir Paul said appealed to everything he held dear. Everything that had enticed and driven him ever since he could remember. Everything he had been taught by the father he worshipped. He wanted to run out shouting he had seen his dream.

Then a horrendous image of a land of skeletons floated before his eyes. But Sir Paul went on before he could rationalize the disparity.

"The character of the leaders of a nation determines whether it will prosper or wither. George, long may he rule, is England's King, but, providentially, he is not her leader. Pitt is. For two centuries, seaborne commerce of the East India Company and her sister firms around the globe have led England toward ascendancy. But ascendancy is not empire. You, Morley, have discovered a market dynamic of such staggering proportions that it could lead to empire. *However...*" Sir Paul smashed his fist on the desk making Joy jump in his seat. "However! You are *not* the conscience of China. That is the business of imperial rulers of Cathay. If England does not advance on this opening, Portugal will. Portugal will capture the strategic advantage. And with it Portugal will recover its global pre-eminence. D'ye hear?" Joy nodded. "Opium *will* go to China, Morley, even if *you* refuse to take it there. It is for China to reject the drug. Not us."

Joy kept nodding. The logic was irrefutable. Sir Paul stopped pacing and looked steadily at Joy with red-rimmed eyes.

"And, Morley, if you still continue to believe you are China's conscience, *listen to this!* Have you wondered what brought warfare out of medieval times? D'ye know what changed battles from storming of castles with crossbow and ladder and defending them with hot oil? What changed them to grand encounters like the Spanish Armada? The Seven Year War? The American Mutiny? With untold lives lost? You do not? Gunpowder, man, gunpowder! Powder that makes muskets pop and cannons bang. And d'ye know who gave gunpowder to the world? China! That very China you so nobly defend. Gunpowder, a simple mixture of saltpeter and nitrate that, as long as mankind inhabits this earth, shall take innumerable millions more lives than opium can ever hope to."

Joy sat mesmerized.

"Don't you wish there was a man, say a councilor in Cathay, as high-minded as yourself? A man who wanted to prevent gunpowder from reaching 'poor' sufferers in the West? Well, strangely Morley, *there was!* The emperors of China's Song dynasty resisted the change in usage of gunpowder from fireworks to weapons for over a century because they understood its destructive power. It stayed a secret until the Arabs found out about it. And then, presto, the world had its popguns. And like gunpowder – with or without you, my friend – be assured opium will reach its victims."

Sir Paul sat down and mopped his brow. Joy stared at him, unbelieving of what had just happened, unbelieving that his own idealism was so abysmally petty on the immense canvas of global sovereignty and the inexorable march of history. The two men remained sitting silently for a long time, each lost in his own thoughts.

BOOK TWO

THE TIGER'S MOUTH

10

To Joy Morley, leaning on the starboard gunwale of *HMS Albatross*, the passing of Malacca brought on a rush of nostalgia.

During his apprenticeship at the Company's grimy London offices, Malacca had been a symbol of a new era in world history. The small coastal town epitomized the ascendancy of Portugal and the expansion of Europe into the Orient. Only two decades after Vasco da Gama rounded Cape of Good Hope at the end of the fifteenth century, Malacca was established as the first bastion of an emerging European world, led by the legendary Portuguese Governor, Afonso Albuquerque. Very soon Portugal's 'State of India' stretched from Angola to Mozambique and from Goa to Borneo and Timor. For a long time Malacca remained the crown jewel in this chain until it was eclipsed in the seventeenth century by the establishment of Macau at the portals of China. And now, thought Joy, Portugal itself would be eclipsed if Sir Paul's vision came true.

As Joy ruminated, Malacca faded astern.

Albatross and two shallow-bottomed Indian ships, *Satpura* and *Gulab,* carrying opium, were traversing the narrow strait between the Malay Peninsula and the big island of Sumatra. Here and there, little islands with rocky crags jutted upward from the sea, their pink and yellow coral reefs foaming under breakers. Thousands of aquatic birds: gulls, terns, cormorants, pelicans, nested on impossible cliffs. There were constant take-offs and landings. Joy wondered why there were no collisions in the congested air around the islands. Were there avian police in feathered uniforms on duty? The wake of the ships attracted more flurries of birds that swooped and settled in the water aft.

Joy's attention was drawn to an especially unruly commotion on a passing island. As *Albatross* drew near he made out men agitating bird life halfway up a treacherous cliff. He climbed up to the quarterdeck and picked up the glass. Squinting, he discerned four fuzzy-haired natives, sarongs tied between legs, clambering among nests on ledges on the rock face. Clouds of indignant birds milled around them. Joy could imagine their outrage. But the men paid them no heed and methodically picked up nest after nest. They tipped eggs over the cliff and stowed the nests in sacks slung on their shoulders.

Looking at the scene, Joy remembered a long troubled night when he had searched for a solution to stem the tide of silver. 'Soups made from fins of sharks and nests of sea-swifts,' Cranmer-Byng had told him and turned his world upside-down. Joy wondered if the disturbed birds were sea-swifts.

Wherever you are, little bird, when I write my memoirs, I shall remember you.

The island of nest-gatherers receded and *Albatross* plowed ahead of a freshening easterly breeze.

Five weeks had passed since *Albatross* began her voyage from Calcutta under Captain Winkley's command. Her passenger manifest listed Joy, Sir Paul, Vikram and five others. They were a congenial lot and included two clerks returning to jobs in Canton, a young bride on her way to join her merchant husband in that city, and a missionary couple on the long journey to Japan.

Albatross and her two charges had sailed from Calcutta along the silt-laden Hooghly River, picking her way through tortuous the fever-ridden marshlands of the Sunderbans mangrove delta. Prior to departure, Joy, with Sir Paul's exhortation ringing in his ears, had thrown himself into a frenzy of activity. It had been a mammoth operation to procure two shiploads of best quality opium from the Patna market even with Vikram's help in time for *Albatross's* sailing. Fortunately for the operation, Lord Cornwallis had rallied around and personally funded *Gulab* and *Satpura* for the cause.

During this busy period, Joy was dismayed by more displays of Jerome's unpleasant nature. He found the captain to be supremely arrogant and bigoted with no subtlety. His mindset was exclusively military and he detested the idea of shepherding a commercial and contraband consignment. It had taken a direct order from Cornwallis, the supreme military commander, to secure his compliance. To make matters worse, bad blood quickly developed between Jerome and

Vikram. Because of his knowledge of sources and intricacies of opium, Joy was convinced the prince was an asset and wanted him to travel to China with them. The captain on the other hand considered Vikram, despite his royalty, a 'blackie' and a heathen in British society. On sailing day, he refused Vikram access on his ship. A standoff occurred, resolved by more orders from Cornwallis and Miller. Luckily, while the captain simmered, Vikram accepted the degrading treatment with equanimity, raising him immeasurably in the eyes of Joy and Sir Paul.

From the moment they cast off from Calcutta, the contrary wind coupled with the heat and the humidity were mind-numbing. The normal run from India to China usually occurred later in the year when rain-sodden monsoon winds blew down from the Himalayas across the plains and into the sea. But the present adverse northerlies forced them to abandon the direct route down the coast of Burma and Siam. Instead they struggled southwest for two weeks following the Indian shoreline to the town of Madras where the Company maintained a large presence. Malaria and heatstroke took their toll and the ship lost eleven hands by the time they reached the town.

A brief but very welcome stop at Fort St. George in Madras allowed fresh fruit and meat and rest under nodding palms. With replenished supplies, Albatross beat eastward across the Bay of Bengal and embarked on the most uncertain part of the voyage. They threaded through the southern Nicobars toward the western tip of the long and narrow island of Sumatra. Jerome spent his days anxiously testing the wind and examining position readings on instruments on the binnacle. If they were not forced too far south, they would be able to enter the

Straits of Malacca, work round the tip of the Malay peninsula, and traverse the South China Sea to the Pearl River Estuary and Canton. If they failed, they would have to go all the way around Sumatra and their voyage would be longer by a month or more. They might be able to slip through the hostile Dutch-controlled and pirate-infested Sunda Strait between Sumatra and Java. Or, preferring prudence to valor, they might sail the entire Indian Ocean to the northwestern coast of Australia before turning north in the Celebes Sea to pick their way through the Philippines archipelago to their destination.

Their luck held.

Albatross managed to enter the Straits of Malacca, a passageway that became narrower as they approached the tip of the peninsula on the port bow. The weather became impossibly hot at their southernmost point, the island of Singapore, only a degree north of the Equator.

On the day after the encounter with nest-gatherers, Sir Paul and Joy sat fanning themselves on deck chairs in the shade of the mainmast. They were discussing the mystery of the Middle Kingdom and its Celestial Majesty, the Manchu Emperor.

Joy was intrigued by land he was about to see. He had brought aboard his chest of books, read voraciously and grilled Sir Paul about the new country. Every little thing that he learned made him look forward more to what lay ahead. Like his father, Joy was as much an explorer as a merchant and yearned for novel experiences in new and unfamiliar places. He lived to find the unknown and learn from it. His soul rejoiced as much from marble poetry of the Taj Mahal as it did from conversations with headmen of Bengali villages. In this he shared a like disposition with Sir Paul. And as the Governor of Canton articulated his own adventures over four decades, a world as different from India as India was from England, unfolded for Joy.

The first thing he learned was that China was old. China was much older than England. Older even than India. Civilization had reigned unbroken in China for thousands of years. Scholarship was worshipped to the elimination of commerce and warfare. The Middle Kingdom between Heaven and Earth, as the Chinese thought of their land, had existed through all time in supreme superiority. China considered other earthly states tributary to herself, populated by barbarians. In China, courtesy was paramount and crimes of passion nonexistent. Family and community were above the individual, any individual, even the Emperor. Faced with oppressive rulers through eons, people of China rose *en masse* every two or three hundred years to dethrone them and place other monarchs and other dynasties on the throne.

Today Sir Paul was reciting Confucian theology.

"Confucius preached five virtues," he said.

"Just five, sir?"

Sir Paul ignored the weak attempt at levity.

"He believed the five virtues constituted humanity in totality. If practiced rigidly they would make a man whole. Courtesy, magnanimity, faith, diligence and kindness. 'He who is courteous,' taught Confucius, 'is not humiliated. He who is magnanimous wins the multitude. He who is of good faith is trusted by the people. He who is diligent attains his objective. And he who is kind gets service from the people.'"

Joy digested this.

"Jolly good stuff, sir!" he assented. "We English could benefit from a dose of Confucian philosophy."

Sir Paul shook his head.

"Only if we have the mindset of the Chinese."

Joy looked at him questioningly.

"Y'see, Morley, the Chinese are complete *in their world.* This makes them impossibly content and patronizing to others. An isolated, unadventurous, and uncurious lot. Following millennia of conformity, their society is at long last being buffeted by winds of change and pressures of foreign influence. I am convinced China is easy game for hostile subjugation. Why? Because they firmly believe God has made them invincible. They cannot conceive that the outside world might not *kow-tow* to them. This is China's fatal weakness."

Joy moved to another topic.

"If they denigrate commerce, sir, how do we trade with them?"

"With great difficulty, Morley. It's a one-sided trade. We pay money to buy their wares. On their terms. In places they designate. At the times they prescribe."

"Meaning?"

"The Chinese emperor has decided to push the unwholesome business of trading with barbarians – that's us – as far away as possible from the temples of learning in Peking. Thus Canton, in southernmost China, is where we foreign devils must go. There is an all-powerful imperial representative in Canton who sets the terms of trade. He is known as the Hoppo. In Canton each foreign country deals through one, and only one, designated Chinese merchant. These merchants, called *hongs*, are collectively members of a society called the *co-hong*. Like our London trade guild. You'll see all this after we arrive. Our own *hong* is a remarkable fellow named Howqua."

"Howqua, sir? I'll remember that. But given its clandestine nature, how shall we dispose of the opium on the Indian ships?"

"Circumspectly, Morley. And, using your admirable word, clandestinely. Very clandestinely. If news we're carrying a large consignment of opium gets to the wrong ears – which essentially means *any* ears – we shall be completely undone. Our nation's trading license will be revoked. Every corsair from the China seas will be at our throats. Our cargo is a gold mine floating on a powder keg."

"So what should we do, sir?"

Sir Paul laughed heartily.

"Well now, I'm glad I found you in that swampy fort, my dear boy. A thinker *and* a man of action."

While Joy blushed under his tan, Sir Paul became serious and looked at the triangular sails of *Gulab* and *Satpura* trailing astern.

"I believe we have to take Howqua into our confidence. It will cost us dear but without him we are powerless. We have to do this carefully and extract a price for the opium. And have it offset against our tea payments."

"Who else should I know about Canton, sir?"

"Well, let's see. Irving Macardle's my number two. Our logistics man is a Chinese fellow named Liu, formally Compradore Liu. He is an employee of the Hoppo. Now that's a remarkable fellow, the Hoppo. Represents the Emperor in Canton. Oh, good morning, my dear!"

The men hurriedly got to their feet as a smiling Margaret Andrews bowed to them theatrically.

"Good *afternoon*, gentlemen. The sun there has passed its zenith. Captain's compliments. Lunch is served in the galley."

Joy beamed at Miss Andrews. The young woman, dramatically red-haired and green-eyed, was betrothed to some lucky writer in the Canton factory. She was cheerful and energetic and had a knack of making people feel at ease in her presence. She had told them she would be married the very day *Albatross* docked in Canton.

"Captain's compliments no less, Morley," said Sir Paul. "Hurry up now. Can't keep the great man waiting."

11

Alone in the bows, standing idly for hours, watching the ever-changing patterns of sky, sea and land, Prince Vikram Sena occupied himself marveling at the sights and sounds of his first sea voyage. After the two Governors had come to his rescue in Calcutta as he was being summarily put ashore by the captain, Vikram had resigned himself to *lascar*-class travel aboard *Albatross*. He was not allowed to mix with passengers and had to eat and sleep with the polyglot deckhands. With visions of ultimate wealth and power and with Buddhist tranquility, Vikram accepted his lot, regarding the irate captain and crew with aloof disinterest.

Prince Vikram had led a regimented existence. His adult life was filled with work and meditation. In the time left over from estate administration and commerce, Vikram worshipped the Buddha and studied Buddhist scripture. He found the activity-free voyage fascinating and had examined the unfamiliar people of Madras during the stopover and tried to understand their strange language, Tamil. He helped in treatment of malaria sufferers. He endeavored to fathom how the intricate rigging and innumerable sail combinations worked. He was entranced by whales and dolphins and flying fish of the Andaman Sea and the spectrum of birds off Nicobar reefs and Sumatran islands.

As the ship rounded the cape of Singapore one afternoon, a whaleboat docked briefly and handed over a mail packet. Soon thereafter, Vikram heard a shriek from the sterncastle followed by a loud wailing. Within the hour, the crew were talking about the fiancé of the woman passenger who had died of meningitis in Canton. The keening continued through the rest of the day until it died away as the sun was setting. Vikram stayed where he was, wondering how heart-breaking the news must be for the woman who had come all this way to start a new life.

Darkness fell and a strong northerly wind whipped the sails as *Albatross* changed heading and stroked untidily into a heightening South China Sea. The increased roll of the ship made it impossible to stand without holding something fixed to the deck. First Mate Fenwick issued orders for sail to be shortened. Hands climbed the rigging and adjusted fore- and mainsail. While descending, they looked down curiously at the statuesque Indian.

Hours passed. A sliver of moon went behind rain clouds and the wind howled among the yards. Four bells clanged and the first watch changed. Passengers and non-essential crew had long since gone below. Still Vikram remained on the deserted deck. He moved amidships where the rolling motion was least, unwilling to descend to the violently swinging hammock that awaited him.

Suddenly he saw a silhouette appear framed in the lamplit sterncastle opening, fifty feet from him. He made out a woman's form before she moved away from the light and became lost in the darkness.

Why would a woman come out on deck alone on a stormy night, he wondered? He recalled the scream and the sobbing and his heart beat faster. Intuitively he guessed it must be the woman whose fiancé had died. After a moment's hesitation he slowly moved aft in the direction the woman had gone, being careful to avoid tripping over hatches and coils of rope. After a while he made out a dim figure near the stern, standing by the port gunwale, looking intently out to sea. Abruptly, it stepped back from the guard-rail. Vikram knew at once what was going to happen and shouted a warning. The woman did not respond and stood clenching and unclenching her fists by her sides. He saw her chest heave and began to run. He was three yards away when she took a running start and leaped over the gunwale. With a despairing cry Vikram flew the remaining distance and grabbed frantically as she vaulted over the railing.

The next moment she was over the side, suspended in space, while, holding her by the wrists, Vikram hung half over the gunwale.

A primal cry for help burst from his lips.

"Bachao!"

He held on tenaciously and shouted again, this time in English. They were not far from the quarterdeck. The stern watch was near. But the wind howled and the sheets flapped loudly and nothing happened.

Vikram raised his head and shouted again but no one came.

He heard a moaning whimper from below and tried to stand straight to see her but could not, as he had to have the edge of the gunwale under his armpits to support Margaret's weight.

"Hold on, Memsahib!" he called down.

Vikram felt he could pull up the woman if she would grip the edge of the gunwale for a moment and relieve him of her dead weight. Only then could he get into position, grasp her under the arms, and pull her to safety.

"Memsahib! Memsahib! Hold the railing, Memsahib!"

Margaret was beyond hearing and flopped like a rag doll swinging with the roll of the ship. Vikram looked around frantically. Nobody was in sight. No one was there to help. He had to save her himself. But try as he might from his doubled-over position, he could not bodily lift her straight up and over. His arms began to hurt terribly. He screamed again and the wind whipped away his cries. He could not hold on much longer. He *had* to try something different. And it had to be now. He put his knee against the gunwale, gritted his teeth and, using every bit of strength, began to lift her up. He had raised her a foot when his strength gave out. With a sob his armpits settled back against the gunwale and he almost let go. Tears of anger, frustration and fear blurred his vision.

"Memsahib!"

It was a frenzied entreaty, but there was no response.

Suddenly, the ship rolled heavily to port on a higher than usual beam wave. The woman's body swung out, then came back and slapped sickeningly against the ship's side as *Albatross* rolled in the opposite direction.

A desperate idea came to Vikram.

He waited for the ship to roll completely back to starboard with the inert woman pressed tightly to the side. Then, as *Albatross* began her next roll to port, Vikram waited for the precise moment when the sideways motion was at its greatest and, using every ounce of muscle, he swung her out into the air. Then he pulled upward as hard as he could and jerked her inward, toward himself, as the ship began to roll back. With the rolling momentum of the ship, Margaret's body, swayed out almost horizontally, landed on the edge of the rail and Vikram, terrified he would lose her when the ship rolled back, heaved her in mightily. She slithered the rest of the way inward and collapsed on him, knocking them both to the deck. They lay there, lacerated, wasted, as drops of warm rain began to fall.

Margaret was the first to stir. She moaned, squirmed, and rolled off her savior onto the scrubbed boards.

Vikram sat up painfully, feeling his aching and bleeding forearms and armpits. He looked around. There was still no one to be seen. A lantern swung on the quarterdeck and another by the companionway hatch. He leaned forward and helped the woman sit up, resting against him.

"Memsahib!" he ventured.

She started, trembled for a moment, and was still.

"Memsahib. You are safe. Do not worry."

She moved and he felt her hands tighten around his arm, her face invisible in the darkness. After a while he felt her shoulders shake and her body jerk in spasms. She began to shiver and shake uncontrollably even though he was holding her as tightly as he could. He looked around worriedly, realizing that she was cold with shock. Where should he take her? Back to her cabin? Which *was* her cabin? Should he shout to attract Morley-sahib or someone else? What would the captain do if he saw them together? But he *had* to get her out of the rain and wind and make her warm. He got to his feet shakily. Lifting her unresponsive form, he staggered toward the overhang of the quarterdeck, wondering whether or not to carry her into the cabin area of the sterncastle. His failing strength decided this and he shakily lowered her into the dry, wind-free space between the sterncastle bulkhead and the rear gunwale. Then he settled down, supporting her weight against himself. They were sheltered by the ship's superstructure with the lantern on the quarterdeck dimly lighting their little niche. No one challenged them. The only sounds were the whine of wind, slap of sail, creak of timber. Briefly Vikram wondered whether the watch was asleep. Then he composed himself to meditate, willing his warmth to flow to her.

After an eternity Margaret moved, coughed, moaned deep in her throat, and slowly raised her head. She turned around and looked at the person supporting her. As Vikram watched, she buried her face in her hands and began to cry. Gradually, her sobs quietened and she lay back propped against the bulkhead, her eyes shut, her face ravaged. Presently her breathing became regular. Her muscles twitched spasmodically and relaxed as she slept.

The stern watch on the quarterdeck above shuffled his feet, yawned mightily, hawked and spat. His footfalls sounded as he got up to check their heading. There was another yawn and then silence.

Vikram decided not to raise the alarm and continued to sit protectively by the sleeping woman, cushioning her head from the hard planks with his arm, unmindful of his own growing numbness. An hour passed and another. The rain stopped but the wind continued strong. The sailor on watch moved about every so often but did not come down the ladder.

Margaret awoke in the hour before dawn. She stirred but stayed in the same position. Abruptly she sat up and faced Vikram for a long time, her eyes enormous and wide. Then in a low scratchy voice she said, "What shall I *do?*"

The anguished question broke something inside Vikram. A voice spoke and with a start he realized it was his own.

"Memsahib! Do not be afraid."

Whether she heard him he did not know, for at that moment there was a babble of many distant voices. They heard shouts, then a crash of breaking glass and a scream from the opposite end of the ship. The sailor above them did not awaken and the clamor subsided. Margaret and Vikram continued to sit silently, watching the receding cloudbank in the uncertain light.

Abruptly heavy footsteps rang out close to them and the glow of a lantern lessened the gloom.

"Miss Andrews!"

It was Captain Winkley's agitated voice.

"Where are you, Miss Andrews? I went to check your room."

Hastily Margaret got to her feet, looked down at Vikram for a brief moment, and turned toward the sterncastle opening.

"Oh!" gasped Jerome as she brushed past him. "There you are! Why did you go out on deck?"

Margaret did not reply and disappeared.

The footsteps came in Vikram's direction and he started up with his hand instinctively going to the sheathed knife inside his robe. The light of the lantern fell full on him before he could rise. There was a sharp intake of breath as Jerome saw him and then a mighty roar.

"Ye bloody nigger!"

Vikram drew his knife.

"Drop that!"

Jerome lashed out with a boot and the knife skittered away. Vikram wrung his injured hand and struggled to get to his feet. Another boot crashed into his ribs and knocked him on his back. Then a pistol was at his head.

"Captain! No!"

Margaret threw herself at Jerome, trying to deflect the pistol. The captain staggered, recovered, and pushed her away roughly. His furious face was beetroot red and his cheeks were puffed out.

"I'll kill the bastard!"

The tousled head of the watch showed furtively from the

quarterdeck.

"No!" screamed Margaret.

"The goddamn nigger! Pull a knife on a navy officer, will ye? I'll shoot him like a dog!"

There was a click as the pistol's safety catch came off.

"No, Captain. I'll...I'll tell Sir Paul! He's his friend."

Jerome looked around. His chest was heaving with fury but the pistol stayed steady.

"You'll tell, will ye?" he snarled. "Go ahead. This is my ship. I won't have ye hobnobbing with niggers. I'll deal with you in just a moment after I..."

He turned back to Vikram.

"He saved my life!"

Startled, Jerome lowered his pistol and Vikram got to his feet. For a minute the three stood in a frozen tableau while the watch looked down breathlessly. Then Jerome rounded on Margaret and a crafty look came into his rugged visage.

"All right, off to your cabin, my lady. Your blasted prince lives. But he'll pay."

When Margaret hesitated, Jerome grabbed her shoulder with an oath and pushed her inside the sterncastle.

An hour later from the open window of her cabin, her heart in her mouth, her fists sore from beating on a locked door, Margaret watched as a lowered jolly boat fell away astern. In it were two men. Even from the distance she could make out one of them as her rescuer.

She reeled back with a strangled cry and fainted dead away.

12

"*Deck there! Lights to starboard!*"

A seaman perched high on furled yards of the foremast, called excitedly down to the deck of *Albatross*.

"*Lights to starboard. Two o'clock on the starboard bow!*"

It was five days since Prince Vikram was offloaded into the South China Sea.

When he first heard the news, Joy had had a titanic row with the captain and only Jerome's stature as master of the ship prevented Joy from physically assaulting him. And then an absolutely livid Sir Paul ordered him to come about to search for the prince. When Jerome still did not comply, Sir Paul grabbed his lapel and read him the riot act. He would be summarily relieved of his command and his commission, and would be chained in the brig for the rest of the voyage. Captain Winkley, in all his years at sea, had never been ordered to do anything by a civilian or a passenger. A test of temperament ensued. Finally, Jerome dropped his gaze.

The sails were quartered and *Albatross* back-tacked to the area where Vikram had been cast off. They searched for hours in widening circles, but no trace of boat or survivors were found. The search was called off at nightfall.

The next day they continued on to Canton.

Margaret was not seen on deck again.

ž

"Deck there! Lights to starboard at two o'clock!"

Midshipman Harry Newbond, chief of the evening watch, heaved a sigh of relief and scanned the horizon through his glass.

They had arrived in China!

Albatross was making slow headway in darkness under mizzen sail in anticipation of landfall. The convoy would normally heave-to at dusk. But, as the light was fading a Chinese junk had drawn alongside, redolent with fragrance of ginger and, based on its information, Jerome had ordered an extra hour's sailing.

Nineteen-year-old and well-built, Newbond hoped the lights spotted by the masthead did not belong to another group of junks. He squinted through his glass and after a few moments saw the lights himself. He whistled in surprise as more flickering points entered his field of vision. Soon an entire row of lights twinkled, jumped, and swayed like fairy spangles.

"What in hell?" he asked of nobody in particular. But he had been ordered to look out for lights and these *were* lights. He closed the glass with a snap and leaving his position in the bows, rapidly walked aft and climbed the ladder to the quarterdeck.

Captain Winkley, hands clasped behind his back, turned from a conversation with his first mate. He nodded curtly as the young midshipman touched his cap.

"Permission to report sighting, Cap'n."

"Go ahead, Mr. Newbond."

"String of lights at two o'clock, sir. I'd own they be three miles ahead. Ne'er seen the likes of them afore."

Jerome opened his own glass and looked in the direction indicated. He seemed satisfied by what he saw.

"Thank you, Midshipman. Mr. Fenwick!"

"Aye aye, sir!" replied Mickey Fenwick, first mate of *Albatross*, a leathery veteran of the Company's flag for over three decades.

"Order all ships to heave-to, Mr. Fenwick. An extra tot of rum for the hands, if you please. And signal landfall to the Indian ships."

"Aye, aye, sir!"

Earlier that day, nearness of land was first indicated by appearance of fruit flies and dragonflies. A warm, indolent aroma of vegetation was their next indication. Later, three fast-boats of the Hoppo's patrol drew alongside while crew and passengers crowded the railing. A black-robed inspector came aboard and greeted Sir Paul with a great show of humor. From the background Joy studied his first official representative, his very first *mandarin* from the land of Cathay.

The visitor seemed not to notice the attention he was getting and jovially examined bills of lading – the cargo of *Gulab* and *Satpura* had been declared high-quality silk – and offered to take messages to Canton. Sir Paul accepted and penned quick letters to Macardle and Howqua. Moments later, the Chinese boats skipped away.

Just before nightfall a pair of magpies alighted on the bowsprit. Hands peered hopefully into the gloom, but when the seas disappeared in darkness they were still out of sight of land. The excitement waned while the ship plowed on, until the galvanizing call of the lookout.

After giving the order to heave-to, Jerome turned around, and stopped abruptly. The midshipman was still there.

"Yes Mr. Newbond?"

"B...begging yer pardon, sir..." began Newbond, then his courage failed.

"Well?"

"Begging yer pardon, sir. I dinna mean to intrude, sir..."

"Great Neptune, Midshipman! Stop driveling and speak up!"

"Yes sir. Sorry sir. I was jus' wondering about them lights, sir."

Jerome frowned and Newbond quaked.

The captain's first reaction was to tell the young man off. It was unheard of for a lowly midshipman to ask a question of his captain, let alone remain in his presence unordered. Then his brow cleared. For all his intolerance, Jerome was a good naval leader. Newbond had distinguished himself on the voyage and marshaled his gun crew efficiently. He must be intensely curious to risk the wrath of the master. It showed courage and a healthy thirst for knowledge, traits necessary in the intense competition belowdecks.

"Those lights, Mr. Newbond," explained Jerome, "are oil lanterns. They line the sandbar at the entrance to the Pearl River and guide ships in. Chinese pilots have them set up to indicate dangerous sand shoals." He peered at Newbond to see if he was following. "Mr. Newbond, do you know what the river entrance is called?"

"Canna say I do, sir."

"It's called the Boca Tigris, meaning 'Tiger's Mouth' in Portuguese. And do you know what's in the Tiger's Mouth?"

"Yes, sir. Leastways I think so, sir. That Chiny city, Canton's the name. Up the Pearl River, ain't it? Like Calcutta's up the Hooghly."

"Quite correct, Midshipman. Now off you go."

Newbond saluted and slithered down the ladder. He noticed Joy standing at the gunwale and went over.

"Evening, sir."

Joy turned and smiled. A friendship had developed between the two during the voyage. It was the reverse of Joy's relationship with Sir Paul. Here Joy was teacher and young Newbond the student. Joy had found in Newbond a bright mind, a veritable sponge for information.

"Midshipman! Glad you're here. Look now. Away east to port. Can you see that light blinking faintly? You do? Can you tell me what it is?"

"Macau, sir?"

"Yes it is. Your geography's first-rate, young Newbond. That's the Guia lighthouse in Macau. The beacon for Jesuits in the Orient."

"Sir?"

"This place has history, man. History soaked with more blood of Christians than fell in the Holy Land during all the Crusades. Imagine that for a moment."

Newbond imagined that and waited for more.

"For the last two hundred years, Newbond, Japan and China have beheaded untold hundreds of Catholic priests. Yet, legions of Loyola's Society of Jesus still follow St Francis Xavier into China. Mostly to horrible deaths. They all begin their journey inland through the Macau you see there. Well, young Newbond? Any questions?"

"No, sir! Leastways not now, sir. Thankee kindly."

A spontaneous smile got through Newbond's control before he disappeared.

A little later, Jerome called for his first mate.

"Pass the word to the other ships, Mr. Fenwick, if you please. We shall make for Macau under reduced sail on the morning tide."

Fenwick debated whether to signal this important information to the Indian ships and decided against it. The lascars were notorious for misinterpreting light signals and semaphores, even assuming they were awake enough to notice them in the first place.

"Mr. Newbond!"

The young midshipman reappeared and touched his hat. Fenwick gave him quick directions and in a few minutes Newbond was being rowed across in a whaleboat to *Gulab.*

13

Five hundred miles east of *Albatross's* position, in the ancient kingdom of Annam, decades of upheaval had reached a climax.

It had begun in a small way.

Three brothers from a nondescript village called Tay Son formed a small band of desperadoes, rebelling against heavy taxes and corruption, and captured the provincial town of Bin Dinh. Against all odds, their gains grew as the brothers defeated the Nguyen chieftains of Hue in the south and Trinh leaders of Hanoi to the north. In quick succession, Saigon, Old Hue and Hanoi came under Tay Son dominance. Chinese armies, sent to bolster the fallen Annamese monarchies, were defeated. Finally, the Ch'ien Lung Emperor of China, recognizing that the Tay Son had become masters of their country, invested the eldest brother as King of Annam.

How could three impoverished brothers become rulers of a

country the size of Annam?

A key reason was the active support of a fierce and opportunistic confederation that habitually sensed the wind and moved with it: the league of pirates that preyed on a huge stretch of coastline encompassing Malaya, Annam, and south China which included the rich ports of Johor, Da Nang, Macau, Canton, and Amoy.

The leader of the pirate confederation was a small, wispy-bearded man named Wu, a former pearl diver from the cliffs of Hainan island. No one knew his given name. After several explosive forays in the service of the King of Annam, he earned the nickname of *Cha-tan* which in Cantonese means 'bombshell'. As his fame grew, the pirate chief came to be known universally as Wu Cha-tan or Bombshell Wu.

ॐ

Early on a sunny morning, Wu was wrestling with a difficult problem. As he was wont when in deep thought, he fingered the hammerhead shark's tooth that hung round his neck on a string. His brows were wrinkled, his feral features were pinched more than usual as he tried to decide on a course of action never before contemplated by the corsairs of Indochina: action against a barbarian ship.

Chiang-p'ing, Wu's headquarters village, was situated two miles up a river that flowed into Annam's Ha Long Bay. The village straddled an invisible line drawn by mandarins in faraway Peking and Hue to demarcate their countries, a line that pirates recognized only when fleeing from one government's forces or the other's. Nestled behind myriad islands of the Annamese coastline, Chiang-p'ing lay innocuously but strategically on the shipping lane that connected Canton with Hanoi.

Last night, just outside the narrow strait between Lei-chou Peninsula and the big island of Hainan, Wu's marauding fleet had come across a convoy of ocean-going junks carrying a fortune in Sumatran rhino horn and Siamese ivory. The pirates fell upon the defenseless craft and slaughtered the cowering traders. On one of the junks they came upon a very unusual creature. It resembled a human being. But it was bigger than a normal human being and made guttural noises like an animal. Its skin was very dark. Its head and face and chest had matted black hair like a monkey's. On looking closer, the pirates concluded it *was* a human being. But none among them had seen anything like it. Its eyes were large and round like a woman's. However, it was evident since it wore no clothes, the creature was male. The half-man half-beast was covered with burns and bruises and it smelt vile. It lay on its back on the bottom of the boat with eyes cast up to the sky. Sometimes its body jerked fitfully and it made harsh sounds during which it clasped and unclasped its hands. The pirates spat into the sea and debated whether to throw the creature over the side. Then the leader of the raiding party suggested that Honorable Wu might be interested in keeping it in a cage or selling it as a curiosity to a nobleman. His companions agreed there was a bonus earning possibility here and went to look for other spoils.

On another junk, the raiders found a heavily pock-marked captive dressed in outlandish clothes. Upon questioning him they learned he was a Chinese sailor and had been set adrift by a barbarian ship and picked up, parched and sun-scorched, by the traders. In Cantonese, the pirates asked the scarred man if the strange creature was in any way associated with the barbarians.

"Which creature?" the Chinese asked.

"The black subhuman with the big *yang* and ox-like hair who smells of offal."

"Oh, *that* creature! It is a man. He was on the barbarian ship. He ran afoul of the barbarian warlord and was put overboard with me."

"What sort of man is he?" one pirate asked.

"He is a prince."

At this the pirates chorused their incredulity and cast outraged looks at the boat that contained the object of the conversation. A prince? Their sense of dignity and order was violated.

"He says he comes from Meng Chia La," continued the pock-marked man. "The land the barbarians call Bengal. I do not understand his language. Even when he attempts to speak the tongue of the barbarians I can barely comprehend." He paused and added, "He is mad!"

The listeners nodded in unison for it had to be so. What other explanation could be there for the impossible appearance and gross nudity of the creature. They gave the Chinese sailor some cooked rice and fish in a banana-leaf. Then one of them asked, "Why does the barbarian say he is a prince?"

The other pirates looked at the speaker irritably.

"Feng Sheng-chi," said one. "Is the tiger not fierce? Does it not go about naked? And is it not the king of the jungle?"

But Feng Sheng-chi would not be diverted. He was brighter than the others and more observant. The alien apparition interested him and he repeated his question.

"I do not know *why* he says mad things, *heya,*" answered the pock-marked man. "I only know he *is* mad. On our little boat he first wept like a girl." The others spat. "Then he took oars and rowed like a maniac and tried to catch the departing barbarian ship with big sails. When the ship disappeared, he raved and shouted. I was afraid he would fall into the sea. That is if he did not capsize us with his dancing. Then he noticed me and ordered me to pull for the ship." The speaker's scarred face wrinkled in outrage. "Imagine me, Tau-pei, ordered about by a lowly Meng Chia devil. Of course I refused."

The ugly face of Tau-pei warped into a grotesque grin.

"Hei wang-zi tried to reason with me," he said using the description, *hei wang-zi* or dark prince, when he referred to Vikram. "It was horrible. He said he was a prince from India. He insisted that the barbarian ship carried a precious cargo from his land. This I believe, O Lords. From the beginning of our journey to Canton I have suspected this. There was much secrecy on board. The dog-offal, red-headed devil barbarians did not tell us what the cargo was. They kept us ashore until the ships were fully loaded. After we came aboard we were ordered to stay below and the hatches were padlocked until we sailed. There was bad blood between Hei wang-zi and the warlord of the barbarian ship. And..." Tau-pei waved his chopsticks dramatically, "...Hei wang-zi trifled with a red devil female. That is why the warlord dropped him into the sea."

At this Vikram's standing among the pirates improved by several degrees. They regarded him with renewed interest while Tau-pei dug into rice and continued his narrative.

"After his voice failed from all the screaming, Hei wang-zi fell to the bottom of the boat. He refused to talk and lost all interest in life. As you see him now."

"What was the cargo?" Feng Sheng-chi asked.

"I do not know, Lord. The barbarians would not tell us on the ship. And anyway the ship has gone. So what good is it knowing about the cargo? Good riddance I say. *Eee-yah!* It had more big guns and devil soldiers than the Hoppo has in Canton."

The pirates contemplated this fact and asked for more information about the ship. As they prepared for the trip to Chiang-p'ing they thought about how much they could achieve if they had a ship like *Albatross* and her guns.

Feng Sheng-chi had another thought.

"Did Hei wang-zi go about naked on the barbarian ship?"

Tau-pei cackled in remembrance.

"No, Lord. He wore clothes. Outlandish clothes but of very good quality. Expensive clothes. Silk. The trader pigs fought over him and tore his clothes away in their covetous frenzy. They kept him alive in the hope of selling him as a novel slave in Canton."

The listeners nodded.

The traders on the captured boats had been Punti tribesmen from Canton. The avarice of the Punti was well-known in the Pearl

River delta and slavery was rife along the Cochin-china coast. Vikram's ill-treatment at the hands of Punti traders made him more acceptable to his present captors who were Tanka fishermen turned privateers who despised the Punti.

The talk of the strange foreigner and intriguing cargo had absorbed the men's attention. Suddenly there was a shout of alarm. A man pointed to the eastern horizon and everyone saw, a long distance away, white sails above a high prow gleaming in the setting sun.

"*Ai-eeeee-ahhh!*" screamed Tau-pei. "It is the barbarian ship! It returns for Hei wang-zi. Its guns will kill us all!"

The description of *Albatross*'s armament was fresh in the pirates' minds. With one accord they raised sail and melted into Kuingchow Strait.

For Vikram, memories of the hours after his precipitous departure from *Albatross* were hazy. He remembered the rapid succession of events as if he was a bystander: the suicide attempt of the English lady and her agonizing rescue, the time he had spent with her behind the quarterdeck, the captain's sudden and belligerent appearance, the knife, the pistol, the kick in the ribs, Margaret saving *his* life, incarceration in a roach-filled brig. When three British sailors came to take him from the brig he had struggled desperately, but a blow to the head knocked him unconsciousness. He recovered in a tiny boat as *Albatross* was floating away, haloed by the rising sun.

As he regained consciousness, it took several moments for the awesome implications to sink in.

He was adrift in the open sea. A cork, bobbing in an immensity of sea and sky, a million miles from anywhere. His world came crashing down. His mind snapped and he collapsed into a welter of anguish. He was lost. How would he get back to the ship? How could he get home? What could he do? He groaned and cried and tore his hair. Suddenly it dawned on him that with every passing moment the ship was getting further away. He looked up and saw *Albatross* had become tiny against the vast horizon. He grabbed an oar and frantically paddled the boat, making it slew around in a circle. Realizing his error, he fitted both oars into rowlocks and pulled as hard as he could toward the ship until he collapsed from exhaustion. Then rage hit him. He stood up and raved at the injustice of it all. He raved at his helplessness. He raved at the captain's cruelty. Then he began to plead. He implored the Captain-sahib to come back for him. He promised the Captain-sahib he would leave the Memsahib alone. He beseeched Morley-sahib and the *Laat*-sahib to rescue him. He promised to take all sahibs to the tree under which the Buddha attained enlightenment. Nothing happened. Slowly he sank to the bottom of the boat, his shoulders shaking in abject misery. After he knew not how long, he felt someone prodding him and sat up in consternation. Astonished, he realized for the first time he was not alone on the boat. He stared bemusedly at his companion's bizarre features: the grinning eyes, the wide nose, the countless smallpox craters.

"*Kay tumi?*" he demanded in Bengali. Who are you?

"*Nǐ zai zuo shenme?*" the man replied in Cantonese. What are you doing?

Vikram had never spoken to a Chinese person before. Distractedly, he turned back to the ship but could see nothing against the horizon. *Albatross* was gone. A gigantic sense of loss came over him, a feeling so strong it hurt his chest. He was in the middle of an ocean in a small boat with a strange man. Which way should he go? Which way was land? What was *on* land? The bleakness of his situation paralyzed him.

Tau-pei watched him curiously.

"*Nǐ shì shuí?*" he said. Who are you?

Vikram, on the verge of complete panic, stared at Tau-pei. Who *was* this man? Why was he here? A thought struck him. Perhaps the Chinese man was a guide assigned to take him somewhere. Vikram was overcome by remorse. He had misjudged the Captain-sahib. Perhaps they were not far from shore.

"Who are you?" he asked with wild hope, this time in English.

Tau-pei understood this and a big smile suffused his face. In spite of his distress and the man's bizarre appearance, Vikram smiled back hesitantly. Tau-pei jabbed himself in the chest.

"*Ngoh hai Tau-pei!*"

Vikram understood. With communication established, they continued in an innovative patois. Vikram gathered that Tau-pei was a sailor and a chronic trouble-maker who hated and habitually needled the ship's officers. His favorite target was tyrannical Bos'n Kelsey who was especially brutal and apelike. Tau-pei had been thrown in the brig on three occasions during the voyage. At dawn today he had refused being rousted out of his hummock for artillery drill. He proudly repeated to Vikram the profanities he had used against his tormentors. Going for impossible glory, Tau-pei relieved a gunner of a bottle of rum and brought it down on the Bos'n's head. A near riot resulted with white and Chinese seamen shouting in anger, about to go at each other with knives and bottles when Captain Winkley appeared. Through sheer force of personality and lungpower, Jerome averted a major brawl and Tau-pei was offloaded with Vikram.

In the end, considering what could have happened, Vikram and Tau-pei were lucky. The next day, with night clouds gone, they suffered through a day of dehydrating sun before a flotilla of seagoing junks came upon them. It seemed to Vikram the world was empty at one moment and full of quarter-circle sails the next. Lines of round faces, male and female, under bamboo-hats, stared at him as the twin-masted vessels came closer. The people pointed and jabbered excitedly. Vikram regarded them dubiously. Then the first junk came alongside and four bamboo-hatted men deftly crossed over. They made straight for the Indian prince and fell on him in a screaming clawing frenzy. The boat rocked violently. Vikram, without his knife, hit out, knocked one man overboard, and retreated as far as he could. But he was quickly overpowered. Tau-pei backed away to the opposite end of the boat. Within moments Vikram's clothes were pulled off. When they let him go, he was bleeding and scratched. Shocked by the suddenness of the violence, Vikram tried to cover his nakedness with his hands and withdrew into himself in mortification. There was a violent interrogation of Tau-pei and then the traders turned back to Vikram. A big argument among the aggressors developed after which he was bodily lifted from *Albatross's* little jolly boat and transferred to a junk.

The following hours were blank. The subsequent capture of the Punti traders by Wu's pirates and the ensuing rape and murder had not registered on him. He came alive when a searing pain shot through his shoulder as someone shook him. He pulled away and opened his eyes. A Chinese man was holding a leather bag and a black cloth out to him. The bag dripped water. Drops fell on his chest. The effect was so supremely blissful that Vikram reflexively snatched the bag away, drank three large gulps and poured water on his head and chest and over his burnt body. Then he drank some more and poured more water on himself. Within seconds the liquid on his skin was absorbed and his body was bone-dry.

Feng Sheng-chi poured more water onto a cloth and rubbed Vikram's back with it. Vikram screamed as the scorched skin peeled away in scales.

"Hai! Hai!" exclaimed Feng.

He changed tactics, wetted and wrung out the cloth on the suffering prisoner.

Vikram's sanity returned.

He got to his feet shakily. Realizing that the wet black cloth was a set of drawstring pants, he snatched it from Feng and put them on. Even its minutest contact with his hypersensitive skin hurt. He rolled up the legs as high as he could. Then he noticed it was daytime. They were in a large junk at sea. All around were Chinese-looking men, all watching him intently. Among the men he recognized Tau-pei. Giving up the effort to make sense of his surroundings he sank back and closed his eyes. Soon exhaustion overcame anxiety and, crouched on a thwart with his forehead braced against the gunwale, he fell into a deep sleep.

And so, when *Albatross* reappeared and the pirates fled precipitously, Vikram was spared further distress.

While Vikram slept, Feng Sheng-chi thought.

The pirate fleet had sailed close to land and was tied up for the night among many fishing boats typical of Annamese coastal villages. Cooking fires were lit on board. Rice was boiled and eaten with dried fish. When snores of sleeping men blended with the growl of waves, Feng stared into the falling darkness and reviewed the day's events.

Feng Sheng-chi, like his colleagues, was from the Tanka clan, a dispossessed, landless, fishing community of floating villages along the long coast of southern China, living lives governed by shifting monsoon winds and migratory shoals of fish. Feng's childhood home had been a small boat where he lived with his parents. Unlike most Chinese, the Tanka did not dwell in large lineal families. They could not. Life was too perilous for more than two generations to exist at once. Typhoon, famine, Punti oppression, official persecution, lack of land and means, left the Tanka at the lowest stratum of China's coastal populace. A rich Tanka owned at best two junks and employed twenty people. A small natural disaster was enough to put a Tanka beyond the pale of honest livelihood and turn him to crime.

Feng was an orphan and atypical because he had been attracted, not driven to piracy. He was a natural fighter amid the forty thousand boat people of the Pearl River. As long as Feng could remember, ethnic rivalry between native Punti, migrant Hakka, and riverine Tanka, was continuous and vicious. While Canton prospered as the single port where barbarians could trade, Tankas were the worst sufferers. The city grew rapidly. Before long the cultivated land around it failed to support the city's exploding population and people were pushed into the river. Feng's water-world was buffeted by interlopers. Farmers, artisans, salt-gatherers came into conflict with boat people.

For most Chinese, childhood is a loved and protected haven. No so for little Feng. From his earliest memory, he and his parents ran errands for a pittance, stealing and cajoling for food, starving when there was none. When he was eight, his parents were horribly tortured and killed in a battle of retribution with the Punti. And so, at that tender but world-wise age, little Feng joined a brotherhood called the Kuan-yin Tui. This was a triad that, while worshipping a Buddhist goddess of mercy, was the most active defense force of the Cantonese Tanka. Little Feng's knowledge of the violence-infested lanes of floating villages made him well suited to delivering messages to members of the sect. He was small and elusive, an invisible urchin, dependable and innovative in ways to avoid the enemy. And he never forgot his parents' murder. As he grew he trained Tanka youth who did things for him, terrible things. Presently the Punti came to fear a new demon, a man they called Feng Sheng-chi or Angry Feng. By standards of a shockingly short-lived society, Angry Feng would have his throat slit before long, had he not met Bombshell Wu.

When Feng was a battle-scarred fifteen-year-old veteran, his triad chieftain, Tat Au-yong, told him Tay Son rebels of Annam were recruiting Chinese mercenaries for their final thrust into Hanoi. Feng found this very surprising. Why should anyone pay for what he did just to survive? But the man before him was his mentor, his protector, and adopted elder brother. When Honorable Au-yong spoke, everyone listened. Au-yong told Feng that the infamous Wu Cha-tan was in residence on Lan Tao island near Canton and his band of pirates was on the verge of winning the battle against King Le of Hanoi. Feng listened with his eyes courteously downcast but his heart on fire. That afternoon he boarded a sampan for Lan Tao.

The meeting between the wizened pirate and stringy gangster occurred on the sands of a hidden cove. Later it was said that the tempestuous father had on that day found a turbulent son.

Through simple words and gestures and Tau-pei's shaky translation, Vikram and Feng managed to learn something of each other. Vikram was told that his captors were pirates of the south China coast and that he was about to meet their great king. Soon the attitude of his captors ceased to worry Vikram. They were contemptuous. They snapped irritable comments when he was near and treated him like a diseased dog. But they did not physically harm him.

One evening, during the run to Chiang-p'ing base, Feng probed Vikram about the barbarian ship and its important cargo. As soon as Tau-pei translated the request Vikram was on guard.

"Which important cargo?" he hedged.

"Impo'tant ca'go on big red devil ship go Canton," said Tau-pei.

Vikram was dismayed. Who had told Feng the cargo was important? Vikram did not want *Albatross* to attract attention. Especially from pirates! Feng's face was inscrutable, but Vikram knew he was being studied closely. How much did the brainless Chinese sailor know about the opium? How much had he told the pirates? Whose side was he on? He looked at his scarred face and decided it did not matter. Tau-pei would sell his children for a coin.

"Oh, *that* cargo! It is valuable. Very valuable."

"What in ca'go, *heya?*"

"Silk."

"Si'k, *heya?*"

"Yes, silk. A new quality of silk for the Chinese people. From Murshidabad. In Bengal. Near my home. Silk from Bengal is best in the world."

This longish explanation appeared to satisfy Feng and he changed topics.

"You are a prince?" he wanted to know.

"Yes."

"Prince from where?"

"Rajmahal. In Bengal also."

"What is Bengal like?"

Even in a hostile world among ferocious people who had torn away every shred of his dignity, Vikram had to tell his glittering family legend complete with 12th century warring kings, Muhammed-bin-Khalji and Laxman Sena, whose names were destroyed by Tau-pei in the telling.

When night fell and his captors were asleep, Vikram stared up at a luminous sky hung with brilliant stars and wondered whether the woman whose life he had saved was looking at the same dazzling display. Though aware they were approaching the pirate lair, he knew he was lucky to be alive. Which was all he wanted. A stoic determination had set in him to live out each day with the hope that somehow he would return to his people.

The pirate flotilla weaved its way through a muddle of coastal islands and sailed into a beautiful bay. Vikram looked around in awe at dramatic limestone outcrops that jutted from azure water. Then they carefully entered the mouth of a river that was hidden by overhanging foliage. After a while the river widened and twisted and turned between high banks that were thick with trees and shrubs. Then the vegetation opened out and their flotilla was surrounded by a mass of boats of various shapes and sizes.

They had reached their destination.

Vikram followed his new friend and tried to make sense of this alien world. Each boat housed a family and was also a place of business. Incongruously, chickens scampered on the boats while cats stalked them. People on view were elderly men, women and children who stared at him with unblinking intensity. Though he was of medium height in his own country, Vikram was tall in comparison to the Annamese. And dark while they were fair. His large eyes, chiseled features, bushy beard and thick, long, curly hair were in stark contrast to their uniform orientalness, lack of facial hair, shaven heads, and braided queues. Vikram felt a freak. *And no wonder,* he told himself. A Chinese visitor in Rajmahal, say Tau-pei, would be a public spectacle. With his peeling skin and bruises and scars, he must be quite a sight.

It was mealtime.

People were eating or feeding children rice, vegetables and fish using the eating sticks he had grown to recognize on the pirates' boat. The air was aromatic with the fragrance of sesame oil, ginger and soya. Vikram could not remember when he had eaten last and felt ravenously hungry.

Skipping and scrambling from boat to boat behind Feng, he finally came aboard a large black-hulled, double-masted, pennant-decked junk. Without question it was the flagship. Several men in black trousers sat on deck in a circle, eating from bowls. They jumped to their feet on seeing the outlandish visitor. Feng spoke rapidly to a man who hurried inside the boat's small shack. Vikram wondered what he should do. He looked around and was startled to see that behind him, Tau-pei was shaking like a leaf.

A reedy unsmiling man with a thin beard emerged from the shack. He was dressed like his people with black pantaloons as his only garment. His face was pinched and sinister. The big tooth around his neck added malevolence to his bearing.

Suddenly Vikram realized that he was the only man standing. Around him, everyone had dropped to their knees in front of the chief, their foreheads touching the deck. Suddenly, Wu screamed out a torrent of words in a high falsetto. Startled, everyone looked up and gasped when they realized Vikram was not kowtowing. Feng jumped up and tried to pull him down to his knees. When Vikram resisted, two of Wu's men violently pushed him to the deck and banged his forehead on the boards.

There was a silence.

In his position of subjugation, his eyes an inch from splinters in the wood, Vikram's mind went completely blank. He watched a drop of blood fall from his forehead to the board, flatten itself, spread into a dark stain. Then another drop fell on the stain. And another.

Abruptly he was hauled to his feet.

Vikram listened without comprehending while Feng gave Wu what must be an account of their trip. Every now and then Feng would clasp his hands together, raise them above his head and bow deeply as though hinged at the waist. The chief nodded and grunted in satisfaction as he looked across to where the captured Punti junks were tied. Vikram felt warm blood run down to his eyes and tried to blink it away. Something made him refuse to wipe it with his hands. He stood as straight and as disdainfully as he could. From Feng's manner of speaking and the way he was being pointed at, Vikram understood that Feng had got to the part that concerned him. Wu transferred his attention to Vikram and shouted an impatient order. One of his men flourished a wet cloth with which he reached up and roughly wiped the blood from Vikram's face. Feng turned sideways and nodded, indicating he should come forward.

Vikram did not move.

Wu looked him up and down and yelled at him. Vikram waited for Tau-pei to translate but nothing happened. Wu screamed again, this time at something behind Vikram's back. He turned and saw Tau-pei groveling helplessly on the deck. In his terror the unfortunate man had quite forgotten *pigdin* English. A pirate pulled him to his feet and shook him. At last Tau-pei was able to interpret.

"This ca'go? What is it?"

Though expecting the question, Vikram's heart beat painfully.

"Silk," he said. This was translated to *sichou.*

There was a hurried conversation during which the quaking Tau-pei was interrogated and Vikram watched in apprehension. Then Tau-pei faced him and spoke laboriously.

"Tau-pei listen along ear belong him. Listen big voice along number one shiplord belong red devil ship. Shiplord, him say ship he carry impo'tant ca'go for Guangzhou."

This speech took time and two repetitions to get the point across. Vikram knew that Guangzhou was the local name for Canton.

"Yes," he agreed. "Important cargo. Silk cargo. Good silk."

Tau-pei translated and Wu flew into a rage, bawling at Vikram in his jarring voice.

"No he can be silk," Tau-pei quavered. "Number one shiplord, him say Hoppo, him no likee this impo'tant ca'go. Why Hoppo no likee silk, *heya?* What is ca'go, never mind?"

When Vikram insisted the cargo was silk, Wu lost his temper and screamed at his men deliriously. They closed in on Vikram who hit out and sent two spinning. But it was no use. He was dragged struggling and fighting to the mast. His hands were tied together and in minutes he hung by trussed wrists from the yardarm. His feet dangled inches above the deck.

The rest was a blur.

The first blow landed between his exposed and burnt shoulder blades, making a sound like a horse stepping in a puddle. His anguished scream sent the gulls squealing.

Wu screeched at his victim.

"Shuo!"

The blow from a rod of braided rattan broke and tore into the already chafed skin of Vikram's back. The suddenness, indignity and impossibility of what was happening made the shock of the blow fill him with disbelief. It could *not* be happening to *him!* He was a Sena. A prince of the famous land of Rajmahal. But it *was* happening. The second blow landed. The pain was infinitely worse than anything he had ever imagined. Every nerve-end in his body, from his tied fingertips to his hanging toes, cried out in agony.

Wu screamed again.

"Shuo!"

What was did the madman mean by *shuo*?

Tau-pei's lurid face floated into Vikram's misting vision.

"Hei wang-zi! *Shuo!* Say! Say what is ca'go?"

Panic-stricken, Vikram clamped his teeth shut and desperately looked for Feng. He whimpered an entreaty to the only man who had been kind to him. But he could not see Feng.

The third blow landed.

"Bachao!"

The cry for help was torn from his core by the exquisite shock. He swung defenseless from the yard while earth, trees, people, boats spun around him. His body throbbed. At the next blow he lost control of his bladder. His tormentor's savage face faded in and out of focus with red and purple colors. Another blow and his body jerked away.

"Ahhhhhhhh!"

Tears sprung from his eyes as the scream turned into a wail. It was too much. He could not stand it. It was too much. But no! He would not. He would not tell. He would not sacrifice his friends. He would not let them near her.

Another blow.

The cry died in his chest.

It was too much.

He felt consciousness slipping away.

"Shuo!" howled Bombshell Wu.

After the next blow Vikram told him.

The moment of Vikram's capitulation had a remarkable effect on Wu. He did not at first understand the English word and his victim suffered two further blows before he cried out so loudly that all of Chiang-p'ing heard.

"Opium! The ship has opium! Opium! Opium!" And then in Bengali, with all the venom wrenched from his abused soul, "Take the opium and taste cannon, you fornicating son of stinking swine!"

At this point Wu and his men realized they had a confession but had not understood it. But Tau-pei had. The pirates were astounded by his exclamation.

"Aaah-eee-aaah!" cried out Tau-pei. *"Yapian! Yapian!"*

Tau-pei used the Cantonese word for opium, then fervently wished he hadn't! Wu froze, gasped, swallowed, choked, and had a coughing fit. He glared for a moment at the slumped prince who was being lowered from the mast and then rounded on Tau-pei with his face twisted in an extra-feral snarl.

"Opium, dog-dirt? The barbarian ship carries opium?"

Tau-pei fell down and almost died of fright. Prostrate on the boards, he nodded his head pitifully.

"And the barbarian ship is sailing for Guangzhou?"

Tau-pei nodded again.

Bombshell Wu did not miss a beat.

"Attack boats ready! Out of the river and along the bayshore."

His men scrambled.

Even in his traumatized state Vikram recalled he had concealed the fact the Indian ships, not *Albatross*, carried opium. He felt confident *Albatross* could repulse any attack mounted by the pirates.

Then the suffering took its toll and he fainted dead away.

14

The attack on *Albatross* came at dawn.

Four sampans, concealed by swirling fog, closed on the clipper as she swung under anchor in the Tiger's Mouth.

The pirates climbed hand over hand up the fore and aft anchor chains. Their chests and legs were bare. Knives were sheathed under their arms, musket and cutlass slung crosswise over their backs. Their faces were suffused with an unholy glow from the hallowed battle-tonic of rice wine laced with gunpowder.

Wu Cha-tan loomed behind the foredeck watch and slit his throat from ear to ear and the man died without a sound. Four pirates made for the quarterdeck while four others secured the foredeck. Several took up station by hatches by which the ship's company would have to come from below. Two stood on each side of the sterncastle opening below the quarterdeck. More pirates came up the chains.

Their presence was discovered when an intruder stumbled over a cargo hatch and his cutlass made a clattering noise on the boards.

"Action stations! Action stations!"

The bullhorn voice of Bos'n Kelsey, officer of the watch, roared out from the quarterdeck. Someone jumped to the ship's bell and clanged out an urgent summons. Kelsey slithered down the ladder to the deck below. He saw a sloe-eyed figure approaching out of the fog, raised his musket and fired. The figure vanished. Suddenly he felt a sharp stab in his back and yelled in agony. The massive Irishman turned and flailed wildly with his musket, but his slight adversary rolled easily with his action. Then Wu stepped back and swung his cutlass. Bos'n Kelsey died instantaneously, decapitated.

There was a short and fierce hand-to-hand battle. More muskets fired in the gloom 'tweenmasts before the boarding party prevailed. Six of *Albatross*'s sailors had scrambled up companionways and had cutlasses run through them before those behind realized what was happening and remained below.

Joy and Joshua Piper, *Albatross's* second mate, shared a tiny sterncastle cabin next to master's quarters. The early morning tumult woke them both. Together they rushed into the narrow outside corridor. At the same moment the captain's door opened.

"Belay there!" rapped Jerome in a voice that brooked no argument. "Mr. Piper, watch the passengers. We have been boarded."

Joy looked on as Jerome, wearing a loose shirt over cotton breeches and hastily donned boots, took four measured steps into the sterncastle tunnel and stopped just before it opened onto the maindeck. In a loud voice he announced "I am master of this ship!" to someone Joy could not see. In the lamplight a cutlass appeared at Jerome's throat. Then a strange man – to Joy's surprise, a Chinese! – wearing frayed black pantaloons and gold earrings, led him away and out of sight.

After a few moments a musket shot shattered the silence and Joy's face turned ashen. Should he go to the captain's aid? Was someone waiting by the opening with a raised sword? He turned indecisively and saw Sir Paul standing beside the second mate, and then, through the last cabin door, he glimpsed the white face of Margaret peeping out. Piper, unmindful of Jerome's order, pushed past Joy and out to the deck. The next moment he shrieked and staggered back into their corridor as a cutlass from an unseen hand thrust at him. Piper moaned and reeled back against the bulkhead, blood already seeping from a chest wound. He slid down to the deck as the others hurried to help him.

Joy was trying to expose Piper's wound when a shrill Chinese voice rang out. It had spoken for a few seconds when Sir Paul gasped and muttered an oath. Joy turned to him and saw dismay in his face.

"It's Wu! Oh my God, it's Wu! Why did Wu attack *us?*"

Joy stared at him.

"Who, sir? Wu, sir?"

No one found this funny. Margaret looked up, horrorstruck by the agony of the man dying in her arms.

"That shouting was one the pirates telling us we've been captured by Wu's men. Bombshell Wu. The most notorious pirate in the South China Sea. But...but why? Pirates don't attack European ships. They prey on local traffic."

Joy looked at Sir Paul, bewildered by the unexpectedness of the calamity. They had been boarded and attacked before they had even set foot in China!

Sir Paul was incoherent with rage.

"...unheard of...Chinese pirates attacking a British target. And anyway, what infernal kind of a watch did we have?" He stopped and his face paled. "Great heavens! They'll unload the bounty and sink us."

Margaret gasped but Sir Paul, unmindful, continued.

"They'll have to. They'll have to eliminate all trace of us or cause a terrible stink with the mandarins. The Hoppo has guaranteed us protection. Why in heaven's name did they attack us?"

The answer hit them both at the same time.

"There's been a leak," said Joy.

Margaret turned back to the recumbent Piper. His limbs hung slackly. His entire shirt and her dress were red with blood. Joy felt for a pulse, found none and they laid the unfortunate man on the deck.

Several minutes passed.

Joy rose and moved gingerly along the passageway to the opening, ready to spring back at the first sign of menace. The sky had lightened slightly and he could discern ghostly shapes moving about outside. He was debating what he should do when there was a tremendous crash. *Albatross* lurched mightily and heeled sickeningly over to port. Joy went spinning to the opposite bulkhead. His head banged hard on the wooden wall and he collapsed in a heap. Bright yellow stars sparkled in his blurred vision as he felt the ship slowly right herself with a splintering, tearing sound. His head hurt unbearably but, strangely, his mind continued to work without a break. He pushed away the miasma of pain and sat up. They must have run aground at speed, he thought. But wait, how could they? Weren't they hove-to? He struggled to his knees but fell over on all fours as the ship jerked again sideways. Then he heard screams and shouts and clashing of steel and banging of muskets and sounds of people running. What on earth was going on?

With his head pounding and his eyesight alternately clouding and clearing, Joy crawled back to their corridor and saw Sir Paul, lying on his face on the floor. One of his legs was bent at an unnatural angle. The dead second mate lay beside him. Margaret, apparently unhurt, was kneeling beside the old man. Together, they made a tentative attempt to straighten the crooked leg but stopped when Sir Paul, clutching his chest, cried out in pain. The cry changed to a moan of distress. It was obvious the leg was broken and there were probably internal injuries. Joy realized they had to have the Governor looked at by the ship's surgeon at once and provide morphine to lessen the pain.

"Got to get help," Joy said, getting unsteadily to his feet.

"Oh my God, Mr. Morley!" burst out Margaret. "Look at you."

Blood was pouring down Joy's face, but unmindful, he stumbled to the maindeck quite forgetting the possibility of a cutlass thrust. Nothing happened. Staggering forward, he reached the galley companionway and groggily grasped the railing. Hearing his name called, he looked around and discerned Fenwick standing with his shirt tattered and blood on his arm. Next to him was a mountainous figure that he recognized as Captain Fernandes of *Gulab*, one of the Indian ships. Wondering how Fernandes could be aboard *Albatross*, Joy saw, hanging a gunwale railing, a Chinese man whose bare chest and black pantaloons were awash with blood. Then his vision blurred and he reeled with a roll of the ship. Recovering, he felt something soft at his feet and looked down at the body of a British seaman. The sightless eyes stared back at him. He looked around in horror. There were dead and wounded strewn over the deck. There was blood everywhere. A wave of nausea passed over him. He staggered and squealed in pure terror as the separated head of Bos'n Kelsey rolled toward him. He could not fight the nausea anymore and hung grimly to the railing as bile rose in his throat. The ship swam and he felt himself falling into an enveloping blackness.

15

After his ordeal in Chiang-p'ing village, Vikram lay semi-conscious for several hours. He had first been severely burned by exposure at sea and bruised dreadfully by lashes of rattan. When he revived, his leathery throat and pain-wracked body cried out for water in the darkness. It hurt everywhere. An incessant rustling and fluttering indicated the presence of vermin among the sacks he lay on. Vikram's thirst grew and he groaned loudly. A light came on and he opened his eyes and saw a round face peering down at him.

"*Jol!*" croaked Vikram through cracked lips. He turned his face sideways and mimed the act of drinking. Feng shouted over his shoulder. Invisible feet scuttled away and came back with the life-giving leather bag. Before long Vikram was gently sponged clean and being helped to lie on his stomach on a fresh blanket. A woman applied salve to his wounds. With his thirst satisfied and the cool feel of the ointment, his mind stilled and Vikram drifted off to sleep.

A sad-faced woman appeared in a pool of light. Rust-colored ringlets in her hair gleamed in the nimbus. She gazed at him with a rapt expression. He reached held her hands and told her he would save her. The pool of light extinguished and the woman disappeared. A thin-faced man materialized out of the darkness, white and bare-chested, and leered at him. The hanging tooth gleamed and came close. Then Captain-sahib appeared from nowhere and brandished a cane. He heard the woman pleading *"Bachao!"* from far away. But he could not help her because his hands were tied to the mast. Then Captain-sahib screamed *"shuo!"* and hit him with the cane.

Vikram awoke with a start.

When his heartbeat slowed and the perspiration cooled he began to think logically. He looked around. He was on a boat and it was still dark outside. He had no idea what day it was. He knew he was in a pirate village. Where was the village? On the Chinese coast obviously. But the coast of China was very long.

Suddenly, an unnerving panic began to fill Vikram's mind He pushed it away with an effort and a curse, and continued to think.

Their ship had been bound for Canton. Canton was on the China coast. Was it far away? Vikram knew little of charts and maps. But even if Canton was near, how could he escape to his friends? There were cruel men holding him. He did not know the language of the country. He would stand out because of his appearance. His situation was impossible. Again the nameless fear churned his stomach. On the verge of terror, he checked himself. As long as he was alive, he told himself, he had to think of escape. The legends of India were awash with daring escapes of royal prisoners. *He* was royal. He was a warrior prince. A Sena. Strong and intelligent. He *would* escape. His oppressors were harsh, but uneducated and greedy.

Greedy!

The word stuck in his mind. What had he that would appeal to Chinese greed? The answer was abundantly clear. Opium! Not just a bag of opium. Not a ship of opium. Not a field of opium. A *mountain* of opium! The hills of Bihar could supply opium forever.

With that reassuring thought Vikram drifted back to sleep.

⤸

"Hei wang-zi! Ni hao!"

Vikram stirred on the rough blanket. The sun was glinting through a dense grove of trees on the riverbank.

"Ni hao!" called the voice again, louder this time.

A murmur of sounds came from all sides mixed with an enticing smell of cooking. Vikram opened his eyes slowly against the sunlight, turned over with a grunt and gingerly tried to sit up. His body hurt dully and was extremely stiff, but he managed to sit. His senses stabilized and he examined his wounds. As he did so he recognized the ingenuity of his captors. Considering the inconceivable agony of torture, when every pore and every nerve-ending of his body had revolted and screamed in protest against the braided rattan, there were bruises but no cuts, no broken bones, and apparently no internal damage. It was a torture system for extracting information without maiming or killing. He found that all the blood and grime had been washed off and he was wearing a fresh pair of black pantaloons. A pungent healing odor hung in the air. He put his hand to his back and it came back sticky with eucalyptus liniment. His mouth felt vile and he felt he felt he could drink half the river. Then Angry Feng came into his line of vision. The pirate nodded and the leather bag was offered. Vikram drank eagerly and let the water run down his face and chest. Then, spurning Feng's offered of help, he held tightly to the lean-to frame and in stages, with a huge effort, got to his feet. He saw a silent crowd watching from surrounding boats. In their expressions was a mixture of sympathy and curiosity but no hostility. His wounds hurt, but with the stimuli of surroundings, people, birdcalls, water, and the prospect of food, he pushed the pain to the back of his mind. Later, eating rice and fish with his fingers, having declined the ubiquitous eating sticks, he saw he was in one of a cluster of boats on the river. There were a few shacks on shore, but the village was mostly riverine. The fast-moving brown water carried clumps of leaves and sticks away from the village. The far bank was in shadow.

Feng waved inquisitive bystanders away and sat on his haunches before him. Vikram wished he had a mirror and check his reflection. After all his travails – he had lost count of the days since he was cast off – he must look quite a sight. When he finished eating, an old woman came to rub more ointment on his back. The sun rose higher and it became hot and steamy. The woman went away. After a while Feng said something to him in Cantonese. Vikram shook his head uncomprehending. Feng turned irritably and rapped out an order. In a few minutes Tau-pei appeared.

The young pirate got down to business.

"Feng Sheng-chi, he ask how much opium," opened Tau-pei.

Vikram felt a moment of pique. Feng had not even bothered to ask how he was feeling. Then he put aside his annoyance. The pirates had probably seen, caused, and suffered enough mayhem to immunize themselves to the vilest forms of human suffering. And anyway, why should Feng care how he felt? He, Vikram, was only another captive.

The plans – or were they dreams? – of the night came back. He remembered the mountain of opium. He was a Sena prince. This man Feng was just a lowly covetous pirate. With a start he realized Feng had given him his cue right away.

"How much opium?" Vikram countered. "How much opium does Feng want? Where is his leader?"

There was a pause after Tau-pei had translated. Vikram took another look around and saw that Wu's flagship and most of the able-bodied men were gone. But Feng was still here. Why? His now hyperactive mind pondered if it was a deliberate slight.

Ironically, Feng was thinking the same way. Of late he had had the feeling his chieftain was keeping him away from important action. He could only ascribe this to his own growing popularity among the pirates. This was not a good sign. Ever alert to danger signals, Feng knew that rivalry of this nature ended with one winner and a body for the sharks. He had not dared question the pirate chief's order to stay behind and guard the black prisoner while he went after opium. Feng's disappointment was not lost on Vikram. He filed away the information and concentrated on the dialog. Things were happening fast. He had not thought he would be negotiating for his life so quickly.

When Feng did not reply, he said "Feng likes opium?"

Yes, Feng liked opium.

"Why does Feng like opium?"

Chinese like opium, Tau-pei translated. They like it a lot. Not just to smoke it but also to sell it. There was money to be made in opium. Much money. Did not Hei wang-zi see how swiftly Honorable Wu went after the barbarian ship?

Yes, Hei wang-zi had seen.

"Where are we?" he enquired.

Tau-pei's fractured translation involved unknown names and places and directions to which Vikram listened carefully. Most made no sense but he gathered that he was not in China but in a country called Annam. Annam was next to China. They were in a waterway called the Bach Dang River, near a small town called Hai Phong. Vikram was not interested Hai Phong. Where was Canton? Or Guangzhou, to be precise.

At last he got the reply he wanted.

"Guangzhou, *heya?* Six day boat he sail there there," Tau-pei pointed east, "along coast belong China, then he come Guangzhou."

Just six days? Vikram's heart raced. He was closer than he had dared to hope. He made sure he kept his eyes downcast and the excitement out of his voice. He could not afford to lose his advantage.

"Does Feng know the way to Guangzhou?"

"Feng Sheng-chi him know way along Guangzhou ve'y well."

After a pause, Feng asked directly "How muchee opium?"

This time, confident with information about his whereabouts, Vikram was ready. And as he spoke he unconsciously fell into the *pigdin* English of South China.

"Too muchee opium! Feng Sheng-chi want too muchee opium?"

"*Shi, shi!*"

Tau-pei danced in a frenzy of translation, beginning to see spoils for himself too.

"Feng Sheng-chi him wantee too muchee opium never mind. Mo'! Mo'! This fellah Tau-pei he he'p Hei wang-zi, *heya?*"

The tables were turning!

Vikram kept a straight face and said, "Opium, very good opium, he come from my land, Bengal...uh...Meng Chia La."

Tau-pei stared at him reverently while explaining this to Feng, whose eyes inadvertently lit up then hooded over. Vikram watched him warily. The critical moment could come at any moment.

"Why devil ship take opium along Guangzhou?" Feng asked.

"Same reason. Chinese like opium. English lord wants to sell opium to Chinese. English want to buy tea from Chinese. Trade."

Feng thought about this.

"How red devils sell opium to Chinese fellah?"

Vikram shrugged and winced at a stab of pain.

"English sahib sell to Chinese merchant. Merchant sell to Chinese people. Easy."

"No, *heya,* not easy. Not easy. Not easy. Opium no can sell to Chinese *hong.* Hoppo him say no can do, never mind."

Vikram knew opium was banned and tried another approach.

"Why pirate leader he want opium?"

"To sell to Chinese fellah."

"How *he* sell?"

"Honorable Wu, he ve'y wise. Many f'iends, never mind. Wu he sell through f'iends belong him. Wu he sell rice and pepper and silver and ivory to Chinese fellah."

Vikram took the plunge.

"Does Feng want to sell opium?"

There was dead silence. The abrupt question got past Feng's self-control. His face reflected incredulity and interest. Vikram looked away to give Feng time to collect his thoughts. He watched women dipping clothes in buckets of soapy water and thrashing them on boards reminding him of Bengali girls at work beside village ponds.

At last Feng spoke.

"Feng, he likee sell opium," Tau-pei translated. "Hei wang-zi give opium for sell?"

Vikram was about to answer the question but Feng motioned him to be silent and follow him. The three men boarded a small boat and Tau-pei poled them away. In the end it was easier than Vikram had hoped. A hundred yards upstream, under an overhanging branch, they closed the deal. It took much gesticulation and many pictures in the mud, but finally a plan emerged. Vikram told Feng about the poppy fields of Bihar. Feng told Vikram about the triads of Canton. With a shock Vikram realized that his new business partner had access to a network independent of both pirates and officialdom. His own suffering had not been in vain. He had stumbled onto something that might enable Morley-sahib's dream. If only he could find his English friend.

He need not have worried. Feng soon offered to help Vikram reach Canton in exchange for a promise of a year's supply of opium, enough to make him rich beyond measure. Vikram had no idea if this was possible, but agreed with just the right amount of reluctance.

ॐ

The next day, while a woman spread medicinal herbs on his back, Vikram sat on the pebble-strewn beach and studied the limestone pyramids of Ha Long Bay, thanking his stars that, in spite of the entirely different worlds in which they had evolved, he and Feng followed the same religion, Buddhism. It elevated their alliance of convenience to the beginnings of rapport. The dramatic setting was a fitting backdrop for the growing exhilaration that filled his breast.

Framed by nodding palms, the sprawling vista included placid green waters, broken by impossibly-shaped islands, towers, cones, monuments, arches, pillars, porticoes, and dotted among them, double-masted fishing trawlers hanging motionless like pairs of snails.

A voice called out to him over the gentle waves. Taking a deep breath, Vikram walked along water line, leaving the woman behind. He stopped, took a final look around, then hurried to where Feng waited under the trees with their arrow-boat. It really was happening!

Suddenly he was overcome by a rush of gratitude for his two unlikely friends. They were taking him to Canton. He clasped his wrists together and bowed in the Chinese way.

"*Hsieh, hsieh!*" he said. "*Hao pengyoumen!*" Good friends!

Tau-pei grinned proudly. Even Feng smiled. Hei wang-zi's rendering of their language was quite unexpected. The dark prince had certainly learned much. He even behaved like a civilized person!

"Ready?" asked Vikram.

The two Chinese nodded enthusiastically.

"We shall be rich!" Vikram said.

They chorused assent.

"Then let us go, Honorable Feng!"

Their crew of two stony-faced, black-robed Chinese women raised sail and poled the small arrow-boat into the bay. The sails filled and the scenery rolled by, magnificent and stark. White cliffs. Cascading waterfalls. Rock sculptures. Calm water. Gamboling dolphins. Leaping fish. Little islands with surf-decked beaches.

The panorama had differing effects on the travelers. The Indian prince dreamed of ruling Bengal after centuries of exile. The Tanka pirate glowed. *Honorable Feng!* No one had ever called him that. He dreamed of others who would address him so. The pock-marked sailor tallied the number of courts he would build in his new house in Fo-shan and counted the wives he would fill them with.

During the week-long journey Vikram learned enough Cantonese to understand Feng without Tau-pei's assistance. They discussed Indian and Chinese renditions of Buddhism. They recounted their frustrated aspirations to power. The more they talked the more animated they became. After the fourth day Vikram felt he could trust the Chinese pirate. He told Feng of the English goal of bringing opium to China in high volume. Feng in turn told him about the violent politics of the Chinese underworld.

The great island of Hainan fell astern and mountainous headlands of Macau came into view. As they neared the Pearl River Estuary, Vikram made out a very big ship, anchored with its mast broken. His heart beat faster. Was it *Albatross?* What happened to its mast? In a welter of anxiety, he debated whether to go in close and discover the ship's identity. But what would he do even if it *was* their ship? If he was identified, its irate Captain might fire a musket or even a cannon from the deck. Reluctantly he decided to press on for Canton.

For the rest of the day the crew-women navigated the endless bends of the Pearl River through cultivated fields on either bank. As the city's landing pier came into view, Feng pointed out the English 'factory.' It was situated near the end of a prominent row of warehouses bordering a large square which extended all the way down to the waterfront. Vikram watched the milling crowd in the square as the women tied up alongside other boats. Vikram, who had not exchanged a single word with them during the entire trip, nodded farewell and received flinty stares in return. Smiling unabashedly, he followed Feng across eight intervening boats until they reached the stone steps of the pier and climbed to the square to be were surrounded by a sea of babbling humanity. No one took notice of Vikram's foreignness. Porters jostled him for the privilege of carrying his belongings. In borrowed pantaloons and vest, he had none. Peddlers thrust a bewildering array of things, even a baby pig, in his face.

"Hei wang-zi!" Feng clutched his arm. "We go Chow-chow factory, *heya?* Many Eeendian fellah he belong Chow-chow factory."

"No," said Vikram. "We go English factory."

16

While Vikram recovered from his wounds and sailed eastward with his Chinese friends, Joy hovered in the murky space between life and death while the fever induced by his head injury mounted. Hallucinations and thirst tormented him as they had Vikram. Often during those terrible days, he started up and cried for water. Each time a gentle hand caressed his face and an angel bent over him and touched the edge of a cool metal to his lips. He held on tightly to the angel's hand while nightmares plagued him filled with frenzied scenes from the embattled ship.

Then the demons receded and Joy slept, dead to the world.

When he awoke, a darkened lantern flickered dully and threw yellow shadows in the room. From outside he could hear men's indistinct voices. A dog yelped mournfully.

He opened his eyes and tried to recollect what had happened. There were no dogs on the ship. A cow for fresh milk yes, and goats, and the ship's cat, but no dogs. And then he realized with a shock the constant rolling motion of the ship had ceased. He was not at sea but on solid land in a bed in a room with walls. He tried to sit up but the effort was too much.

Something stirred close to him.

Joy flinched and shut his eyes as memories from the beset *Albatross* returned. The hellish visage of Bos'n Kelsey's head rolling on the deck stared up at him. Joy perspired, groaned and squirmed, and tried to retreat into the depths of the bed. Then he felt the soft hand on his cheek and relaxed. The paroxysm of fear stilled and the hand pressed his face and lips and gently massaged his chest. He opened his eyes and tried to focus on the angel. She said something reassuring and her soft fingers continued to sooth away his desperation. The tension ebbed. His throat and tongue were bone dry. He tried to speak and only managed a horrid rasping sound. The angel understood and the cold rim of a tumbler pressed against his lips, and he drank thankfully. The effort was exhausting and he fell back.

The room brightened as the lantern was turned up. The angel looked down at him, her eyes wide with concern.

It was Miss Andrews. He stared at her dumbly.

"Where?" he managed to croak at last.

"Macau," said Margaret, wiping his perspiration away with a clean perfumed cloth. "Sleep now, Mr. Morley. I'll stay with you."

Macau!

Joy's thought processes began to function. He was in Macau and he was alive. But why Macau? Was he a captive? With Margaret? What had happened to the ship? Where were the others? Before he could voice the questions he slipped back into slumber.

The next time he awoke the fever had broken.

Motes of dust floated in myriad sunbeams that penetrated through a bamboo-curtained window. His head felt heavy as lead. Carefully he touched his forehead and found it was bandaged. His throat felt papered over. He was alone but could hear people talking as if an assembly had gathered just outside his window.

Presently he heard heavy footfalls approaching from opposite the window. He turned to see, and at once acute pain shot through his head. Joy gasped and closed his eyes. The pain lessened. Someone entered the room and Joy opened his eyes warily.

"Ah, back among those present, are we?" It was the voice of Captain Winkley. "How're you feeling, old boy?"

Joy looked up, keeping his head still this time. Jerome peered at him.

"Feeling better?"

Joy almost nodded but caught himself.

"Yes," he croaked. "What happened?" He swallowed and managed "Water."

"Su Siao!" Jerome called out. "Water!"

A moment later an elderly Chinese woman entered carrying a tray. Her ancient face resembled a prune. She hobbled towards him and put the tray on a small table and handed him a brass tumbler. Jerome sat down on an ornate chair and watched as Joy drank two tumblers of water and the woman delicately fed him soup and rice from porcelain bowls. Joy was ravenous. The thick soup was delicious and, distractedly, he wondered if it was made of sea-swifts' nests.

The *amah* suddenly spoke to him.

"Massa likee go *su-su?*"

Her voice was painfully shrill. Joy did not understand and stared at her blankly. On his other side Jerome chortled.

"Su Siao wants to know if you require the chamber pot."

Joy's face grew red in embarrassment. He found that while he *did* require the chamber pot, he'd be damned before he used it in the presence of a woman. In his discomfiture he wondered unhappily what had happened while he was comatose. He realized Su Siao was placidly waiting for him to answer. He shook his head, gasping at the resultant pain. The *amah* collected the tray, patted a corner of the sheet and left. Joy had an urgent need to know what he was wearing. He surreptitiously felt around and to his relief he found he had on a vest and loose trousers.

Jerome cleared his throat.

"Well, Morley, do you want to know what's going on?"

"Yes."

"All right then. I'll tell you my story and you tell me yours. We found you out cold below the quarterdeck with your face covered with blood and a hellish gash on your skull. Why, for a while we thought you were beyond the pale. That was a week ago. After three days,

Surgeon Morefield said you were out of danger. Ye know, you'll have to thank the sharp eyes of young Newbond for delaying your appointment with your Maker."

Jerome settled back in the chair and stretched his booted legs.

"It's lucky for everyone on *Albatross* that morning – well, *almost* everyone, not the ones who died – that Midshipman Newbond happened to be aboard *Gulab* and excited about going to China. So excited that he came on deck at first light to watch anchor being raised. And it's also lucky that he had the lights of Boca Tigris on his mind. When flashes of light came out of the dawn mist from the direction not of Canton but of *Albatross*, it immediately caused him concern and he raised the alarm. *Gulab* lit signal flares. *Albatross* did not respond and Captain Fernandes decided to approach and investigate. The flashes could mean only one thing. Musketry or pistol fire. And because *Albatross's* cannon had not sounded, Fernandes correctly guessed there had been a boarding party and hand-to-hand combat was in progress. So with great presence of mind, Fernandes raised sail fast and bore down on our ship."

Jerome mused for a moment.

"That *was* quick thinking for an Indian, was it not? But wait, Fernandes is mostly Portuguese." Having solved the imagined discrepancy, he continued. "Where was I? Oh yes, Fernandes was investigating. He had to know whether the ship was in friendly or enemy hands. So keeping his flares going he brought *Gulab* closer. If a lookout was at station, *Gulab* would have been seen and signaled. When there was no reaction, he decided to ram *Albatross* to effect maximum surprise on her attackers and board her in the resulting confusion. Ye know, that big fellow would make a good navy man."

Joy lay still, engrossed. Jerome rose to his feet and paced the room as though it was his quarterdeck.

"They were Chinese pirates, Morley, with a real daredevil in command. In the initial attack they slew nine of my men and would have killed more if they could." He stopped and looked down at Joy. "You with me, Morley?"

Joy affirmed by blinking his eyes. He now remembered Sir Paul had referred to the pirates as Wu's men. The daredevil Jerome was referring to must be that same Wu.

Jerome went on.

"We discovered they'd approached us in lightweight sampans hidden in the mist. Must be frightfully good navigators to have found us with the fog bearing down so hard. Their failure was they had not realized we were a convoy, nor had they expected help to arrive so quickly. Back on *Gulab,* at the last moment Fernandes ordered the helm hard over so that she hit *Albatross* a glancing blow. But hit her she did, and strong enough to bring down her foremast and cause severe damage to her fixtures. Newbond, Fernandes and thirty armed sailors came aboard and easily retook *Albatross.* The mist cleared and we turned our guns on the sampans as they scattered. Right then and there we strung up the pirates who were still alive on board. All but their accursed leader. A strange mousy fellow with a bloody great shark's tooth round his neck. Ye'll not believe this, Morley, but just as we thought we had him cornered on the afterdeck, the man threw his cutlass in my face and leaped backward clear over the rail and into the sea. Oh well, I'll wager he never made it out of the water alive and the shark used his other teeth on him. To cut a long story short we limped into nearby Macau with our dead and wounded."

"How is Sir Paul?" Joy asked anxiously, remembering the precarious state of the old Governor when he had last seen him.

Jerome paused and said gently, "Sir Paul Miller died of his injuries five days ago."

The words hit Joy like a physical blow.

"Commiserations, Morley," continued Jerome. "I know you were close to him. His age went against him. Sir Paul had both his legs and several ribs broken when *Gulab* rammed us, and we suspect he had a spinal injury."

A great emptiness filled Joy as the captain ended the story with little of it registering on him.

"Man, it was a disaster. We lost a total of twenty men in the attack and in the battle to retake the ship. Among the officers, First Mate Teixeira of *Gulab* missed his footing in the crossing and died 'tween ships. From *Albatross's* company, Second Mate Piper took a cutlass in his chest and died in the passageway of the sterncastle. Midshipman Hearst and Bos'n Kelsey died in the first attack. And Sir Paul. We buried them with all of Macau turned out. Twenty-one guns saluted the Governor as he was lowered into Loyola Cemetery."

His mind far away, Joy watched the sunbeams marching along the wall. A single massive tree that dominated all others had crashed to the forest floor. A true servant of the King had died in action. Sir

Paul was the symbol of a courageous England. A visionary England. A leader who waged war against greed and mediocrity. Joy recalled King George's command to Sir Paul: *"It is thy sacred duty to turn the tide of silver."* He closed his eyes to cover the prickling that was beginning behind them. Without Sir Paul the opium project was finished. A huge emptiness filled him.

Then a strange thing happened.

A tall angular figure appeared at Joy's bedside and frowned down at him for his weakness. Joy lay back squirming, trying to avoid the piercing eyes. But they transfixed him like a pinned moth.

"I can do it, sir" Joy heard himself say softly. "You can depend on me to carry on. I shall not fail the King."

Jerome looked at him in surprise. He bent and brought his ears close to Joy's lips in an effort to make out what he was mumbling, but gave up. The poor sod must be hallucinating again.

౿

A week later, Margaret sighed and lowered a book of Milton's verse she was reading. Joy smiled at her from the bed.

"Thinking of the future, old girl?"

Margaret nodded and looked wistfully out of the window.

Joy was propped on pillows, his head swathed in bandages. He was still weak, but the fever was gone. Surgeon Morefield had proclaimed him on the road to recovery. Margaret looked at the emaciated form of the once-vigorous young man, the only person left as a buttress against the yawning chasm that was her life.

Margaret felt she had departed England seemingly eons ago, when her mother, her only surviving relative, died just days after Stephen Farloe proposed to her. After that, in quick succession, Stephen's own death, the prince's disappearance, Sir Paul's end, the mayhem on the ship, had shattered her.

Only Joy remained.

Hailing from a poor but genteel family, Margaret grew up helping her widowed mother run a tailoring shop in east London. The match with Farloe was made through an acquaintance when the East India Company clerk was visiting England to find a wife. Stephen was twice her age. Mum was apprehensive about her living in distant China but, since the alternative was spinsterhood, she accepted Farloe's proposal. They were to marry in London in March and travel together to Canton. But tragically, Mum contracted pneumonia after being caught in an ice-storm and was gone in a week. That changed everything. Farloe's leave ended before the mourning period and he left for China. Margaret stayed on to sell their shop in Stepney before embarking on *Albatross*.

In Macau, she would not normally reside in her present lavish accommodation. Seeing her obvious association with the beleaguered party, the authorities had allotted her a room in the British Residence.

Since the fateful shipboard confrontation with Vikram, Captain Winkley's attitude toward her had changed. From aloof and disinterested, he became spiteful and haughty. Fortunately, after the pirate attack he had been immersed night and day with repairs and the protection of his ships. During this time Margaret began to understand the magnitude of responsibility now resting with her. On his deathbed, Sir Paul accurately gauged her intelligence and knowing his end was near, took Margaret into confidence. She learned about the value of the cargo and understood the vast national stake in the venture and its stupendous importance for England's future.

Jerome had not understood, though he had been privy to the operation from the beginning. To the captain the opium business was an irritant. The East India Company had assigned him to police the seas between India and China, not to mollycoddle contraband cargo. The pirate attack had, in his opinion, vindicated this view and his primary responsibility was to repair *Albatross* and seek vengeance.

Once, while Joy lay comatose, Jerome had needled her about Vikram. At first Margaret listened with eyes lowered. Encouraged by her silence, Jerome had mocked her again.

"Well, what say you? Which one did your blackie in? The sharks or the sun or the thirst? Perhaps Siamese corsairs got him. Now what would they do to him, eh?"

Slowly Margaret's chin came up and she looked her tormentor square in the face. Dead-green arctic eyes in a lined gray face bored into the captain and Jerome shivered involuntarily. A wilting scorn added itself to the iciness of the woman.

Abruptly, he left the room.

Pushing Jerome out of her mind, Margaret submerged her personal sense of loss and threw herself into caring for her two grievously injured men. When Sir Paul succumbed in spite of her efforts, her anguish mounted. Panic-stricken, she willed, prayed, and fought for Joy's survival. She remained at his bedside around the clock, sitting motionless by his recumbent form, ministering to his slightest need.

Margaret sighed again and put Milton away. When she was not worrying about Joy's health and the opium venture, she was beset by the disappearance of the foreign stranger who had saved her life. Try as hard as she could, Margaret could not understand how in a matter of days and hours, her world was devastated by bolt after bolt of lightning from cloudless skies. Her soon-to-be husband's death. The bid to end her life of which she could remember only the vaguest detail. The strange closeness she had felt with her rescuer on the ship's deck. His cruel abandonment. The catastrophe of the pirate attack. Sir Paul's violent death. Joy's injury. The fight for his life. If once, only once, the prince returned she would thank him from her heart. But it would not happen. No one survived in a tiny rowboat in a huge ocean.

Margaret wiped away a tear for Vikram and looked around. Joy had fallen asleep. She yawned, stretched, and after a moment's thought, walked to an outside balcony. The warm sunshine lifted her mood. She crossed to a low wall and looked down into a large and very crowded square, two floors below her. It was enclosed on three sides by majestic buildings and a magnificent cathedral dominated the fourth. In the brilliant light it was a glorious view.

Someone touched her arm. Margaret spun around with a gasp.

"Oh! It's you, Mrs. Mac."

"Och, lassie! I dinna mean to scare ye," Alice Macardle

squeezed her arm apologetically. "Right splendid ye be aboot at last."

Margaret impulsively gave the Scottish woman a hug. Alice, the roly-poly wife of Sir Paul's second-in-command, was a doll.

"And how be his lordship feeling?"

Margaret almost said 'who?' before she understood. Didn't people refer to a peer by his title only when he actually inherited it? She knew Joy's father was still alive. Lord Morley in England must have an awesome reputation for the Macardles to be so subservient.

"Actually Mr. Morley is better," she said. "He is speaking coherently. In fact, that's why I'm out here. Oh, Mrs. Mac, isn't that church simply grand?"

"Aye, lass. Sao Paolo Cathedral. That down there is Macau's main *largo*. *Largo* means town square in Portuguese. Ye should see them Chinese dragons on the cathedral walls."

Margaret pointed to two-wheeled vehicles moving rapidly along one edge of the *largo*.

"What are those, Mrs. Mac?"

"*Jin-rickshas,* lassie. Ye sits in it like in a cart and a *coolie* in a bamboo hat, he runs along pulling."

Margaret was impressed by the sights. The *largo* was full of activity like market day in an English town, only on an immensely larger scale. Hundreds of peddlers stood behind wheeled carts with large umbrellas as protection from the strong sun. Crowds of shoppers surged among them. Chinese grandfathers, housewives, bow-legged porters with baskets slung across their shoulders at the ends of poles, children dwarfed by wide hats, little donkeys carrying impossible loads. Tall and swarthy European men walked among them in high brown boots. There were no white women on view. Margaret thought this rather strange on market day but decided not to ask. Instead, she took a long breath and stretched.

The air was exciting and enervating, a rich mixture of sea and salt and fish and tar and cooking. The arched Mediterranean mansions around the *largo*, the angular colonnaded church with its broad flight of steps with dozens of people sitting on them, sharp voices peppering the drone of commerce, all of these made her forget for a moment her desperate situation. She was in China! No, not exactly China. There was a lot of Spain here...no not Spain, Portugal! The Portugal that Sir Paul wanted to outshine. And it was now her charge. With that somber thought her face clouded over.

Oh, Mr. Morley! she thought. *I'm just an ordinary girl. Do get better and take over. I cannot carry this much longer.*

"Poor lassie." Alice sense the mood change and put an arm around her. "Come in out of the sun."

Margaret allowed herself to be led into the cool interior of the British Residence. Alice fussed and cooed and finally Margaret relaxed and ate her first real meal in a long time.

 formula

"*Gentlemen! Gentlemen! Yer attention please!*"

The commotion in the big room quieted.

"Gentlemen, may I have leave to present Lord...er, begging yer pardon...the Right Honorable Joy Morley of Ashford and Calcutta?"

Joy concealed his amusement.

Two days later they were in the Committee Room of the British Residence in Macau, a building that bore the grandiose name, *Britannia*. It was a large Mediterranean mansion situated on the main square of Macau, the Largo de Seneca. It was the low period of commerce and the Company's Select Committee of Canton had relocated to Macau per the Hoppo's regulations. On a dreary afternoon with oil lamps already lit by Chinese servants, Irving Macardle, deputizing for Sir Paul, took the chair and introduced the still weak Councilor from Calcutta to the assembled members. As they were presented in turn to Joy, the men sympathetically studied the young aristocrat with swaddling around his head and the strain evident in his pallor and unsteadiness. But the steely glint in his eyes and the sense of purpose were unmistakable. Why is he here, they wondered? What was his relationship with their departed leader? What about the broken ship in the bay? None of them had been told what had happened and it was bad form to ask outright. So they commiserated with Joy's misfortune and waited expectantly.

"Thank you for your concern, gentlemen," Joy began when everyone was seated. "I knew Sir Paul Miller for only eight weeks. Those eight weeks for me were a lifetime of learning. He was my teacher and my mentor and my hero. It is my unhappy legacy that despite being at his side, I could not shield him from hurt, from death."

He told them about the assault on *Albatross* from his recollections and from what Jerome had told him. When he finished there was silence. The men, varying in age from stooped fifties to an eighteen-year-old scribe, looked at him with hopeful expressions. Suddenly Joy knew the reason for their excessive anxiety. They were rudderless without the commanding presence of their Governor, and were hoping to hear from Joy something that would help them cope.

"Why did Chinese pirates attack the ship?" someone asked.

Joy took his time to reply.

He had told no one of the opium cargo. Only Jerome, Margaret, First Mate Fenwick and the masters of the Indian ships knew. Joy was worried about the Indian ships in Macau Harbor with their vulnerable load, and fervently hoped that Macardle's assurance they were well-guarded was accurate. Jerome had told him that crew of the three ships had been confined aboard. But word could spread. Word *would* spread. The pirates would return.

"It could be for one of many reasons," he replied as convincingly as he could. "Perhaps her formidable appointments drew attention. She is a new breed of ship as you must all have observed, a taller and stouter vessel, with bigger cannon and more gun ports. Perhaps the pirates wanted to hijack a warship to their lair."

The conversation moved to piracy. The corsairs' association with the Annamese revolt and their depredations on local shipping were known. But European shipping had never before been harmed. There was controversy over what the attack on *Albatross* might indicate. Listening to increasingly abstract arguments and unsubstantiated theories, Joy was reminded of never-ending bickering of the Executive Council at Fort William. His head began to hurt and he was feeling tired and depressed when Macardle came to his aid.

"Sir! This Committee is thankful for yer kindly meeting us e'en with yer infirmity. Oh, and by the by, sir, Howqua has arrived in Macau and waiting for ye."

Joy brightened at this news. So Howqua had come over from Canton. That was very good of him. But he did not feel mentally prepared to meet the man Sir Paul had described as a wily negotiator. As Macardle led him out of the Committee Room, Joy asked that a message be sent saying he would meet the Chinese merchant in two days' time.

They emerged from the Committee Room into the second story landing from which long flights of marble steps curved gracefully down to the main rotunda and up to the living quarters.

A small intense-looking man in expensive robes rose from a velvet chair beside the door, clasped his hands together and bowed.

Macardle stared at him in astonishment.

"Liu! What brings *ye* here?"

"*Ni hao*, sar."

Compradore Liu bowed as Macardle introduced Joy.

"Mr. Morley, sir, this here is Liu, our chief-of-staff. I was not expecting him. All bonny in Canton, eh Liu?"

Hearing this, Liu became very agitated.

"Morley-*hsien?* Morley-*hsien?*"

"Yes, Liu. Here rightly is Mr. Morley. And what might be yer problem?"

"*Ai, ai!*" said Liu, much excited. "Morley-*hsien!* Hei wang-zi!

Him come, f'om Guangzhou."

The two men stared at him blankly.

"Hey mon, yer raving!" Macardle exclaimed. He looked at Joy apologetically. "He's quite sensible usually..."

"*Hei wang-zi! Hei wang-zi!* Him wantee see Morley-*hsien* very much, ne'er mind."

"Looks like ye've a visitor, sir," elucidated Macardle.

"Yes but who on earth is Hey Wang whatever?"

"Beats me. Where he be, Liu?"

Liu energetically pointed down the stairs. They all went across to the balustrade and looked down to the circular entrance foyer, but there was no one in sight except an English soldier on sentry duty.

Macardle squared on the compradore.

"What's the game, mon?"

"Outsidee! Outsidee! Feng Sheng-chi, sar, he blingee fellah Hei wang-zi f'om Eeendia."

This made an immediate impact on his audience.

"*India?*" said Joy in astonishment.

"*Shi! Shi!* Eeendia, sar. Hei wang-zi. Plince from Eeendia."

"*Plince!*" Joy felt the blood rush to his head. "Prince! From India! Prince Sena is here? Praise the Lord!"

Without another word, Joy hurtled down the lamplit stairs. He slipped twice in his haste and weakness, but managed to save himself by grabbing the banister. Macardle and Liu followed at his heels shouting in wild confusion. The soldier saw them coming and smartly pulled the big double-door open. Joy rushed out and found himself on a broad terrace. The light was very poor. A long flight of steps led down to the invisible *largo*.

Joy looked around frantically.

"*Namaskar,* Morley-sahib!"

The everyday Bengali greeting in a familiar voice in an incongruous setting heralded the emergence of two strikingly dissimilar figures from the shadows. One was tall, the other was short; one was dark, the other fair; the tall dark one was dressed in white; the short fair one wore black.

Joy and Vikram embraced spontaneously. Simultaneously, they cried out in anguish and stepped back.

The enterprising soldier held up the lamp he had taken from a wall sconce and the two comrades studied each other. Vikram was dressed in a rough cotton shirt and trousers that were several sizes small for him. His usually clean-shaven face was covered with a fuzzy black beard. The torchlight fell on discolored bruises and scars on his neck and forehead. But his eyes were triumphant. Joy felt a wave of happiness. It was good to have his friend back.

"Morley-sahib, this is Honorable Feng to whom I owe my life."

Joy nodded to the small Chinese and turned back to Vikram.

"We were worried to death about you. What happened?"

"It is a long story, Sahib. Your turban becomes you. Perhaps we have many interesting tales to exchange?"

Joy laughed heartily.

Meanwhile, Margaret, drawn from her top floor room by the commotion, had seen Joy's precipitous downward rush. While the conversation on the entrance landing was going on, she came down quickly to the foyer and hesitated inside the doorway, trying to decipher the words. What on earth could make Mr. Morley laugh so uproariously? She looked back over her shoulder and found, crowded behind her, several members of the Select Committee.

Joy's group began to troop back in, Macardle first, then Liu. The soldier held the torch high and steady. Joy came next, his face decorated by a smile whose ends seemed to disappear into his askew bandage. Margaret controlled an impulse to shake him for news.

"What...?" she began and Joy interrupted her.

"Miss Andrews, did you know that..."

Then Vikram stepped into the torchlight. Joy stopped as he saw her expression change. Margaret blinked and her eyes widened. Her hand moved jerkily to her throat. Her mouth opened. No sound came. Then she began to fall, and the big soldier, without dropping the flaming torch, caught her as she pitched forward in a dead faint.

Eventually, things sorted themselves out.

In the drawing room of *Britannia*, Margaret recovered with the application of Mrs. Mac's smelling salts. The first thing she saw was Joy's white face with his bandage all crooked. He was breathing hard.

"Mr. Morley, off to bed with you," was her first words as she sat up straight.

Joy tried to protest, but soon the soldier was helping him up to his room. Margaret followed them and after completing two long flights of stairs Joy stopped grumbling.

"You'll tell Mac to take care of the prince, won't you?" Joy said while Margaret tucked him in and adjusted the dressing. "He's a good friend, you know."

"I know. Of course we shall take care of him. You relax now."

Joy sank into the goose down pillow with a sigh. Margaret brought the sheet up to his chin. Joy pushed it back, reached out, and squeezed her hand.

"Margaret, can I call you Margaret?"

"Why certainly. It's my name. Now it's time for you to sleep."

Joy looked at her dreamily.

"Dear Margaret! Did anyone ever tell you that you are very beautiful?"

She looked at him in surprise, but before she could say anything his eyes closed and he was asleep. Margaret thoughtfully readjusted the sheets and slowly descended the marble stairs. Halfway down, a warm radiance spread inside her, and she stopped herself from running down the last flight.

In the drawing room she found the Macardles, husband and wife, and Vikram sitting woodenly on opposite sides of the room with a wide expanse of carpet separating them. Margaret bit back a grin. How British! They had not been introduced!

"Mrs. Mac," she said as she walked between them, "have you had a moment's peace since we arrived?"

The Macardles regarded her nervously. The change in Margaret was unsettling. They were used to the melancholy woman whose only interest was care for the injured men.

"Mr. and Mrs. Macardle, please meet Prince Sena from India, a close personal friend of Mr. Morley and Sir Paul, may he rest in peace."

The effect of this statement on the couple was so electrifying that Margaret had to summon all her control and not burst out laughing. The Macardles sat up straight. Their wooden looks changed to servility. Hurriedly, Margaret explained, "Oh, he does not usually dress so. He was on *Albatross* with us, when...when, he was...well, when he was lost at sea." She turned to look at Vikram. "It's a miracle. He has come back from the dead."

They were all quiet for a while.

Alice broke the spell by heaving herself off the sofa.

"Lassie, will ye help me make everyone a nice cuppa tea?"

Margaret reluctantly accompanied Alice from the room, irrationally afraid that Vikram might disappear as soon as he was out of her sight. Left behind, Irving Macardle cleared his throat. He had a problem. He had no idea what to say to the strange visitor sitting across from him. Macardle was a career merchant of the East India Company and went by the rule book. The man was Indian, therefore of lower social class and should be condescended to. But he was a prince and therefore a social equal. And he was a friend of Joy Morley, a peer, and the great Sir Paul, and thus belonged to a class higher than his. Contravening all this, the man was visibly bruised and wore soiled native garments. What the devil should he do? Macardle decided he needed a drink.

"Whisky, yer...yer..." poor Macardle stopped in confusion, unable to resolve between highness, honor, and excellency, and lamely ended, "...sir?"

Vikram shook his dark head slowly and smiled urbanely and Macardle subsided with the feeling that he had somehow effected a breach of etiquette. What an irksome situation! Perspiring, he looked fixedly at a point above Vikram's head and wished Alice would come back. Then, unable to bear the silence he pulled out his fob watch, and raised his eyebrows in astonishment. It was past eleven o'clock. What *was* going to be done with this...this prince? What had Miss Andrews said? *Back from the dead.* Jesus! Where would the man stay?

Under his suave exterior, an anxious Vikram was thanking the Buddha for every tranquil moment that passed as he sat with dreadful expectation of the captain walking in at any time.

The women returned bearing trays.

Alice did the honors and Margaret served. As she served him, her fingers touched Vikram's and she almost dropped the tray when an unexpected shock jolted her. Shakily she took her own cup and sat down. She looked at him again and her heart began to race. *What was happening?* Her gaze fell on the angry weal on his neck and she yearned to reach out and soothe it. Suddenly she realized the room was silent. Everyone was looking at her. She blushed furiously and lowered her eyes and took a sip of tea to get her thoughts in order.

Macardle cleared his throat. He had had enough. He wanted to go to his bedroom but could not leave his wife with the problem of settling the visitor. And obviously they both could not go away and leave Miss Andrews alone with a strange man.

He got to his feet.

"Miss Andrews. Alice will see Mr...His...His Highness to the Blue Room. That be aright with yerself?"

Vikram put down his cup, stood, and spoke for the first time.

"Thank you, Sahib. Honorable Feng waits outside. He has a place for me."

Macardle was relieved.

"But," Margaret fought to control her dismay. "H...how will Mr. Morley find you?"

"I shall return tomorrow, Memsahib."

He nodded and walked across the central rotunda. Margaret followed him to the door in acute disappointment. She desperately wanted to thank him for the night on *Albatross.* As she was closing the door behind him she heard a whisper.

"I shall wait. Until you come."

An hour later the Macardles were asleep in their second floor apartment. Su Siao, snoring with her mouth open, was sprawled in a chair on the landing outside Joy's room when Margaret, a coat thrown over her clothes and a pair of shoes in her hand, emerged from her own room and noiselessly stepped around the *amah.*

Wild horses would not have held her back.

She went down the stairs in bare feet without a sound. The

sentry in the rotunda was gone. She carefully lowered the heavy bar on the front door and pulled as hard as she could on the handle. After initial resistance it opened with a rush making her step back with a gasp. It was pitch dark outside and a strong sea breeze blew in. She stepped over the threshold and struggled to close the heavy door against the wind, the shoes in her hand getting in the way.

There was a slight noise and someone reached out and closed the door for her. She felt about in the darkness and found him. At once, all the foreboding that haunted her, mysteriously vanished. She felt completely, foolishly, safe.

Minutes later, Feng was leading the way with a lantern across the empty *largo* onto the harborside promenade of Praia Grande. A medley of boats bobbed on the esplanade. Margaret hurried to keep up with Vikram who held her arm. She had no idea where he was taking her and did not care.

A short man with a savage scarred face materialized at the deserted dockside and Margaret faltered. But her companions hailed him softly and Vikram helped her down to a waiting boat. Tau-pei followed. From the pier Feng cast off the lines, jumped aboard, sat in the prow with his back to them and lit a cigarette. Tau-pei pushed at the wooden pier with a long pole and in seconds they vanished in the blackness of Macau Bay.

Vikram and Margaret crawled into a tiny reed-covered space in the middle of the boat. It was a very warm night. He helped her as she shrugged off her coat, laid it flat and sat on it. Then he lowered himself next to her. For Margaret, everything faded except his nearness.

"How are you, Memsahib?" he asked.

"I am well," she replied without hesitation, "but sad. I grieve for my fiancé. For my mother. For Sir Paul. My heart was broken when the captain threw you off the ship. It was so, so unjust."

"Here I am, Memsahib. A little damaged. And a lot wiser."

"How did you survive?"

"Because of you."

"Me?"

"You, Memsahib. And my friends from the ship. And the dream we shared. *Laat-sahib* Paul has attained *nirvana*." He paused with the memory, then continued in a low voice. "When they took away my dignity and my honor and even my clothes, when they tortured me to near death, one thing kept me alive. The hope I would see all of you again. You most, Memsahib. For I had left you alone in the world"

Margaret swallowed and reached for his arm and felt the weal where the rope had bound him to the yard. When he cringed in pain, even though he tried to hide it, she whimpered in empathy. She gingerly felt for the remembered wound on his neck with her fingertip.

"Did it hurt very much?"

"Yes, Memsahib. It hurt very much. But it does not now. No matter, it is past and it will heal."

"Tell me what happened."

Vikram spoke slowly with his woolly face close. He told her about his trial in the open sea. About the greedy traders. The floating pirate village. About the cruelty of Wu and his pirates. The wisdom and friendship of Feng. The beauty of Ha Long Bay. The voyage along the

Chinese coast while he learned Cantonese. His anxiety after seeing the dismasted ship. The frantic trip to Canton, then back to Macau.

When he finished she was silent, caressing his neck, and thought about the things he had told her. His beard felt soft against her fingertips. He smelled of suffering and of strength. Like a faraway hard-to-grasp dream, she remembered when she emerged from her suicidal trauma and saw him sitting next to her, supporting her much like today. Then her heart turned over as she remembered the captain's boot crashing into his ribs and the pistol jamming into his head. With a sob she traced the outline of his chin until her finger came back to the bruise on his neck. She touched his arms, his chest and then his back through the open vest and recoiled, horrified by the feel of the scars.

"Oh, sweet mother of Jesus! You poor, poor thing."

Tears cascaded down her cheeks.

"How could they hurt you so? Oh God, how can people do this? I nearly died again when the captain put you overboard. I saw you in the little boat on the enormous sea but my door was locked."

Vikram sighed.

"It is all right, Memsahib. The Buddha brought me back."

Vikram tried to brush away her tears. Then he stroked her hair and her sobs subsided. Her senses overloaded, Margaret abandoned herself to his touch in the gently pitching boat.

Suddenly a warm drop fell on her cheek.

"Oh, you poor dear." Margaret's heart melted. "Come to me! It's all right, don't worry. It's all right. We're together."

"You will not do it again, Memsahib?"

"What?"

"What you did on the ship. I worry for you."

"What I did on the ship? You mean...?"

She shivered and he held her close.

"How did you save me?"

"I will tell you one day, Memsahib. But now, promise me?"

"Only as long as I have you."

Instinctively realizing the perils and impermanence of life in what they had each experienced, Vikram and Margaret sat silently huddled in their tiny den, lulled by the cradle-like rhythm of the boat, striving to banish away the hostile world.

It was still dark and an early rooster was crowing an overture to the coming day when Vikram led Margaret back to the Residence.

17

Howqua marched on top of the world.

Splendid robes of gold-embroidered silk rustled as he strode to and fro around the lofty ramparts of Fort Guia. His long jade necklace clattered against his knees. The seal of office laced on the front of his costume glinted in the sun, as did his golden nail covers. He impatiently adjusted his brocade cap which the playful mountaintop wind trying to snatch away while it blew his long drooping mustache in all directions.

Howqua was an elite *hong* merchant of Canton. His real name was not Howqua, but Wu Guorong. Being a *hong*, the head of a business house that dealt with Europeans, he had taken, as custom dictated, the title Howqua from his father. The *qua* honorific indicated his calling as a trader for the foreign barbarians. During his last pilgrimage to Peking, Howqua had paid enormous sums of money toward ravages of the Yellow River, to bid or, as his many detractors would opine, bribe his way through the obstacle course of Chinese officialdom for a contract for the business of the English Company for full ten trading seasons.

Howqua did it all.

The commerce of Canton was a complex system where everybody needed everybody else and paid or extracted as much as market forces would bear. Howqua arranged for pilots to guide English ships up the Boca Tigris. He arranged for *stevedores* to unload ships at the Whampoa Island berthing. He arranged *compradores* to look after domestic needs of the merchants in the city and the recruitment of their servants. He selected and offered to English merchants, samples of categories of tea brought from the interior of China, where no barbarian was allowed. He ensured that bills of lading, manifests, and clearances for loading and unloading of cargo were prepared correctly, and duty payment cleared with the Hoppo.

Howqua was especially worried that morning.

In Canton, he had received a message from the English *tai-pan,* sent by fast boat while *Albatross* was still offshore, that a new and important cargo was arriving which would need special holding facilities. He had rushed to Macau on hearing about the attack on the English warship, only to receive the crushing news that the *tai-pan* had died in the hands of the pirates. He ordered he be taken to

Britannia. Arriving there, he had been further shocked to learn that a lowly Councilor from India would handle the cargo transaction. Why from India? Was this man English, or, heaven forbid, an Indian? Howqua had smitten his brow. Only his curiosity about the shipment kept him from storming away from Macau at the insult. Why did not the dead *tai-pan's* second-in-command handle the matter as was customary? But this was impolite to ask, and further, it would weaken his negotiating position if he showed too much interest.

He *was* interested. Very interested. Howqua did not imagine the *tai-pan's* message and the attack on the ship were unrelated.

A week after Howqua arrived in Macau, Juan Menezes, linguist of the East India Company in China, brought news that the English Councilor would meet him today at Fort Guia.

Howqua had held previous meetings in the big fort that rose above the town and the panoramic view from its ramparts had long ceased to impress him. When his pacing took him northwards he could see the long, sandy isthmus that joined the hilly four-square-mile peninsula that was Macau to the bulk of Heung Shan, an island in the Pearl River delta. When he retraced his steps, he was looking seaward. Two outer islands, Ilha da Taipa and Ilha de Coloane, emerged from the blue-green of the South China Sea. Hundreds of junks bobbed in the water, but the scene was dominated by the big barbarian ships. Conspicuous among them was *Albatross*, battered, foremast still down, its smashed bow a patchwork of repair, listing unhappily. She was the center of much traffic. Small craft clustered around her with men and material for her restoration. Further east, junks, sampans, and a schooner seemed to be hanging motionless in the distance as they wound through channels of the Pearl River.

Joy Morley came up the stairs with Menezes and stepped onto the aisle behind the crenellated top of the fort walls.

Juan Menezes had a remarkable heritage.

He was a Nhon, descended from the Portuguese, but bearing little resemblance to his swarthy ancestors. In his veins ran Portuguese, Chinese, Japanese and Malay blood with some admixture of Spanish from *conquistadores* of the Philippines. He had explained the reason for this mixing of blood to Joy. The much-travelled Portuguese who brought no women to Macau, married and had intercourse with local women all across the East Indies. Their mixed-blood offspring were treated as equals in Chinese and Portuguese societies of Macau, and the Nhons thrived.

As he walked along the rampart toward the Chinese merchant, Joy studied the ornate trappings apprehensively. This man could make or break his dream. Simultaneously, Howqua examined the young Englishman critically.

Two weeks had passed since Joy had learnt of Sir Paul's death. Excellent physique, Margaret's devoted attention, determination to push the opium deal forward, combined to help him battle depression and recover rapidly. Vikram's unexpected return energized him further. His head wound was healing although the surgeon said he would carry the scar under his hairline to his grave.

Away to his left, four men, Howqua's bodyguards, lolled and smoked in an alcove. Joy noticed that while they had laid their spears on the ground, sheathed knives hung from their sashes.

Joy had come to China unprepared to interact, let alone negotiate directly, with the Chinese, knowing that Sir Paul and his local associates would do so. Faced with the frightening prospect of having to bargain with a leading Cantonese businessman, he had questioned Menezes, Macardle and Liu extensively about Chinese body language, manners, protocol, etc. With Sir Paul dead, he was on his own in the opium venture. Being uncertain about local equations, he was afraid to trust the resident Englishmen. He had to do it himself. Vikram's first-hand impressions of the ways of the Chinese had been invaluable for today's interview. He dressed for the occasion in his best formal clothes and worried that the extra-large three-cornered hat sitting tightly on his bandages might at any moment fly away.

The Pearl River sparkled and the South China Sea shone on all sides. The green hills looked like brushed Chinese prints. Nature could not have set a more dramatic stage. It was now or never.

From his learnings, Joy knew he had already won the opening round by arriving last! He came to a stop a few feet from Howqua. Menezes stood slightly apart, his eyes cast down.

"Greetings, respected sir," Joy opened solemnly and bowed in correct Chinese fashion, arms clasped together. "Trade Councilor William Joy Morley of the English East India Company of London at your service."

Menezes converted all this into Cantonese. The *hong* merchant bowed in return and spoke in a startlingly high-pitched voice.

Menezes translated.

"My unworthy name is Wu Guorong. The Councilor may call me Howqua as others do. Has the Councilor eaten rice today?"

Joy stared at Menezes upon hearing the translation.

"Has the...? Have I *what?*"

"Sir, he means 'how are you?'" Menezes said *sotto voce*.

"Oh...yes! Thank you, Menezes. Actually I...I *have* eaten rice today." He turned back to Howqua. "Have you, sir, eaten rice today?"

"The *tai-pan* was a good man," said Howqua, ignoring the question. Perhaps an answer was not expected.

"Yes, sir. The English *tai-pan* was a good man. A very good man. He taught me much."

They stood awhile without speaking, thinking of the English patriarch, then Howqua resumed.

"Guangzhou has seen many merchants come and go. The *tai-pan* was the mightiest barbarian of all."

A singular compliment! Joy bowed to acknowledge.

After a while Howqua said, "The Councilor himself has suffered grievously," indicating the dressing under Joy's hat.

"Yes, it was painful. But I am better now. Thank you kindly for asking."

"The *tai-pan's* ship," Howqua pointed his chin towards *Albatross*. "It has suffered grievously too."

Joy felt a twinge of irritation. The pleasantries were galling. *Patience!* he admonished himself.

"Yes, sir. But the ship, like my head, can be repaired."

For some reason, Howqua found this incredibly funny and

laughed unmusically.

"Are your children fat and healthy?"

Joy was caught off-guard again.

"I have no children."

"It is indeed a great sorrow the Councilor's wife is barren."

This was getting ludicrous.

"I have no wife."

"Oh, is that so? Perhaps the Councilor finds difficulty in copulating and has therefore not married? There are ways in Macau to ease that."

Joy stared at the flamboyant man in amazement, not knowing what to say. Undeterred, Howqua carried on the theme with gusto.

"Howqua will arrange for a consort to help the Councilor perform." He stared at the ground, considering the matter. When Joy did not reply he looked up in consternation. "Perhaps two consorts? Three?" Howqua raised his penciled eyebrows. "The Councilor *must* be satisfied."

Joy got hold of himself and drew a deep breath and decided to play the game. Menezes had told him that the Chinese took their time in getting to the main issue. The more important the issue the longer the preamble. He was getting used to Howqua referring to himself in the third person and unconsciously began to adopt the style.

"Thank you for inquiring, sir, but be assured the Councilor has absolutely no difficulty in copulating. There is a simple explanation. The Councilor has not found the right woman."

"That is unheard of! The Councilor must select his *tai-tai* at once. Otherwise his juices will dry up."

They discussed Joy's sorry sex life and Howqua's prolific one. Then they discussed the quality of tea and the price of silk, and after that they lamented the depredations of pirates of the South China Sea. An hour went by. Joy's head hurt and the frailty of the past days strained by a three-hundred-step climb, returned.

"Perhaps Howqua would like to sit?" he said at last.

Howqua was immediately contrite.

"*Aa-eee-ah!* Howqua has done the Councilor great wrong! Please make yourself comfortable." The merchant wrung his hands and fussed over him. "What has Howqua done! The Councilor is recovering from serious injury."

He screamed at his men and waved his hands like a windmill. Joy subsided on the parapet with a sigh of relief. Magically, porcelain cups of aromatic tea appeared. Delicacies from steaming panniers were offered. Joy understood that unchallenged, Howqua would continue the inconsequential talk forever. It was all a by-play to get the Englishman to make the first move. Conceding that the superb food and tea made him feel better, he put down his cup and took the plunge.

"The English have brought important cargo on this voyage."

Howqua instantly dropped the banter, his joviality was replaced by a hard look.

"*Shi. Shi.* Howqua has heard so."

"It is a new thing, this cargo."

Joy was unconsciously falling into the Chinese way of speech. And he found he was actually beginning to enjoy the cat-and-mouse game. *Be careful,* he reminded himself, *just don't finish as the mouse!*

"If this cargo is accepted," he continued, "English trade with China can double."

Howqua stared at Joy for a long moment. His forehead trembled and his eyebrows went up very slightly. Was it disbelief, Joy wondered. Or interest? Howqua's expression did not change as he waited for the Englishman to go on.

"Is Howqua interested in such cargo?"

Joy decided to delay revealing the cargo's identity for as long as possible – as he had with Vikram and the Jagat Seth in Calcutta.

Howqua did not mask his irritation.

"Does the concubine swoon at the mention of the *yang?*"

But Joy would not be brow-beaten. Despite a mounting headache, he waltzed around the subject until even Howqua could stand it no longer.

"The Councilor hides his cargo as he would the pleasure box of his *tai-tai*...when he has one!"

Juan Menezes did not translate this verbatim. He had dealt with Howqua before and knew about the man's departure from traditional politeness when incensed, especially when he knew his words would not be understood. Menezes blithely substituted the politer "Honorable Howqua hopes that when the information is revealed he will not be disappointed."

Joy judged that this was the closest the merchant would come to asking him outright.

"Is Honorable Howqua interested in opium?"

Both Menezes and Howqua recoiled violently. There was no need for translation. Howqua clutched his ample stomach and looked around to see if anyone else had heard.

"*Yapian!*" Howqua exclaimed.

"Yes sir, there are two ships with opium in Macau harbor."

"Why?"

"*Why?*" Joy was confused. "I don't understand."

"Why have the English brought opium?"

Joy stared at Howqua. What an odd question! Was there a problem in the translation?

"Does not Howqua realize the English have brought opium to trade?"

Strangely, Menezes did not translate but gazed into the distance. Joy was at a loss as to what was going on and looked around for inspiration. Meanwhile, Howqua called his servants and spoke rapidly. Three men disappeared down the steps and one took a position at the top of the steps.

"What's happening?" Joy asked uncertainly as Howqua returned to stand and stare at him impassively before speaking.

"Who else knows of the opium cargo?"

"In Macau?"

Howqua nodded.

"Only the captains of the three ships. The cargo was loaded in Calcutta while crews were ashore. The captains are under strict instructions not to reveal the secret."

Howqua looked long and hard at Joy, his eyes hooded, his

mustache blowing.

"Someone has revealed the secret. Chinese pirates do not attack English ships. It is a bad thing."

Why is the man not excited? Joy wondered.

Reading the thought, Howqua said, "The English have two gold mines in the harbor. But they also have two kegs of gunpowder. Howqua is certain the secret is not widely known, or every pirate from Borneo to Siam would be arriving in Macau. The secret must have leaked out to Chiang-p'ing or Lan Tao because Wu Cha-tan was seen in the pirate attack." He mopped his brow. "The English are lucky." After a pause he said, "if only Howqua had known before."

"The English are not lucky," Joy said pointedly.

Howqua was at once apologetic and did a dance of embarrassment.

"A thousand pardons, Honorable Councilor. So sorry. So sorry. The ramifications of the cargo have made Howqua ill-mannered as a street peddler."

He resumed his pacing.

"The opium is from India?"

"Yes, actually from Bengal. From Patna."

Howqua beamed.

"It *is* Patna Opium?"

"Yes, sir."

Howqua thought some more. Then he asked matter-of-factly, "Does the Councilor know how much the cargo is worth?"

Oh no, you won't get me that easily! Joy thought. *Never be the first to name a price – basic dictum of negotiating.* He pretended to think. He had two hundred chests of opium, a hundred to a ship. Cornwallis had paid Vikram 750 Spanish dollars per chest for a total of 150,000 dollars, partly from the Company treasury and partly from his own wealth, expecting proportionate returns. Each chest contained 140 pounds of the powder. Sir Paul had said they could get ten times this amount in China, but Joy thought this unlikely. However, it was somewhere to begin. He feigned ignorance to Howqua's question.

"No sir, I do not."

The merchant went back on the offensive.

"Howqua cannot believe the Councilor is negotiating without knowledge of terms."

Joy was ready for this one.

"Ah, sir, that is shameful but true. The Councilor did not anticipate having to establish the trade pricing. The *tai-pan* would have done so. His sudden passing has left our Company bereft."

He said this in earnest innocence.

The *hong* merchant's eyes narrowed and Joy could read his thoughts. This could be his deal of a lifetime. Howqua felt an orgasmic anticipation about the possibilities before him. An unprepared, inexperienced young trade representative, unused to the ways of China, dealing for a cargo of untold value, with no one he can trust. Howqua stopped himself from rubbing his hands together and decided to adopt a big brotherly attitude.

"Considering it is the Councilor's first venture in China, his Company's most unworthy *hong* Howqua will try to make the best arrangement. What quantity has the Councilor brought?"

Joy had thought this through and utilized his newly-learnt art of self-deprecation.

"The Councilor is ashamed before Howqua for not being completely certain. We have, perhaps, eighty chests."

"In three ships? That is difficult to believe."

"The *tai-pan* advised us that foreign traders are not allowed to carry opium in their ships. So opium is only in the Indian ships." Joy rambled on deliberately. "But maybe we have a little more. I am not quite sure. Since we were uncertain of the outcome of the transaction, we did not wish to take up hold space that could be used for spice purchases in Java. Howqua must know opium is an unknown commodity. The English in India, uncertain of the market, are risk averse to the point of..."

Howqua was forced to interrupt this flow.

"It is dangerous to bring opium to China. Its entry is banned by the Emperor no less."

"Really, sir?" Joy made his eyes round. "I am so dismayed. Shall we take it back? But we have been told it is in great demand."

"Certainly it is. But distribution is perilous. All cargo unloading at Whampoa Island in the Pearl River is monitored by the Hoppo. If Howqua is discovered dealing in opium he shall be beaten one hundred strokes and forced to wear the *cangue*[2] around his neck. And the English shall be banned from China."

---

[2] A device used for public humiliation in China until the early 20th century, occasionally used for torture. As it restricted a person's movements, it was common for people wearing *cangues* to starve to death as they were unable to feed themselves.

Joy made a show of clutching his bound forehead.

"Oh! Oh! The Councilor is devastated to hear this."

Howqua continued his pacing. They had been talking now for over two hours. The sun had climbed directly overhead and it would have been very hot had the steady breeze not cooled the hilltop.

"The unloading of the cargo will be difficult," Howqua hypothesized. "We shall need boats for up-country distribution. One cannot brazenly enter Whampoa and unload opium."

He laughed at the humor he saw in the imagery. Joy knew all this but let the other man carry on with his lamentations. Finally, the offer came.

"Howqua has decided to accept the cargo. Keeping his own profit non-existent, Howqua can give one thousand dollars per chest."

Joy bit his tongue and hid his chagrin. 200,000 dollars in return for Corny's investment of 150,000? This was a much lower starting bid than he had expected.

"If the Councilor will arrange delivery."

Joy stared at Howqua and fought hard to control his temper. It was ridiculous. He might as well pack and go back to Fort William.

"Sir!" he protested. "The *tai-pan* would be desolate had he been alive. We paid more to *buy* the opium in India. The East India Company are traders not missionaries. Surely Howqua jests."

"Tausan' five hunner'!"

Howqua broke into *pigdin* in his excitement. Joy looked him in the eye but did not respond. Howqua returned to Cantonese.

"Two thousand." Menezes translated. "Howqua has expenses.

Great expenses. Howqua faces immense risk."

Joy looked at him sadly.

"Sir, the English face immense risk. This Councilor is overcome by the mistake he made in bringing opium to China. The *tai-pan* had false information. How unfortunate it is that we faced peril and loss for so pitiful a return. I am convinced now it is unwise to proceed on this venture. Howqua may be in danger of wearing the *cangue,* but the English King will execute this councilor for getting England barred from China for nothing. It is better we return the cargo to India, or sell in Siam where there is no imperial edict."

Howqua was unmoved by the long speech. Joy knew the wily Chinese negotiator had seen clearly through his lamentations.

"Howqua cannot go beyond twenty-five hundred. Any more and Howqua will be destroyed!"

Saying this, the Chinese merchant stared at Joy challengingly. The implied message was explicit. This was as far as he would go without a counter-offer. Joy had managed to get the starting price raised two and a half times without showing his hand. His aura of innocence would not stand up any longer.

"Sir, merchants of the East India Company are extremely poor businessmen. We had expected to sell chests of opium in China for seven thousand dollars at the very least. This is the minimum incentive for the Company to bring more quantity of opium. Perhaps the demand for opium is exaggerated?"

Howqua twirled in a complex jig and pulled at the sleeves of his robe in vexation.

"Seven tausan' dollah! Seven tausan' dollah! *Aah-eee-ah!* What is this? Madness! Impossible. Ve'y impossible."

Joy said nothing.

Howqua raved and ranted. Abruptly he stopped and asked in *pigdin,* "Quality, he good?"

Joy stood up.

"Fortunately, sir, we have a sample."

The *hong* merchant took the leather pouch and undid the thong. There was a yellowish-white powder in it. Howqua sniffed the powder and, with his head still bent, looked at Joy with an unusual expression, a mixture of suspicion and grudging respect. Then the mask dropped back.

"To judge its quality Howqua has to simmer the powder in water and strain it. Only then can the relative weight of the opium be compared with impurities."

"Howqua has this Councilor's assurance it is best quality Patna Opium. During procurement, our representative checked the quality thoroughly. But, of course, Howqua must assure himself."

The merchant of Canton paced anew.

"There is indeed demand for opium in China. Increasing its import will bring great reward. But risks are great. How shall the unloading be effected without luring outlaws? Without attracting meddlesome *mandarins?* It is indeed a problem. But...," he sighed mightily "...Howqua must do it since the Councilor must return feeling justly rewarded. Howqua now offers thirty-five hundred dollars per chest, subject to the quality being excellent. After all, eighty chests of opium are not much return for this trouble."

"*Oh!*"

Joy dramatically thumped his head with the back of his hand, squeaking at the resulting stab of pain. Keeping up the charade of gullibility he said, "Oh, sir! I may be thinking of one ship's cargo. Perhaps we may have more chests. The captain who waits below will know the exact tonnage. Have the kindness to wait."

Without giving Howqua a chance to react, Joy turned on his heel and walked past the Chinese guard, down the steps to the next level of the fort and onto the courtyard below. He left the open-mouthed merchant watching his retreating figure.

Captain Zal Irani, master of *Satpura*, and two armed English soldiers started forward as Joy came toward them. They had expected his return long ago, but had been ordered under pain of dismissal not to interrupt the meeting. One of Howqua's guards stood nearby. Another could be seen by the main gate of the fort.

Joy told Irani to keep waiting. Then he climbed laboriously back up the steps. When he reached the top he was breathing heavily.

"I am terribly sorry, sir," he puffed to the impatient Howqua. "One of the ships had additional cargo loaded at the last moment. We have two hundred chests of opium in total."

Howqua's eyes widened. Then a broad smile lit up his face.

"Ve'y good. Ve'y good."

"But the English are unable to sell for less than fifty-five hundred dollars."

"*Aa-eee-ah!* Am I made of money? Where will Howqua find that

DIPAK BASU

much money? It is impossible!"

Joy said nothing. Howqua came close. Menezes' translation became rapid-fire.

"It is impossible. When he has done business in China as long as Howqua, the Councilor will know how expensive it is with *squeegee* and *cumshaw* and all the other bribery Howqua must put up with."

"Five thousand two hundred and fifty!"

"Four tausan'!"

"The English will depend on Howqua's help when the new *tai-pan* takes charge. For that reason, we shall sacrifice this opium at five thousand dollars per chest. This councilor will not go lower."

"Five thousand dollars per chest? Two hundred chests at five hundred dollars is ten *lac*[3] dollars. Where will Howqua find ten *lac* dollars of money without causing suspicion?"

"Money, sir?" Joy acted as though that money and profits were the last things he had in his mind. "Howqua will not give us *money!*"

Taken completely aback, the *hong* merchant goggled at him.

Joy continued the innocence act.

"No, no. The English strive to please. Howqua will face no monetary inconvenience whatsoever for this transaction. He only has to credit our tea purchase for this year for one *lac* dollars."

Howqua's mouth fell open. His expression became a curious mixture of astonishment, anger and admiration. He stared at the boyish emaciated figure with the strapped head and realized he had been outwitted at his own game by a novice. No, here was no novice.

---

[3] Lac = one hundred thousand

Do not take the English lightly, he reminded himself for the hundredth time. Had not the old *tai-pan* proven that? But, Howqua told himself, it really was all right. If not a killing, he had a good deal. No, it was a great deal. He had thoroughly enjoyed the bargaining. And of course, he would get back twice the price he was paying when the opium was distributed retail.

Joy, on the other hand, was completely drained, feeling sick and faint. He turned away unable to keep the facade up any longer.

Suddenly Howqua's shrill laughter rang out across the ramparts of Fort Guia and Joy found himself enveloped in a bear hug. Howqua slapped his back heartily.

"*Hao shen! Hao shen!*" Howqua crowed. Very good! "Without question, this Councilor from India will be *tai-pan* one day!"

Joy looked closely at Howqua in surprise. He first thought Howqua was being facetious. Then he saw the compliment was genuine. He began to feel good. Very good. A million dollar return on Corny's outlay was most welcome. Impulsively he tightened his arms around the plump Chinese and the two men laughed and yelled and staggered around Menezes like a pair of wrestlers.

Howqua waited until the last moment to drop his little bomb.

"Of course, the Councilor who will be *tai-pan*, should have no trouble arranging the unloading and delivering the cargo to Howqua."

18

The Select Committee of Canton had at last been told about the opium venture. Reactions of members went through the entire spectrum of emotions. First there was stunned silence, then exclamations of disbelief, followed by oaths of outrage. Then there was pandemonium. Members went at each other with verbal hammer and tongs, delighted to have so monumental a topic to debate.

Sitting beside Vikram, Joy slumped tiredly and closed his eyes. A single phrase played over and over in his mind. *Déjà vu. Déjà vu. Déjà vu.* It was the Executive Committee of Fort William all over again. How many such meetings had he suffered through in Calcutta? Listening to the maelstrom of uninformed opinion of men who were supposedly blazing a trail for English supremacy, Joy could easily appreciate the burden under which Sir Paul had labored. While the senseless, acrimonious polemic raged, he saw how simple it would be for England to slide back to the Dark Ages.

Major Abernathy, the liaison officer, was insisting the opium cargo should be reported to Chinese officialdom.

"You're missing the point, Major," somebody banged the table. "Representation to Chiny authority is exactly what we must avoid."

"Ain't possible."

"Only as it needs courage."

"*What?* How dare ye, ye good-for-nought..."

Irving Macardle jumped up.

"Stop! Ye all listen now. You are both uninformed. When the Turks brought opium to China..."

"Gentlemen, please!"

Macardle stopped in mid-sentence, looking pained.

Joy got to his feet.

"May I speak?"

A committee member opened his mouth to actually contest the question. Joy held up his hand like a gauze-wrapped Moses and the man subsided.

"Gentlemen, negotiations for opium delivery are already underway. But we have a problem with Howqua."

"Aye!" assented Macardle with relish, as if he had just scored a personal victory.

Joy ignored him.

"The problem, however, presents an opportunity that can have major positive impact for us. Gentlemen, opium will come to China in a big way. Opium can become England's savior."

Everyone spoke at once, some in favor, some against. Joy became Moses once more.

"Gentlemen. Opium *has* to come to China. You have no choice."

"But..." began a selectman.

"Sir, I am prepared to spend hours with you on the background and merits of this venture. But not now. Please understand, opium *has* to come to China."

While members came to terms with this, with a little start Joy realized he was unconsciously adopting Sir Paul's confident style of speech. He told them how the bravado of Drake and Raleigh during the Spanish Armada had rewarded England a million-fold.

"Gentlemen, the hardest part of creating history is living it. Look around you. We are, you are, about to create history. Today. What would you like history to record? That England handed the Orient back to Portugal? Or the British Empire grew out of the Orient?"

There was dead silence. It was the very first time they had heard of or even thought about a British Empire.

"Yes?" Joy persisted.

Still no one spoke and the men stared at Joy like children in a schoolroom, scared to speak in case the answer was wrong.

"What is Britain, gentlemen?" Joy continued. "Is it Windsor Castle? Is it the King? Is it William Pitt? They are a Britain of bygone days." He paused, then, "Britain is *you!*" Joy nodded to add emphasis. "*You!*" He pointed to each man in turn. "*You* are the future of Britain. And success, nay survival, of Britain is in *your* hands. You at Canton were fortunate to have a great Englishman as your leader, but Sir Paul has gone to his grave. He cannot be, must not be, allowed to take England's greatness with him."

Joy changed his approach.

"Gentlemen, do you know the reach of the Portuguese Empire?" When no one ventured a response, Joy counted on each of his fingers until all were used up. "Brazil. Azores. Angola. Mozambique. Goa. Cochin. Ceylon. Malacca. Macau. Borneo. A great chain, fifteen thousand miles long, possessing the greatest commercial resources in the world. In comparison, what is the extent of the East India Company? Lost American colonies. Three frail footholds in India, widely separated. A shaky toehold in China. Each one disputed. Each one threatened. How can we aspire to replace Portugal as *the* world's maritime power?"

Joy stopped and looked around at each member as if expecting answers. Most dropped their eyes. Joy continued.

"How can we replace Portugal's maritime power? I will tell you how. First we have to believe. Believe that it *can* be done. Britain *can* replace Portugal. Britain *will* replace Portugal. And then, gentlemen, we have to act. Act to replace Portugal. And the key is opium. Be it insidious. Be it dishonorable. Opium *will* propel Britain forward if we are inventive. Or else, the mantle will pass to nations with greater enterprise. The choice is yours. Today. Now. Decide carefully."

He sat down, drained.

After a silence there were more arguments. Joy thought of his own nights of fighting demons before he understood Sir Paul's call-to-arms and sympathized with the small-minded merchants he was asking to change the world. As the deliberation continued, members of the Select Committee listed the pluses. The opium cargo was here. The cargo had a good price and a confirmed buyer. There were excellent long term prospects. Then they listed the minuses. The cargo was vulnerable. The cargo was contraband. A delivery mechanism was missing. There was no one in charge.

They tackled the vulnerability issue first. There was nothing much they could do beyond *Albatross* and a couple of smaller navy craft guarding the Indian ships, and by preventing word from spreading. But every day that passed would surely bring a crisis closer. Then they discussed the problem of unloading the cargo. Who could do it? Where could it be done? How would Howqua dispatch it onward? When nothing conclusive emerged, frustrated, they started to talk dispiritedly about the imperial decree that prohibited import of opium.

"Sahibs?"

Everyone looked up in surprise as Vikram spoke for the first time. When the meeting began they had not known what to make of the dark Indian who had not been introduced. When he remained a silent presence they forgot him in the heated dialog.

"Sahibs," Vikram said frowning in concentration and speaking as clearly as he could. "I am Prince Vikram Sena from India. The opium comes from my lands. I have been listening to Morley-sahib and may be able to help. I count seven parties to the success of the venture. Or to its failure."

"Seven, eh?" Major Abernathy could not resist a sarcastic dig.

"Sure ye ain't forgotten one or two?"

Joy wanted to strangle the man.

"Yes, Sahib, seven." Vikram said, unruffled. "The producer, the seller, the buyer, the unloader, the distributor, the consumer, the regulator." When he had difficulty with the words, Joy helped him.

"The producer," Vikram continued "is myself. The seller is the East India Company represented by Morley-sahib and you. The buyer is Howqua. The regulator is the Chinese administrator."

"The Hoppo," Macardle added helpfully.

"Thank you, Sahib. The Hoppo is the regulator. The consumers are the Chinese people. The unloader and the distributor are missing. As you have correctly concluded, this is the problem." He paused for a moment. "We shall examine the problem from a military viewpoint."

He had their attention now. The strange accent and the broken words coupled with obvious intelligence and simple and logical speech were a novel experience for the Englishmen.

"Who is in conflict with us? And who is our ally? The Hoppo opposes us on account of his imperial duty. Can he be made an ally? Perhaps, as the Hoppo is greedy. Who else? The pirates of the sea confront us. They are greedy too. Can *they* be made allies?"

Everyone, including Joy, gasped in surprise.

"Through personal experience in their island hiding place I have found the pirates are divided. This is an opening. Remember that. And there exists one other group that must be considered."

Vikram paused to give dramatic effect.

"Who?" asked someone, unable to stand the suspense.

"The triads of Canton."

There was bigger gasp. Selectmen were terrified of triads.

Joy's heart began to beat faster as, before anyone could interrupt, Vikram described his scenario piece by piece while recounting his adventures. He told them of Bombshell Wu, of Angry Feng, and the flowering of their friendship, his respect for the young man's wisdom and organizational ability.

"Feng Sheng-chi who has links to both pirates and triads is highly motivated to help us. He is experienced and, in my opinion, he is trustworthy. Of course for a price." There were loud objections before Vikram could continue. "I suggest we charge Honorable Feng with the task of drawing together workers and boats to secretly unload the opium. That is our first step."

The members looked at each other dumbstruck. What Vikram was suggesting to them was beyond the utterly impossible. Joy's heart went out to his friend for magnanimously using the word 'we' and 'our' through the discourse. Finally, finally, someone had original ideas.

Vikram pointed out of the window.

"From a small boat I have seen the complex system of inlets and islands while I coursed up and then down the Pearl River. Honorable Feng knows that maze of waterways intimately. His knowledge and willingness to help will make him a good distributor."

Macardle found himself agreeing with the prince. He looked Vikram up and down. The well-groomed man in locally tailored robes hiding his scars bore no resemblance to the battered and unkempt native in dirty pantaloons that had appeared on his doorstep. With

Vikram's unbiased and positive attitude, the animosity between Committee members evaporated.

Joy was ecstatic.

"I recommend we examine the remarkable scheme of his Highness," Macardle said. "We be needing Howqua's approval, since the distributor, this Feng, must work with the buyer. Or at least have a close liaison. We have to introduce the two Chinese gentlemen. Hmmm, their backgrounds are quite diverse."

"Three Chinese gentlemen, Sahib."

"Three, yer Highness? Oh, yes. The Hoppo. We have to think that one through. It'll need a right lot of diplomacy. The Hoppo, eh? *Should* he be involved in this?"

At that moment, Compradore Liu entered the committee room and went over to Macardle with a rolled-up scroll.

"Chop f'om Hoppo, sar," said Liu.

"*Begorrah!*" exclaimed Macardle. "This be uncanny, mon. Speak of the man and along comes his letter."

"*Joss!*" said the Company engineer.

Joy and Vikram looked at the elderly man who explained.

"In China, good portents, called *joss*, are important. I think you just had a big dose of *joss* here. What does the letter say, Mac? Oh, it's in Mandarin. Read it please, Liu."

The *compradore* cleared his throat, held the scroll to the light and read the brushed characters. His smiling face became grave.

"This is an Imperial Decree," Liu said. "It is being sent to all Factories in Canton and Macau immediately. It is about Eight

Regulations regarding the behavior of foreigners that have been set in effect from the New Year." He shook out the scroll and translated:

The Eight Regulations that will be strictly enforced are:

1. *Vessels of war are prohibited from entering the Boca Tigris.*
2. *Women, guns, and arms are not permitted in Factories.*
3. *All pilots and* compradores *must be registered. If smuggling occurs,* compradores *shall be punished.*
4. *Each factory can employ up to 8 Chinese for menial services.*
5. *Foreigners are prohibited from rowing about the Pearl River for pleasure. Exceptions for droves of no more than 10 shall be permitted on special days.*
6. *Foreigners may present petitions only through* hong *merchants.*
7. Hong *merchants are not to owe debts to foreigners. Smuggling to and from the city is prohibited.*
8. *Foreign ships arriving with merchandise must not loiter about on the river. They must come direct to Whampoa. They must not rove about the bays at pleasure and sell goods subject to duty to rascally natives so that they may smuggle them, thereby defrauding His Celestial Majesty's revenue.*

"Some fresh air?"

"Thank you, Sahib."

The Hoppo's damning scroll had abruptly ended the meeting and Joy and Vikram walked down the stairs to the Largo de Seneca. Vikram took his convalescing friend's arm and they strolled across the square to the waterfront without speaking, each man mentally reviewing the fallout of the meeting.

"So it will be Feng?" Joy mused. "How appropriate."

Vikram did not follow, but said nothing.

"Oh!" Joy was suddenly contrite. "Are you all right?"

Vikram looked at him inquiringly.

"I am so involved with all that is happening that I don't know where you are staying. Are you comfortable? I am so sorry, my friend."

"Do not worry, Sahib. I am well taken care of. On my first night I stayed with Feng, who has, shall we say, interesting friends in Macau. But later the memsahibs arranged for me to stay with Menezes a short distance from the British Residence. I have learnt much of Macau from him. And from Feng."

"What a fascinating place is China!"

Vikram nodded and they looked out at the waters of the harbor and the busy afternoon scene. Dozens of sampans bobbed in the foreground or made their way from the pier to junks lying offshore. About twenty foreign ships dominated the setting, including *Albatross* whose mast was now upright. They could make out the two smaller Indian ships beside her.

Joy returned to the main theme.

"You have faith in Feng?"

"I owe him my freedom, Sahib, and my life. I have spent several days continuously in his company, on shore and at sea. He has placed his trust in me by breaking with Wu's clan, for which his own life is forfeit. The pirates that attacked your ship are now his blood enemies. They will not rest until they kill him. But Feng is used to living on the run. And he is protected by the triads. He is convinced that dealing with the English for opium will give him the long-term power and wealth to protect him from the pirates and lord it over them. An unsafe life, Sahib. I cannot but admire him."

He told Joy more about the triads of Canton. About Feng's rise in the secret society of the Buddhist goddess of mercy. And the fact that he, Vikram, was a Buddhist, commanded respect in the eyes of the triad chief, Tat Au-yong.

"Yes, I have faith in Feng," Vikram concluded.

"What about the Hoppo?"

Vikram stopped and looked straight at Joy.

"Is not the Hoppo an official of the Emperor's government?"

"Yes, he is."

"Then the Hoppo is a simpler solution."

Joy's head jerked up. The simplicity of Vikram's reasoning was unnerving. How lucky was he to have such a perceptive friend. A slow grin spread over his face.

"Shades of the Battle of Plassey! Robert Clive defeated Shiraj Doula and annexed Bengal without a shot being fired."

"Every man, Sahib, has his price."

"True, quite true." Then Joy's face clouded over. "But how can we bring over one so close to the Emperor?"

He began to brood as they walked past the majestic facade of Leal Senado that housed the Macau government.

"Come my friend," Vikram tried to cheer him. "You worry too much. You have recovered your health and you are on your way to recover your dream. Is that not enough? Life is fleeting."

Joy stared at him. The philosophical attitude was a departure from the businesslike prince of old. His question showed in his eyes.

"Sahib, I have seen the face of death several times and I have returned. I have experienced human depravity at its worst and I have survived. I have gambled with my life and I have won."

About to say something more, Vikram stopped.

"Yes?" prompted Joy.

"I am happy."

Watching his friend's serene face, Joy was intrigued. He waited but Vikram did not elaborate. He took Joy's arm and they sauntered back to *Britannia*. In spite of his qualms, Joy began to feel better.

"Join me for a glass of ale? We can talk more and, by the way, Miss Andrews likes you."

Vikram's face broke into a sunny smile and Joy looked at him in surprise. The cheerfulness was another new side of his friend.

19

Three days later, the click of coins on gambling tables and bursts of excited chatter filled the Baiyun Shan casino. The casino was doing roaring business tonight. It was named after White Cloud Mountain, a landmark that dominated Canton's skyline.

The confluence of Chinese and European gambling passions, a hallmark of Macau, was evident in the eager faces of the hundred and more people jammed into the building. Swarthy Portuguese in bowler hats and bristling beards, Chinese with shaved crowns and queues, light-skinned Parsees from India, all locked elbows at *fan-tan* tables. They placed bets and intently watched the throw of coins. As soon as the shower of silver tinkled onto the table they feverishly estimated the number of coins. They everyone grabbed an abacus or quill and divided the number by four, calculated the remainder and shouted the result. There was a pregnant pause, then whoops of jubilation and groans of disappointment at the dealer's verdict. According to rules of the ancient game, each *fan-tan* player guessing the correct number received three times his stake, less seven percent for the bank.

Cigar and pipe smoke swirled to the ceiling and merged with sooty fumes of lamps hanging above the tables.

Most of the ante-rooms surrounding the casino floor were illegal opium dens operating with payments to corrupt officials. Here, glassy-eyed addicts lay beside one another on divans. Long pipes with smoldering pellets in their bowls, rested by their side. Small pigtailed boys with panniers of coal ran across the *fan-tan* room often under the feet of the men gambling.

Through an archway, the tea-house was visible on the other side of the building. Everyone knew that 'tea-house' was a euphemism for the staging area of the brothel associated with the casino. Men, Chinese and European, sat at small tables and drank tea from exquisite ceramic cups, while prettily dressed *sing-song* girls paraded for their attention. The girls came in twos with mincing steps on tiny bound feet. Their jade and ruby jewelry sparkled in the lamplight. Their white-powdered faces shone in striking contrast to heavily made-up black eyes, blood-red lips, and long dark hair piled with lacquered clips. They played zithers and crooned in penetrating tones. Customers discussed their charms amid unrestrained laughter. After much haggling, a man would leave the casino with a prostitute, or take her up a set of stairs to the floor above.

In one of the ante-rooms, a remarkably diverse group of men were in earnest conversation around a food-laden table.

Joy Morley and Jerome Winkley were English. Zal Irani, master of *Satpura*, gray-eyed and fair, was a Parsee, descendant of persecuted Persians who had fled with their sacred fire to western India a thousand years ago. Joaquim Fernandes, captain of *Gulab*, whose quick action had won *Albatross* back from the pirates, was a Portuguese from Goa. His appearance was quite extraordinary. Fernandes had big bushy eyebrows and a horned moustache. He was a hugely built man, well over six feet tall, weighing more than 300 pounds, dark and swashbuckling. Like Tau-pei, Fernandes had the deeply pock-marked face of a smallpox survivor. Because of his size and appearance, Fernandes instinctively caused fear among those he met. In actual fact, Fernandes had a clever mind and gentle nature.

Juan Menezes had a bit of almost every race in his blood.

Finally, there was Howqua, their host.

Joy had wanted the prince to be present, but Vikram declined. The reason he offered was his Indian-ness would complicate matters. It was a weak argument. Joy knew Vikram was not keen to meet Captain Winkley, and had not pressed him. Midshipmen Kyle and Newbond stood guard at the casino entrance.

The men dug into unfamiliar but delicious food and sat back satiated. Pairs of *sing-song* girls looked in hopefully and were shooed away. The merchant of Canton, his voice now a jolly soprano, asked if anyone would like more to eat.

"*Não, obrigado, senhor,*" Fernandes replied. This was his first visit to China and from what he had experienced, it would not be his last. He thought of the pretty-as-a-picture Chinese girl who had given him hours of pleasure the night before. He had trouble recalling her name. Qio-something. The name meant 'pretty' in Cantonese, Menezes told him later. It fitted her perfectly. What *was* it? Qioli? Qiala? No, Qiaoli. What had she not done for him, tiny thing that she was! Fernandes beamed at Howqua, thinking about Qiaoli.

Howqua watched him in consternation. All foreign devils are ugly, Howqua thought, but this one looked like a hungry tiger! Why did he smile in that horrible manner? Did he have murder in his heart? Howqua tore his eyes away. Barbarians! How *could* he deal with them? Big, evil-smelling men. How could he make them understand their little countries in cold faraway seas were insignificant to China? But, he reasoned, even foreign devils have a purpose and he must suffer them for a greater cause. How much money would he make out of the opium deal? Forty lac taels? Forty-five? Maybe even fifty! If the plan succeeded and opium flowed like water, he would become the richest man in China. With that thought, Howqua's heart beat painfully against his ribs.

"Shaohing chiu?" he announced, holding up a big stone jug.

The foreigners helped themselves to the superb wine of Chekiang province and Howqua clapped his hands. Bus-boys appeared to clear away dishes and wipe diners' faces and hands with wet cloth. He clapped his hands again and the boys scuttled away. Howqua carefully arranged the folds of his robe. It was time for business. Sensing this, Menezes got ready to translate. Unlike at Fort Guia, Howqua got straight to the point this time.

"Has the Councilor decided how to unload his ships?"

"We have ideas, but where can we unload?" Joy countered.

Howqua shook his head in response, but Joy pressed him.

"Where can we unload, sir?"

Howqua thought for a while and said, "The barbarian ships draw attention. The Hoppo always watches the ships."

Howqua stopped and waited, but Joy did not speak. He had not yet decided the logistics of involving Feng's people. As the silence lengthened uncomfortably, he remembered the muddle he had made of his meeting with the Jagat Seth on the ramparts of Fort William. This time he resolved not to show his hand until completely ready.

"By thunder, can we get this over quickly?"

Jerome's outburst broke the silence. Startled, Howqua turned to him and, when Menezes translated, he sniffed in barely-contained disdain. This touched off Jerome's hair-trigger temper and his face began to get red.

"Stow it, Cap'n!"

Joy's voice was low and controlled but contained all the authority he could muster. It had its effect and Jerome subsided.

"Why does the Hoppo watch barbarian ships?" Joy asked, not wanting the conversation to lose its thread.

"An island would be better," Howqua said after another pause. "Isolated. Some Chinese islands have excellent hidden harbors."

Aha! thought Joy. "Can Howqua recommend some islands?"

The merchant of Canton made a long speech, pausing periodically for the translation to catch up.

"Islands, Councilor? There are many islands. There is

Whampoa Island. That is too close to Canton. No island of the Pearl River is safe from the Hoppo's spies." Then he became professorial. "The Emperor has many problems. Famines, rebellions, invasions, plagues, taxes. He has an army of soldiers for military matters and a bigger army of bureaucrats for civil matters. But his navy is weak. The reach of the Emperor ends with *nei-hai*, the inner ocean. Realizing this, pirates have made *wai-hai*, the outer ocean, their domain. On Lan Tao island. The pirates seek to capture the Councilor's cargo. The Emperor and the Hoppo shall want to do the same. And so the Councilor must look for an island between the *nei-hai* and *wai-hai*. It is simple!"

Howqua stopped, believing he had made the issue perfectly clear. Joy looked around at the others who were as nonplussed as he. An island between the inner and outer ocean? Where did one end and the other begin? When he asked Howqua, the answer was devastating in its simplicity.

"One can see the *nei-hai* but the *wai-hai* is too far to see."

Joy stared at the merchant. Then his eyes opened wide as a fundamental naval philosophy became clear. Howqua had just summed up centuries of maritime history in one innocuous sentence. From the quintessential view of the land-lubber, for whom the ocean is vast and intimidating, Howqua had clarified why countries that had ocean-going navies were successful in subjugating those that shied away from the seas or only had coastal power.

His mind snapped back as Howqua clapped once more.

"Hong Kong Island! It is perfect."

Joy sat up eagerly, but was deflated when Howqua stated, "We shall speak of business later. Tonight is for pleasure."

The meeting adjourned. As they made ready to leave, Howqua signaled Joy and Jerome to remain while he escorted the Indian captains and Menezes out of the casino.

Nothing happened for a while.

The two men sipped *shaohing* and watched the diminishing activity in the *fan-tan* room. It was quite late and only three tables were still active. Their attention was drawn to one on which there was a very large pile of coins. The huge stakes were reflected in the tension on the players' faces. As they watched, the dealer threw coins in a waterfall of jingling gold and silver. Joy could not even begin to guess how much the table was worth. For a few moments there was silence as players calculated. Then came a chorus of bets. The dealer began to count the coins amid a breathless hush. Players at other tables stopped to watch. A series of groans grew to a climax as the dealer neared the end of his count. He tallied the last coin and pushed the pile in the direction of the person who had guessed correctly. Joy tried to make out the winner through the smoke. The man was dressed as all the others. He had something hanging from his neck on a string. He had an untamed mouse-like face and did not gloat like other winners while he scooped his coins into a sack. Suddenly he looked up and their eyes met. Joy felt an eerie sensation of unease and involuntarily dropped his eyes. When he looked up the man was gone.

Howqua came back, his expression buoyant.

"Too muchee talk he stop!"

The use of *pigdin* indicated that the time for formality was over.

Joy smiled. After food, wine, and business, it did not take great intelligence to fathom what was next on the agenda.

Beside him, Jerome frowned.

Howqua clapped and two women entered the room hesitantly. At once Joy realized these were not ordinary *sing-song* girls. They were stunningly beautiful in the classical Chinese fashion, fragile enough to break. Their perfect oval faces were powdered snowy white. They wore delicately embroidered silk robes with flowing sleeves. Like identical painted dolls, they bowed to Howqua and stood with bent heads. Howqua put an arm around each and nodded at the one on his left.

"Missee my!" he said.

Then he nodded at the girl on his right.

"Missee my!"

Joy wondered if this meant they were his daughters or his concubines or his prostitutes or his slaves. Joy studied the girls closely and tried to differentiate between them. But other than the color and pattern on their robes, they looked exactly alike.

"Howqua him likee English *tai-pan,* English sea lord too much, never mind. Howqua give English fellahs missees belong him!"

Joy understood. Jerome did not follow but suspected the intent and looked at Joy mutinously. *What's his problem this time,* Joy wondered. "He's making a present of his daughters or whatever, to us, Cap'n. Which do you want?"

Jerome's face turned red.

"Which do I want? Which *one?* Are ye out of yer mind? *Giving* native women to us? Ne'er heard anything so bloody ridiculous."

Joy was not interested in the captain's sanctimony, especially since Howqua's joviality was dimming.

"Not for always. For the night, man. For the night. For Christ's sake, give the fellow credit. Can't you see he's trying to seal the opium deal? Everything in the world isn't run by naval discipline. Let's accept and get him out of here. Then we'll sort it out."

"No!" Jerome said violently.

Joy sighed and turned to Howqua wondering how to turn down the offer. He decided on a convenient untruth.

"The Captain has a pretty wife."

Joy had spoken slowly but could see that Howqua was puzzled. There was no Menezes to translate. Joy had not yet fully mastered Portuguese/English/Chinese *pigdin* argot. Suddenly he remembered the Cantonese word for wife, or rather, chief wife.

"Cap'n has *tai-tai!*" he said triumphantly.

For some reason Howqua thought this was funny, laughed and said something rapidly in Cantonese which Joy did not follow. Switching to *pigdin,* he asked, "Councilor him only takee all two missees?"

"Yes sir, and thank you...er...thankee. Much obliged."

The merchant grinned and nodded in the exact manner of a figurine with a movable head. He said something to the girls and left the room, much to Joy's relief.

There was a long pause.

The two girls stood where they were, heads bowed and eyes lowered. A burst of noise from a *fan-tan* table broke the tableau and

Joy got to his feet. He had a code. A pretty girl, whichever part of the world she may be in, was a pretty girl and commanded a gentleman's attention. Even from a vile character like Jerome. He held out two chairs but the girls giggled, shook their heads vehemently, giggled again, and covered their mouths with their hands. Then they sobered and stared at him with black-bordered eyes, wide and anxious. Finally, they bent at their knees and sat straight-backed, continuing to look at him in awe. Joy was spellbound. They were simply adorable and made him feel protective and masculine. Here was a novel way to experience China. His excitement reached the point of fantasy. How would it be with *two* Chinese girls as Howqua had implied? Then he looked at the brooding captain and sighed.

"These are probably the prettiest girls in Macau, Cap'n. Handpicked by the richest man in the land. What's your pleasure?"

"I am going to my ship. That's my pleasure."

"Well, if you leave, what, may I ask, should I do with two girls?"

"Jesus, Morley! Do what your bloody heart or whatever other filthy part of your body desires! Count me out."

He stood up to go.

"Sit down, Captain!" Joy said, getting to his feet.

"What the devil for?"

The men glowered at each other as the girls looked on in alarm. Joy tried to reason.

"Cap'n, just as it would be improper to refuse Howqua's wine, it's improper and an insult to refuse his women. Will you think of the Company and the deal for just once?"

"What d'ye think I'm here for, you fool? For the Company and the 'deal' as you call it. That don't include mixing it with foreign tarts."

"Why?"

At the question, Jerome blew up like a volcano.

"Mind yer fucking business! And watch yer damned tongue or I'll push it down yer foul throat."

A conspicuous muscle on the captain's forehead started to twitch. He clenched his fists and took a step towards Joy. The girls jumped to their feet and opened their mouths to scream.

"Pax!" exclaimed the flabbergasted Joy.

He decided to back away from the confrontation. Jerome's performance was quite inexplicable and would need later analysis.

"Settle down, man, settle down! Just relax and just...just take one of the little things upstairs. Say something nice to her and leave. Can you do at least that? You can't simply walk out. The girls'll treat us like kings. And you might actually enjoy her after all."

"No!"

Joy stared in astonishment. A normal shy man in the presence of women would be embarrassed, but not so insanely wrathful.

"Just take her up, will you?"

Jerome's face was study in distaste.

"I don't understand a word of their bloody language."

"Trust me, cap'n, you don't need to. This ain't a talking situation. Take her up, be nice, and leave her honorably."

Jerome hurled an oath at him and turned to the girls angrily. They shrank away and almost fell backward over their chairs. For a while nothing happened. Then Joy gently told the girls not to be afraid and that everything would be all right. They did not understand but were reassured by his tone and sat down. He looked at them closely once more. To his European eyes they had at first looked like two peas in a pod, with archetypal Han features and long black hair. He decided they *did* look very similar, which reinforced the theory that they might be sisters or twins or Howqua's daughters. One wore a lime-green robe with a snowy mountain scene embroidered. The other's costume was light pink with a motif of pigeons. Without any other clue Joy would have to decide between mountains and birds. Green Mountains was looking nervously at Jerome. The other girl smiled at him invitingly.

Well, that's that, he told himself. *Joy, chappie, you were always a sucker for doe-eyed smiles. I'll take Pink Birds.*

"What's your name?" he asked her.

The girl stared blankly. Joy repeated the question. When she still did not follow, her companion said something in her ear. Understanding dawned on Pink Birds. She bobbed her head and gave him another big smile.

"*Shi, shi! Wo shi* Lian."

It was the first time either of the girls had said anything. Pink Birds had a clear, faintly nasal voice as she announced her name in an earnest sort of way that Joy found appealing. To make the point perfectly clear he pointed at her and asked, "Lian?"

"*Shi! Shi!* Lian," she nodded vigorously.

He pointed to himself and said, "Joy."

The two women stared at him with their eyes so wide that Joy felt he would fall right into them. He pointed at himself again and said, "*Shi, shi,* Joy!"

"*Ni shi* Joy *ma?*"

"That's right, er...*shi!*"

Joy was pleased with himself. He was actually speaking their language! In much the same way had he learned Bengali. Then he pointed at the sullen captain and said "Jerome."

"*Jay-loam?*" said the girls in unison and dissolved into giggles.

Joy laughed out loud with them but the captain's expression got grimmer. Joy shook his head in exasperation. At this rate even *he* would have a bad night. A sense of humor would help the man a lot. Joy came to a decision. He'd had more than enough of Jerome and it was time to get moving.

"And your name?" he asked the girl in green.

"*Wo shi* Qin-ai."

"Qin-ai and Lian. What lovely names. Lian's mine, Cap'n. Qin-ai's for you. Well, Lian, what do we do next?"

He spread his arms indicating the question. Lian stood up at once and pointed at herself questioningly. Joy nodded.

"*Lai!*" she said, gesturing he should come with her.

"Good night, Cap'n," Joy got to his feet. "Don't wait up for me."

Jerome came to life.

"Eh, what? Wait! What d'ye mean, g'night? Where the devil are ye going? You can't leave me with this, this..."

"...lovely lady. You're on your own now, Cap'n. You've fought the Americans and the Russians. One Chinese wench can't do you in, can she now? Toodle-oo!"

With that Joy followed Lian into the *fan-tan* room. Jerome looked after them angrily. Slowly he calmed down and turned to Qin-ai who gawked at him fearfully. He cleared his throat and she jumped to her feet in alarm.

"H...hello!" Jerome said tentatively.

"Shenme?"

Qin-ai's voice was low and scared.

"What? Why don't you speak English for pity's sake? Damn the blighter, Morley. What in God's name am I to do now?"

"Shenme?"

Jerome considered the situation. He had not the slightest interest in this girl but remembered the tongue-lashing he had received from Miller and Cornwallis about duty to the Company.

"Damn all civilian bureaucrats!"

"Shenme?"

"And damn women!"

"Shenme?"

"And *shenme* to you too. God! How I wish you'd talk a proper language. Bloody heathens! Let's see. What was your name now?"

He pointed at her.

"Wo shi Qin-ai."

"Oh that's right. Qin-ai. I'm Jerome."

"Jay-loam?"

This time she did not giggle.

"Right, that's me. Jerome Winkley, captain. Now we have *that* established, how do we get rid of you?" Qin-ai looked blank. "Oh, never mind. And please don't say *shenme* again. Where do we go now?"

He spread his arms as Joy had done. Qin-ai smiled gingerly and indicated he should follow. They went past the deserted *fan-tan* tables into the tea room. A heavily made up woman was playing a zither for several men sitting around a big table. She wore a black silk *cheong-sam* that was slit to the waist on either side and showed creamy skin of her thighs as she walked.

Jerome turned up his nose.

Qin-ai stopped and asked, *"Chai?"*

"What?"

"Chai." She mimed drinking from a cup.

"Oh, tea! No thanks. It's past tea-time, don't y'know? Let's get this over with."

Qin-ai continued across the tea-room. The train of her robe and long sleeves streamed behind her as she took quick little steps and tripped along like a clockwork toy. She led him up a flight of steps and along a balcony that overhung the street. He looked down and saw the armed midshipmen standing stolidly below. They went past several doors to a room at the very end. A pair of older women waited on either side of the entrance, smiling and bowing. Jerome went past them into the room. He heard the door close, instinctively spun around and violently pulled the handle. It opened easily and the red-faced captain found himself face to face with the astonished women. Sheepishly, he closed the door, turned, and stood still.

The interior of the chamber was simultaneously garish and

snug. It was lit by two oil lamps on chests of drawers on either side of a large brocade-covered bed that dominated the room. An armchair stood beside a barred window. All the furniture, as well as the door and window shutters were lacquered in red and black and hand-painted in floral designs. The wooden floor was covered by a thick rug. The voice of the singing girl floated up from the tea-room with the zither twanging tinnily.

Qin-ai stood quietly by the bed, her eyes on the carpet. Jerome warily lowered himself into the armchair. Nothing happened for a minute or two. After a while, feeling very hot, he stood up and struggled out of his naval jacket. The girl came to life and took the jacket from him. She folded and carefully placed it in one of the drawers. Having completed the task, she turned and looked at him questioningly.

"Listen, old girl. You've been good but I'm not really into..."

"*Chi'ng tso.*"

"What?"

She gestured toward the armchair and he sat back down.

Qin-ai began to untie her robe and Jerome sat forward in consternation. "Hold on!" he exclaimed. "No! Don't do that."

Qin-ai looked at him in perplexed dismay. *"Ai! Ai!"* she wailed, her eyes filling with tears.

"Now belay there. No need to get all worked up. It's nothing personal, y'know."

Jerome decided try sign language and gestured to her to settle down. She stopped crying and looked at him in confusion. He began to perspire and wondered where Morley was. He looked at the door, wishing he was outside it, wishing he was anywhere but in this claustrophobic chamber. What was Morley doing with the other girl?

Qin-ai misinterpreted his look. She smiled knowingly and walked across to the door and barred it. Then she turned and in one fluid motion unclipped her hair. As it cascaded to her waist, the robe somehow came loose and magically billowed around her as it fell to her feet like a lime-green cloud. Qin-ai stood before him like an oriental Venus with one hand in her hair and the other on her hip. Her long silky tresses flowed and shimmered in the lamplight which evoked a golden glow from her alabaster skin.

Jerome gaped at her with his mouth wide open.

Qin-ai came toward him and Jerome recoiled and tried to retreat into the armchair. She came closer and his eyes dulled. All of a sudden, the girl went out of focus, shimmering like a misshapen wraith. Her figure changed and grew bigger and took the form of another woman. An overbearing, all-pervasive woman who tyrannized Father. Gentle Father. A woman who egged Father to an untenable squiredom and an early grave. A woman who dominated each moment of his boyhood, suspicious of deviation from her wishes, suspicious of anything female.

"Mother! No!" he mouthed.

Mother was coming to hit him for looking at a girl.

"No! Please, no!

He jumped up and lashed out with both hands.

Qin-ai screamed.

ço

Joy had just made love.

The girl Lian, so fragile downstairs, had driven him wild with passion. Joy's gentleness and cleanliness, his willingness to learn her ways and his genuine interest in her, transformed Lian's apprehension to admiration. The big barbarians of Macau that she serviced for Howqua smelled fetid, spoke coarsely, and treated women like chattel. For the first time Lian found she actually enjoyed giving pleasure to a foreign devil. He was tender. He explored secret parts of her body as though examining a new and interesting toy. Usually Lian would try to get it over as quickly and painlessly as possible. This time she experienced an exhilaration in the novelty of the strange man. He kissed her lips, her breasts, her stomach, her hips and finally her womanhood with a sensuous wonder of new discovery. No one had done that to her before. Her body caught fire and she completely lost control and abandoned herself to enjoyment of what he was doing. Their passion raged into a climactic fire that burned and dimmed and left them limp and entwined.

As a result, Jerome's first cry of *"Mother!"* did not penetrate their consciousness. Lian heard the subsequent scream and started up convulsively.

"Qin-ai!"

Joy stared at her blankly, then heard another scream and jumped out of bed. Footsteps pounded on the balcony outside as he pulled on his breeches. Leaving Lian cowering on the bed, he tore open the door and rushed along the balcony in the direction of Qin-ai's voice, now reduced to strangled cries. He pushed aside the group that was hammering on the door which he saw was locked from inside. Joy stepped back and threw his shoulder at it and cried out in pain. The shock hurt his injured head more than his bare shoulder, but with a crunch the rod barring the door splintered and it flew open.

Joy stepped inside. The first thing he saw was Jerome. His face was contorted hideously as he coming at Joy with flailing arms. Joy backed away against the press of people behind him. While Jerome's attention was diverted by the crowd, Joy tried to look around him at the crumpled figure on the ground. The crowd shrank away from the madman and before Joy could react, Jerome began to pound and scratch at him. Joy put up his hands to protect his face and his head. He pushed Jerome violently back across the room and into one of the dressers which crumpled and collapsed. A lamp crashed to the floor, broke into pieces, spilling its oil and a corner of the carpet caught fire. Jerome came at Joy again, trying to gouge out his eyes. Joy shoved blindly at the man, then stepped back, bunched his fist, and hit the captain full on the jaw with all his strength, the shock traveling up his arm to his pulsating head. Without even stopping to see Jerome pitch backward, Joy grabbed an edge of the burning rug and pulled it with all his strength against the weight of the bed resting on it. The rug tore and Joy hurled the burning object out of the room. The massed onlookers shrieked as the flaming material landed on them. Someone with a presence of mind pitched it over the balcony rail and on the crowd that was collecting in the street.

Joy was about to jump on the rest of the burning cloth when he realized his feet were bare and there was broken glass everywhere.

He looked around wildly. Smoke was hurting his eyes. He stepped over the two recumbent forms to the bed, pulled the sheets and mattress off, piled them on the flames, and stood on them. The fire went out.

Joy looked down at the girl on the floor.

Pushed violently by Jerome, Qin-ai had fallen sideways and hit her head on the corner of one of a chest. She lay inert, with blood matting her hair. In the light of the remaining lamp, the naked defenseless figure resembled a broken plaything discarded by a child. Joy knelt by her side, vividly recalling Sir Paul Miller and Second Mate Piper lying on the ship's passageway in horrifyingly similar pools of blood. Qin-ai was still breathing, but was losing blood at an alarming rate from her wound. He looked around worriedly. Jerome was out cold. At the door several faces gawked with popping eyes. What should he do? He needed help urgently. Then he remembered the midshipmen. Were they still on the street? He got to his feet just as Newbond pushed his way into the room and stopped dead at the sight of the carnage.

"Newbond! Thank heavens you're here," said Joy. "She's in a bad way. We must stop the blood and get her to Surgeon Morefield."

Newbond turned to go to his captain. Joy grabbed his shoulder.

"Leave the sodding brute. The girl means much more to us. Get her to the surgeon fast. I hope she lives. Oh my God, I hope she lives."

Joy had only just begun to realize the consequences of what had happened. He shook himself and walked out of the room, the assembled crowd making way for him. Catching his breath in the abandoned tea room, he began to pray.

20

Margaret waited impatiently, each passing moment an eternity. At long last Irving Macardle lowered his book of accounts, put down his empty glass, mashed out his cigar and said, "Och! Alice me lass, time to turn in."

The big house became still

Margaret knew Joy was out with Howqua and the captains. There was no guard at the door when she descended the darkened steps carefully. The hinges on the front door did not squeal. She emerged to the *largo* where a sea mist made haloes around the lights.

And then she was in the sanctuary of his embrace.

They broke apart and Vikram led her away quickly through the center of the square. The fog became thicker and the smell of seaweed grew strong as they left the last alley before the pier.

There was a sudden patter of running feet from behind.

"Take care!" shouted Vikram as he released Margaret and spun around, his hand freeing the knife. The next moment they were on him. There was a piercing scream as the knife gouged open the side of an assailant's face. Then his hands were pinned. The knife was torn away. An arm, thrown around his neck, cut off his air.

Margaret was punched in the stomach and pushed aside violently. She fell on her back on hard wet cobblestones. Winded, dazed, sobbing with pain, she heard a struggle and tried to get up to help, but could not find the breath. When she rolled over and raised her head, everyone, even the injured attacker, was gone.

Margaret fell back on the stones with a wail.

৵

"Exhibitionist! Lascivious! Stupid, misguided sham!"

Lifeless Macau Harbor absorbed the vociferous flood of Joy's invective as he walked along the edge of the wharf with Newbond at his side. Phosphorescence-topped waves lapped at the rocks below. A salty putrid odor rose from invisible flotsam.

Two hours earlier, Qin-ai's broken body, covered by a blood-stained sheet, had been brought down to the tea room on a makeshift stretcher by the midshipmen. Jerome was stirring but was ignored. As they made ready to carry the injured girl to *Albatross's* surgeon, Howqua burst upon them. Surveying the situation, he bent over the girl and muttered something to her. Then he stood and issued rapid-fire instructions. The stretcher was lifted by a pair of Chinese men in preparation to being taken away. Joy ran to stop them but the stretcher-bearers pushed past him and disappeared. Completely distraught, Joy went to Howqua and tried to explain and beg his forgiveness in English and *pigdin*. But the merchant of Canton regarded him indifferently, gave no indication of his feelings, and flounced out of the casino.

The crowd dissipated.

Joy stumbled out to the street. Then he remembered Lian. In the tumult following the disaster, he had completely forgotten her. In his unstable state, he decided he had to tell her *he* was responsible for her sister's fate. He staggered back up the steps to the room where a very short time ago he had experienced such pleasure. He saw Lian in her pink robe combing her hair. Her eyes widened in alarm as he blundered in with bandage disheveled, shirtless, blood on his naked shoulder and chest. Joy groped for her hands but she snatched them away and laughed shrilly in his face. Joy stepped back in bewilderment. Why was she laughing? Where was the demure little creature he had left behind? As Newbond, standing outside the door, watched in amazement, she darted past them and disappeared down the steps. Joy made to go after her but Newbond held him back.

"Belay there, sir. Get on yer clothes. Them Chiny folks have strange ways, I says. We've had quite enough o' them for one night."

Now that Newbond said it, Joy felt a huge tiredness while he dressed. Kaleidoscopic emotions washed over him and he hunched over in exhaustion. Then the pain in his head reminded him of Jerome and he made to go to the captain. Once again Newbond restrained him.

"Kyle'll take care of the cap'n, sir. Let's get you home."

Out on Praia Grande, Newbond listened in admiration to the torrent of impressive words.

"Quisling! Imbecile! Traitor! Poltroon! Turncoat! Self-server!"

Joy was going through every private hell that could be wished on a person, bearing all blame for what happened. In every moment when he was not chastising himself, he prayed for Qin-ai's survival.

If only he had not pushed the captain into taking her upstairs.

If only he had reacted quicker.

If only he had not been so enamored in lovemaking.

If only...

Stupid! stupid! stupid!

If the girl died, Howqua would lynch him. *Good!* He deserved to be lynched. The opium deal was dead. A golden opportunity, resurrected from tragedy, was squandered. After his holier-than-thou speech to the Select Committee, he had destroyed everything Sir Paul had striven for. It had all gone wrong and it was all his fault.

"Lewd, irresponsible, incompetent, self-infatuated fool!"

Everything he had done in the past weeks had been unmitigated calamities.

His oh-so-wonderful opium plan had resulted in Sir Paul's death, Vikram's torture, Qin-Ai's injuries, deaths of sailors. When it mattered most, while his colleague was bent on murder, while his sacred mission was falling to pieces, he was frolicking like a deckhand in a whorehouse.

"Who asked you to show off like a grubby adolescent?"

During Joy's outbursts of deranged self-pity, the stocky midshipman, eleven years his junior, became his anchor. Joy threw at him the foulest of oaths, baited him, even hit him, doing everything in his power to push him away and be left alone. Newbond took the punishment passively, spoke to him brightly, and stuck by his side.

Joy suddenly stopped in mid-stride.

"Why did the girl laugh at me?"

"Girl, sir?"

Newbond had been turning the word 'lewd' around his tongue deciding that it felt good.

"Why would the sister of a girl that's just been cruelly beaten laugh like that? Lian was unnaturally happy."

"Lian, sir?"

"Damn you, Newbond. You're absolutely maddening. Why don't you go and do something useful?"

"Me, sir?

Joy snarled an incoherent epithet at him.

Young Newbond looked older than his nineteen years and even at the height of his madness, Joy did not forget the man's keen eyes and quick thinking saved *Albatross* and his own life.

At long last he began to think rationally.

"What time is it, Newbond?"

"I'd warrant it's close on midnight, sir."

At that instant they heard a noise and turned simultaneously. At the mouth of a barely-visible alley on the far side of the empty Praia, a scuffle was going on. Someone cried out in agony. Through the dim light of the stars and mist-shrouded lamps they made out people fighting. Then a group of men entered the square and hurried away, dragging others along.

"Should I check them out, sir?"

"Better not get involved, Newbond. Local gangs. Some poor fellows having a bad night." He smiled ruefully. "They're not alone."

The men disappeared and Joy took a deep breath. "Let's get back, Newbond. There's much I have to do."

They turned into the alley where the brawl had taken place and almost fell over a slumped form on the cobblestones. Joy nodded to Newbond who drew his pistol. Peering through the darkness, Joy discovered it was a woman lying on the street. He bent to look at her face and cried out in horror. An European woman! Her face was grimy and streaked with tears, her hair was askew.

"She's alive!" he cried and pulled her to her feet. "Oh my God! It's Miss Andrews!"

Margaret tried to push him away as her teeth chattered and she shivered uncontrollably. Her breath came in loud heaves.

"Margaret!" He held her tightly. "It's me, Joy Morley. Great heavens, are you hurt? What on earth happened? How in God's name did you get out here?"

"Oh!" she cried, trying to break free and run. "Hurry! Stop them! Catch them. They have him! They're taking him away."

"Him? Whom? Steady, girl."

Margaret breathed is gasps and clutched the side where her hip had hit the stones. In a few minutes she recovered enough to tell them the story.

"Prince Vikram!" Joy exclaimed when she was done. "Why did he come to the house so late?" Margaret hesitated but Joy ploughed on. "He must have had important news. Maybe from Feng."

Holding the trembling woman, Joy came to a decision.

"You can't be on the streets of Macau at this hour, Margaret. And I've had a major disaster myself. What a terrible night. Newbond, can you follow that lot and look for the prince? I'll take Miss Andrews home. Quickly now. They can't be far. And be careful yourself."

"Yes, sir."

The midshipman was about to go toward the wharf when Margaret stopped him with a hand on his arm.

"There's a Chinese sailor who can help," she said.

Joy was amazed.

"Chinese sailor? What Chinese sailor? How do *you* know? What *is* all this?"

Margaret took a deep breath and recovered her poise. Shaking Joy off, she told Newbond, "He should be waiting by a boat on the wharf. His name is Tau-pei. His face is…"

"I know him, miss."

Margaret stared blankly before she remembered.

"Oh, that's right. He was on the ship. Find him and look for them along the wharf. It's got to be those pirates. Hurry!"

"Yes, miss."

Newbond hurried away in the direction of the waterfront. Tiredness and the extraordinary events of the night prevented Joy's mind from working. He leaned against a lamp post while Margaret stood facing the bay. Newbond came back and reported that Tau-pei was not by the wharf at the place she had indicated. The three searched the long pier from end to end. They awoke boat-dwellers who grumbled they had seen nothing, heard nothing, and that the ways of foreign devils were rude and inexplicable.

The first light of dawn was silhouetting the mansions of Largo de Seneca when an exhausted Joy and a forlorn Margaret stumbled up the steps of *Britannia*.

21

It was mid-morning when Joy awoke remembering Lian's scent, a fragrant mixture of jasmine, musk, and an exciting female odor. Dreamily, he recalled their lovemaking. Would he ever experience it again? He tried to keep focusing on Lian, but before long the bedlam of the night forced its way in. All had been undone on a night that began with paradise. He sat up. Little by little he overcame the depression. What was the rational thing to do? His first thought was he should return to Calcutta and Fort William and his former turmoil-free lifestyle. No, he could not run away now. He could not leave Vikram in the hands of pirates. His friend was lost once on this trip, found, and lost again. He *had* to get him back. He *had* to tell Howqua how repentant he was for injury to the other girl. Was Qin-ai Howqua's daughter? She had to be, otherwise why had Howqua been so cold and distant last night, so different from the merry host of the evening? He hoped she was recovering well. He wondered whether he should check on Margaret, but decided against it. She too had had an awful night and needed rest. What on earth had she been doing on the *largo* in the middle of the night, with Vikram? Were they trying to find *him* for some reason? Oh God! Had something *else* gone wrong of which he was unaware? Was the cargo stolen?

Worrisome as this possibility was, first things came first. He decided leave Margaret a note and go at once to Howqua to inquire about the wounded girl.

And he desperately needed a bath.

৯৹

To get to Howqua's Macau residence, Juan Menezes took Joy all the way across the Christian part of town and out through a gate in the city wall. This wall, which protected the Portuguese enclave against attacks from the mainland and the sea, was built in the seventeenth century as part of the massive Monte Fortress which frowned down from above the harbor.

Outside the wall lay Chinese Macau.

Even though he was anxious about the opium venture, the dramatic change in architecture as they hurried through the gates was not lost on Joy. Imposing churches, battlements, Mediterranean buildings gave way to little two-story homes piled on each other.

Partitioned walls, fluted roof overhangs, decorated wooden eaves-fascia testified that Macau was as Chinese as the monstrous Empire to its north.

They came to a stop before an impressive house. It was two-storied like the others, but larger and sumptuously decorated. Blue bricks and openwork timber windows with translucent mother-of-pearl panes formed the frontage. The embellished front door had highly decorative panels. It reminded Joy of the woodsman's cottage made of candy in the Brothers Grimm fairytale, *Hansel and Gretel.*

Menezes rattled a big iron ring on the door. Nothing happened. He banged twice more with the same result. Joy and Menezes looked at each other, wondering whether to give up when then the door was opened, to their surprise, by Lian. A Lian dressed in ordinary robes without the chalky makeup. She looked freshly bathed and wholesomely pretty. Her frown of annoyance faded when she recognized her visitors.

"*Ai-de!*" she squealed. "Joy *shi sheng ma?*"

At the unexpected sight of Lian, Joy's buffeted mind became utterly woolly. *She is glad to see me!* Her sister must be all right then. He forgot the tragedy of the night. He forgot that she had treated him rudely. He looked at the soft dimples and stepped through the door with his arms outstretched and she came into them readily. *She doesn't hate me,* he thought as he snuggled against him full of the musky scent he had woken to.

Then he remembered the open street door and hastily disengaged himself, looking sheepishly at his linguist. Unperturbed,

Menezes spoke to Lian who disappeared into the house.

Before long they were sitting in a front room, studying an ornate marble fountain in the entrance court. Voices of women and shouts of children playing drifted in from the interior, mingled with the smell of cooking. An *amah* laid a tray of food on a table. A second servant brought a pot of tea and cups. Lian returned. Joy tried to focus on business and not look at her as she poured tea and handed him a cup. At that very moment Howqua entered. Joy stood up hastily and hot tea spilt on his fingers. Involuntarily, he yelped in pain.

"*Ya! Ya!*" exclaimed Howqua and discharged a flood of furious invective at Lian who scuttled indoors. Joy was livid with himself. *Damn it! I'm constantly getting girls into trouble!* He started to explain but Menezes shushed him abruptly. Joy stopped in confusion and wished Lian would stay away. But return she did with a pot of ointment and stared lovingly into his eyes while she applied cream on his hand. Embarrassed and perplexed, Joy stood on one foot, then another. Howqua clapped his hands and the girl meekly went into the house. Joy sat down in relief.

"Has the Councilor eaten rice today?" Howqua began but Joy, abandoning niceties, jumped to his feet.

"I have come about your daughter, sir." Menezes translated.

Disconcertingly, Howqua gave a high-pitched cackle.

"Missy my?" he said.

"The two women are his slaves," explained Menezes. "Not his daughters. They perform special tasks for Howqua."

Howqua became serious.

"Did the Councilor not like the woman who bedded him? Howqua asks forgiveness for pain the worthless girl caused his fingers."

"Oh! *No!*" gasped Joy. This was farcical. "I meant your other...er...woman." He could not bring himself to demean the lovely girls by calling them slaves. "When Qin-ai has suffered such grievous injuries, my hurt is trivial. How is she?"

Howqua spoke in a matter-of-fact manner that made Menezes start in surprise. Joy waited, his body going alternately hot and cold.

"The older slave," said Menezes, "died this morning. The herbs did not heal the wound."

Joy felt the ground move under his feet and sat down heavily. In his mind's eye he saw the helpless girl lying defenseless and bloodied on the carpeted floor. He had tried to save her but Howqua would not allow her to be taken to the ship's surgeon. *Damn! Damn! Damn Winkley! Damn him to all perdition!* But was it really the captain's fault? It was *he* who had forced the girl on Jerome. *Damn him, Joy, to all perdition! And beyond!* How could he have known about Jerome's vicious personality? And God only knew what tribal medicines they had tried on the hapless girl.

Suddenly he sensed something was wrong. Very wrong.

Howqua was neither angry nor grieving. Lian had laughed happily upon seeing him and returned his embrace with genuine warmth. This was not a family in mourning.

Shaken, he turned to Menezes.

"What the bloody hell is going on? Why isn't he all cut up by the girl's death?"

Menezes and Howqua discussed something for a long time. Then Menezes turned to Joy.

"Howqua thanks the Councilor because it is right and proper for one business associate to enquire into the well-being of the family of the other. However, the Councilor need not be distressed. It is but a slave. The death of a slave. Nothing more." Menezes silenced Joy's protests and continued. "A man's wife bears him sons or slaves. Upon the arrival of a son, a family rejoices; it laments the birth of a slave. In troubled times slaves are sold to release families from bondage. Are girls not the burden of a family? For whom husbands are bought for outrageous dowry? It is true the slave Qin-ai suffered. Now she is out of her misery. It is but a small loss. Howqua insists the Councilor need not concern himself about a mere slave."

Joy listened to this aghast, then asked almost plaintively, "Insists? Don't you people have feelings for your...your women? Daughters or wives or concubines or slaves? Wasn't Qin-ai a part of Howqua's life?"

Menezes did not translate this. His round face was serious when he answered the question himself.

"Sir, I have experienced the worlds of China and Portugal. Love and affection are not traditional Chinese concepts in the romantic European sense. Chinese parents believe they have a duty to raise and marry off their children. Husbands take wives on dowry or buy concubines or marry slaves to pay off their economic burden. During unrest or famine, at times of great poverty, daughters are sold as concubines or into servitude to wealthy men. Chinese are businessmen first. For parents, unforeseen removal of a daughter before marriage is not a tragedy but the elimination of a liability. The girl Qin-ai was purchased to serve her master. I believe it is unwise to prod Howqua about this, sir. He might take offense."

Take offense! I thought he would have me skinned and decapitated!

Joy could not decide whether to laugh or cry. The gallant and the idealist in him rebelled at the injustice of the Chinese social system. The trader in him rejoiced at deliverance from ruin.

But the summit of paradox was yet to come.

"Howqua has decided," began Menezes, translating a long speech, "In return for the Councilor's commercial wisdom, and for the Councilor's concern for the family of this unworthy Chinese associate, and for his valiant effort to save the dead slave, Howqua will seal a lifetime bond between his *hong* and the English Company. This bond will bring honor to the house of Howqua. The Councilor shall receive as his very own, Howqua's most accomplished concubine. Her name is Lian. She is skilled in lovemaking as the Councilor well knows. She has virtues above those of any other. And she has a one *very* special quality. A quality the Councilor shall discover in time. And out of all the courts of his house, Howqua's best court shall become the Councilor's court. May he be blessed with sons."

৯

Joy returned to *Britannia* with his head spinning.

But before he could settle down he saw Captain Winkley pacing the balcony above the *largo*. He went up and from the balcony entrance watched him briefly, trying to decide how to handle the unpredictable officer. While he waited Jerome reached the end of the balcony, turned on his heel and saw him. He came forward rapidly and rapped out *"Honor!"*

Jerome's features were warped in an angry grimace. A maroon discoloration spread over the jawline where Joy had hit him. The nerve on his temple throbbed. To Joy it was a very unpleasant sight.

"There ye are, ye insufferable puppy. You've defiled my honor. Where've ye been hiding? Man, ye'll pay in spades!"

Joy spoke carefully.

"Come Cap'n, what's done is done. I just learned we're all right with Howqua and damned lucky to get away without hell to pay. You have beaten a murder charge and a Chinese prison. Let's not muck about with dramatics. There's a job waiting."

But Jerome was not listening. His breathing grew heavy.

"Morley, you will apologize for your behavior. Failing which you will oblige me by appearing at the Fort's crest at first light for a duel."

Joy was flabbergasted. The man was mad.

"Since the invitation to duel is mine," Jerome continued tonelessly, "the choice of weaponry is yours."

"Ridiculous!" Joy burst out angrily. "It's suicide. I've shot a charging leopard between the eyes at forty yards."

"And I, sir, have the distinction of winning three duels."

The two men glared wrathfully at each other.

Then Joy was shouting.

"Don't you see what you're doing, you conceited idiot? You've been commanded by the King to keep the sea-lanes clear. I have a duty to the same King to establish the export of opium so that English commerce is not strangled. We're on the same side. And you self-indulgent imbecile, you've got us brawling like drink-sozzled longshoremen and putting our duties at risk."

Jerome glared at him from beneath beetled brows, breathing hard through his mouth. Joy was once more appalled by his unnatural anger. Jerome touched the bruise and this added to his fury. His temple twitched and his voice assumed a dull metallic quality.

"Morley, I'd like to crush you under my heel. I'd like to wipe you off the face of this earth, Morley."

Joy's anger abruptly gave way to a guarded wariness. *Careful!* said a voice inside him. This was not an ordinary irate man. There was manic depression in his manner. A madness. There was no telling what a man made insane by anger might do. In fact, it *was* a madman that had come swinging at him last night. He wondered what quirk in the naval officer's mental makeup had brought him to this. Did the man lose control only when angry, or was he witnessing a progressive decline? Then Jerome's ire ebbed. He regained his composure and his breathing steadied. Seeing this Joy decided to close the episode amicably. Captain Winkley needed careful watching, not antagonizing.

"Settle down, Cap'n. I'll apologize if it means so much to you. If truth be told, I *did* push you into it last night."

Jerome took time to reply. When he did, his tone was anything but amicable.

"Watch yourself, Morley. Ye've got it coming. Just you watch out. If it wasn't for your cousin Reginald in London, I'd..."

He abruptly turned on his heel and strode away.

Joy gripped the balcony rail and exhaled slowly. How much more chaos was there to come? How much more could he handle?

22

Twenty-four hours later, Joy sat tiredly in the drawing room and gazed unhappily at the haggard face of the woman who berated him. Finally, he reached the end of his patience.

"Margaret, calm down!"

From the hallway outside Compradore Liu watched the scene with interest. He was quite aware that Woman Who Shows Her Breasts, as Margaret was unfeelingly named by the Chinese staff, was enamored of Hei wang-zi. Was it actually possible that the *fan kwae*[4] did not see this? Liu shook his head sadly. He was sure there would be a terrible row soon.

He would have given English people more credit had he known that Joy was also thinking of the relationship between Margaret and

---

[4] Fan kwae = red devil. The term was used by the Chinese to refer to Englishmen on account of red hair and beards sported by many of them.

Vikram. Why was she *so* terribly upset? He of course liked and respected Vikram and was concerned about his safety. But Margaret was frantic. Had something happened between them aboard *Albatross*? His mind went back to Vikram's sudden and unceremonious offloading from the ship. Jerome had casually spoken of a 'standoff' with the prince. He and Sir Paul had been too concerned about getting the ship turned around for the rescue to worry about the cause of the argument. But before he could pursue this trend of thought Margaret burst out, "Mr. Morley, *do* something for God's sake! You're sitting around like a stuffed owl." Wearing a low-cut blouse and a hooped skirt with floral patterns, with her hands on her hips she tossed aside an errant lock of auburn hair. Watching, even the venerable *compradore* felt a stab of excitement. What a wild woman!

The agitated Joy had no such feelings and regarded Margaret despondently. All available resources of Macau and English authorities were deployed to look for Vikram without success.

"We'll keep at it until we find him, Margaret," he said. "In the meantime, I've got to see to some urgent business. I will tell Macardle to keep the pressure on while I'm gone. Is that all right?"

Margaret turned abruptly and left the room, almost knocking the *compradore* over.

Joy followed her out and stood for a moment watching her climb the stairs. Then he turned and walked out of the building to a nearby street corner where he found his ride waiting. He pushed aside the curtains and crawled into the waiting palanquin. This time there was no Menezes. He was on his own. The tiny enclosure rose and its four bearers began to move. Flashes of lamplight shone through the translucent muslin drapes as the palanquin swayed through the streets. It was late but people were still about. He heard snatches of dialogue and rowdy laughter. From grunts of pigs he was aware when the procession passed through other *largos*. The *slap slap slap* of the bearers' feet punctuated his thoughts. After twenty minutes they slowed and stopped. Joy felt himself being lowered to the ground and emerged clumsily, looked about. He recognized blue bricks, mother-of-pearl design, and the gaudily decorated door of Howqua's house. His heart beat faster and a heady anticipation grew.

The bearers yelled and thumped energetically on the door and a querulous female voice responded from inside in Cantonese.

"Who is it?"

"Old mother, Bandage Man has come!"

A spirited exchange ensued before the door opened and an ancient woman carrying a lantern led Joy inside with an antipathy she made no effort to hide. They passed through the front court and into the same darkened room where he had met Howqua that morning. Leaving him there the *amah* disappeared. Joy sank into a chair and began to have doubts. Why was it so quiet? Where was everyone? Was Howqua involved in Vikram's capture? Were the opium agreement and the gift of Lian foils for an ulterior motive? Could Howqua be in league with the pirates? Was he about to be taken hostage and held for ransom for the contraband cargo? Perhaps he would never be heard of again. What would his parents do if he was lost in Macau?

The room was unlit but he knew she was near by the familiar

aroma. He felt for her and then she was melting in his arms and his worries disappeared in the warmth and softness.

Lian suddenly pulled away and said "Good evening, sir!"

Joy jumped and let her go as if she had become red hot. She had said the words softly but the effect was cataclysmic.

"Good evening, sir!" she repeated.

The slight nasal accent did not diminish the upper-class King's diction. Joy shook his head, unable to speak. This could not be happening. At the casino, Lian had given no indication she knew English. He felt he was in the longest nightmare and this was another inexplicable turn in a grotesque chain of events.

Lian took her bewildered lover by the hand and led him into the dark silent house. They met no one. After crossing two courts they entered a room lit by a single oil lamp and smelling of fresh varnish. Beside a large satin-covered bed were a padded chair and a straight-backed one. The floor was piled with thick rugs.

"Won't you sit down?" Lian said in the dim light.

This was impossible! It could *not* be her speaking. In complete stupefaction he recalled Lian's absolute Chineseness and the difficulty she had in even pronouncing Jerome's name in the casino. In a dream he sat down heavily on the armchair. Lian removed his jacket, took off his boots, slipping sandals on his feet. Without saying anything more, she wrung a towel from a bowl of cold water and wiped away the creases of worry from his face. Dizzily he watched her doll-like figure skitter about on tiny steps and tend to him with total absorption. Try as he might he could not associate the figure with the posh English elocution he had just heard. Having settled him to her satisfaction Lian stood, bowed slightly, let her hair down, posed and spoke with aplomb of a stage entertainer.

"Wantee jig-jig, sar? Pliss, sar?"

Joy stared with his mouth open.

"Now, sar?"

Joy burst out laughing and Lian looked at him questioningly, then with resignation, as he laughed until his head ached and tears rolled down his cheeks. He pulled her to him and sat her on his knee.

"Jig-jig, eh?" he said, caressing her hair. "You little tease! What in the name of all that's holy is happening over here? Where'd you learn to speak English like that? You could have knocked me down with a feather."

Lian extricated herself and got to her feet.

"Tea-*ah*?"

"Tea would be just fine. Just stop using the slang."

"Yes, sar," she replied, and then "pliss!" and scuttled away before he could catch her.

Tea was brewed and ready in a stone kettle in a corner. Lian poured him a cup, declined one for herself, gathered her robes and settled gracefully at his feet with her eyes on his.

"Joy *shi sheng,*" she opened formally. "I shall tell you a story."

Joy settled into his chair

The first foreigners, Lian said in faultless English, arrived in China more than two hundred years ago. The big sailors, she had heard, behaved arrogantly and violently and were disdained by

Chinese officials who thought they were a new and despicable breed of pirates. Then came the missionaries who conducted themselves with dignity and predicted important events like eclipses. They were allowed to stay and to travel to Peking and establish themselves across the kingdom. Then the merchants arrived. From time immemorial, China prized scholarship and abhorred commerce. And so the foreign traders were denigrated as barbarians and confined far away from Peking, with contact limited to the lowest official class in China, the *hong* merchants."

Lian paused to check if Joy was comfortable.

"Then one day," she resumed, "a strange man came to Canton."

"A strange man!" Joy said. "What was his name?"

This earned him a winsome smile, no answer.

"This extraordinary barbarian was interested in tea where others before him had concerned themselves with silk and spices. Because he was very tall he became known as Tsung-shu Gao or Tall Palm Tree. As the years passed Gao rose to the head of his country's trading station and became a *tai-pan.* Gao was courteous and sincere, qualities which people of China respect. But he could also get very angry. The earth shook with Gao's fury. Those who met Gao treated him with respect and obeyed his wishes. The trade with his country prospered. But Gao was a lonely man."

Lian broke the thread of her narrative.

"Are you a lonely man, Joy *shi sheng?*"

"Only before I met you, love." Joy pulled her back onto his lap. "Tell me," he said kissing her neck. "Is this story going anywhere? Will the tall palm tree live happily ever after with a pretty girl like Lian?"

"Yes, sar."

"Really! How does this story concern us? Can we hurry it up?"

At once Lian became coy.

"You wantee jig-jig, sar?"

"Finish the story quick, woman, 'cause yes, I do wantee jig-jig."

"In time Gao Tsung-shu was assigned to a *hong* merchant," Lian continued. "The merchant was a vigorous man who saw great future in trade with Gao's country and the greatness in Gao himself. It was a partnership that flourished in the face of obstacles."

Joy controlled his impatience.

"And since the *tai-pan* had no *tai-tai* from his land, the *hong* merchant decided to obtain for Gao the loveliest and most accomplished courtesan money could buy. To do this he traveled all the way to Hangchow in Chekiang province which is known for its art and wine and culture and the beauty of its women. And the loveliest courtesan of all Hangchow was Shao Yao whom the *hong* brought back for his friend."

Lian coughed behind her hand.

"Tsung-shu Gao was a *fan kwae.*"

Joy sat up. He knew from Menezes that the Chinese called English traders *fan kwae* or red devils because many had russet hair. He had thought Lian was talking about a Portuguese trader. Now he realized this was about an Englishman who had taken a Chinese concubine. *Tall* palm tree! His heart suddenly missed a beat.

"Gao Tsung-shu and Shao Yao," continued Lian, accurately

judging his thoughts, "were perfect together and Gao was forever indebted to Howqua."

"Howqua? The same...?"

"His father, Joy *shi sheng*. Howqua is an inherited name."

"And the tall palm tree was...?

"...the *tai-pan* who died on your ship."

There was a silence as Lian poured more tea.

"I see. Or do I? So Sir Paul went native? Bloody interesting. Don't blame him if the woman was anything like you. But wait a minute. No, I don't see. What happened to Sir Paul's woman?"

"Shao Yao died in the Black Death after years of serving Gao."

Joy nodded. An infamous outbreak of bubonic plague had decimated China and India fifteen years ago. Tens of thousands had died in Canton and Bombay.

"Did you learn English from her?"

Lian knelt in front of Joy and put her head on his knees. When she spoke her voice was small and vulnerable.

"No, Joy *shi sheng*. Shao Yao knew only *pigdin*."

Joy held his breath.

"Lian learned English from the *tai-pan*." There were bright tears in her black eyes. She waited a long moment before speaking. "Qin-ai was born of my mother and a Chinese husband. She was my half-sister. The English *tai-pan* was my father."

That night, as the palanquin swayed back through dead streets of Macau, Joy thanked his guardian angel for making him select pink birds over green mountains.

23

Margaret was lying in bed with a splitting headache when the door creaked and Su Siao entered. Margaret groaned and sat up, holding her head in her hands.

The *amah* stood for a minute, breathing heavily after the strenuous stair climb and studied her carefully. In opposition to the *compradore,* Su Siao believed that Woman Who Shows Her Breasts would snare unsuspecting Bandage Man and that Hei wang-zi would perish in the clutches of his kidnappers. She believed this strongly enough to lay a twenty-to-one bet in the sweepstakes to which several members of the domestic staff had subscribed.

"Feng Sheng-chi him come," announced Su Siao.

Margaret looked at her blankly.

"Missy, Feng Sheng-chi, him bling chop along Hei wang-zi.

Comee quick-quick."

Margaret closed her eyes and wished Su Siao would go away.

"Feng him come!" Su Siao said as loudly and shrilly as she could. Was Woman Who Shows Her Breasts deaf as well as stupid?

Margaret covered her ears.

Someone had come. That was clear. Who had come?

"Who has come, Su Siao?"

At least she is not deaf, thought Su Siao witheringly. "Feng Sheng-chi, Missy. He come along Hei wang-zi."

Margaret got out of bed and patted her hair. Su Siao hid her distaste. When Margaret first arrived Su Siao had been shocked by the modern European cleavage that Margaret espoused, scandalized by its effect on men, both civilized and barbarian. She came forward and adjusted Margaret's dress and tried surreptitiously to raise the neckline, not wanting the young visitor below to get ideas.

Meanwhile, Angry Feng, waiting in the drawing room, was thinking about his former leader, now gunning for him on account of his betrayal. After the first day in Macau when he brought Vikram to *Britannia* he had gone underground. He had learned of Vikram's kidnapping several hours after it happened. His sense of loss was more due to the evaporation of opium-generated riches than from his closeness with the Indian prince. He made inquiries. The boat people were more willing to talk to him than to Newbond. Feng learned that the kidnappers had taken Vikram to Lan Tao island, which was only to be expected since Wu had a stronghold there. Feng took a long time deciding what to do next. He did not trust barbarians but they seemed to be the only solution. Other than Vikram, who was not a *fan-kwae* anyway, Feng had never met a foreigner and had no idea how to get them to help him. He debated whether he should find Tat Au-yong and convince the triad to storm the island and rescue the Indian prince. But after reflection he decided against such a frontal approach. There were strong reasons against starting an all-out war between triads and pirates which could cause them all to lose ground to the Hoppo. And was not Hei wang-zi the barbarians' responsibility? So, unwillingly, Feng decided to enlist the English in his cause.

Margaret walked into the drawing room and stopped in confusion on seeing the dirty Chinese youth. Feng had been on the boat the day Vikram returned, but she had barely seen his face in the darkness. Feng gaped at the large woman with impossibly red hair, equally impossible green eyes, and skin that was sickeningly pale. Her dress clung to the upper part of her body much of which was visible. He swallowed as he understood why people called them barbarians.

Su Siao brought him back to reality.

"You there, little dog puddle!" she admonished in the local dialect. "Do your business quickly and get out."

"Hei wang-zi in Lan Tao," Feng said to Margaret.

Margaret stared at him and then at the *amah.*

"What is he saying, Su Siao?"

"Oh ko! Hei wang-zi him belong Lan Tao."

Margaret shook her head in perplexity. Su Siao sighed.

"Hei wang-zi belong Lan Tao," she repeated patiently, and added "never mind!" to make it perfectly clear.

It finally registered on Margaret that they were talking about someone called Hei wang-zi. Who on earth was that? The name sounded Chinese. And who was this scared-looking man?

"Who is Hei wang-zi?" she asked.

Feng was disgusted. His grasp of a few English words through Vikram's teaching enabled him to understand the question. What was wrong with the awful woman? He had seen her the night Hei wang-zi had her on the boat and now grasped why the prince met her only in the dark! Had she forgotten her lover already? Feng had an idea. What name had she called him?

"Veek-lam?" he ventured hesitantly, and then he got the fright of his life. The devil woman came at him screeching, her teeth showing, her face all misshapen. Before he could run, she grabbed him by his vest and shook him as a fox might shake a rat.

Feng cried out in terror. Margaret shouted in unison.

"Where is he? Where is he? Tell me. Tell me. Take me to him!"

Margaret shook the unfortunate man until his teeth clattered together. The thunderstruck *amah* dragged her away. With a great effort Margaret recovered her self-control. She walked across to the opposite side of the room with her arms tightly locked around herself to stop trembling. She turned and looked sheepishly at the two Chinese. What an idiot had she made of herself.

"I say! I'm terribly sorry. Are you all right?"

Feng gaped at her, then recoiled as she put a hand up to arrange her hair. This was too much. Margaret burst out laughing.

Feng and Su Siao looked at each other worriedly and edged

toward the door.

"Look. This is ridiculous. Let's all sit and sort it out."

She sat down on a chair. The others remained standing.

"Sit!" she ordered and indicated vacant chairs.

They looked at the chairs, then looked at each other, and sank down on their haunches.

"Where is he?" asked Margaret.

"Lan Tao," answered Su Siao.

"What?"

"Lan Tao," Su Siao repeated with infinite fortitude. "Lan Tao! *Tao, heya?* Land belong water."

After one more iteration Margaret understood.

"Why is he in Lan Tao?"

This took longer. But what emerged was that Vikram was held captive by the pirate Wu on an island called Lan Tao. Margaret sat back with conflicting feelings. He was alive, thank God. But he was in the pirates' lair. How in the world could she get him back?

While Margaret's mind went through all the possibilities, Feng watched her covertly. He wished she would call a white man. For example, the one Su Siao called Bandage Man. Then they could plan a way to rescue Hei wang-zi. While Margaret frowned and tried to think, Feng imagined her and Hei wang-zi making love. Su Siao in turn studied him, following his thoughts unhappily. She reduced her odds in the run-up to Margaret's attachment.

Meanwhile Margaret was looking at Feng worriedly. The young Chinese man and the old Chinese woman stared back from their seemingly uncomfortable positions. She suddenly remembered Vikram telling her about a person who had rescued him from the pirates and of his faith in that person. Could this be him? Her interest quickened.

"Is your name Feng?"

"*Shenme?*"

Margaret repeated the question slowly.

Su Siao looked at her incredulously while Feng again wondered what Hei wang-zi saw in her. Could *anyone* be this stupid? Had not Su Siao told her five times he was Feng?

"Yes, missy," Su Siao said patiently. "Here be Feng Sheng-chi."

"Thank you, Fen...Mr. Feng."

Margaret thought some more.

"Is he safe?" she asked suddenly.

"*Shenme?*"

"Is...what did they call him? Is Hei Wang safe?"

Angry Feng shrugged.

"No can tell."

"Are they treating him well?"

"*Shemne?*"

"What will the pirates...uh, what will Wu do to him?"

"Wu Cha-tan, him kill Hei wang-zi along Lan Tao."

Margaret shrieked and the two Chinese jumped to their feet.

Unknown to Margaret, in the *pigdin* version of English, 'kill' meant 'beat up' while 'kill-dead' meant the slaying of a person. Feng was only describing Vikram's chances of torture. Margaret screamed again and Su Siao tried to run to find Alice, but Margaret grabbed her arm, frantic with worry. They were *killing* Vikram!

She rounded on Feng.

"You have a boat?"

"*Shi.* Boat have."

"Take me to him!"

Feng could not believe his ears. For the hundredth time he wished he had not come to this barbarian den of horrors.

"Where is Bandage Man, old mother?" he urgently asked Su Siao in Cantonese. "And can you *please* take this creature away?"

"All the *fan-kwae* are away," Su Siao replied. "I heard them talking. This crazy woman caused *such* a scene about her lover I am sure they were happy to leave her! Bandage Man, Fat Master, Old Lecher Liu, shiplord, all gone. Shall I call Fat Missy?"

"No, no!" The last thing Feng wanted on his hands was *another* foreign woman. He felt quite defeated and started to leave.

"Hey! Where are you going?" exclaimed Margaret. "Su Siao! Stop him. I want to go to this Lan Tao with him."

Feng accelerated but was too slow. Margaret rushed after him and again grabbed his vest. Feng struggled half-heartedly and subsided in resignation.

At that moment a starry-eyed Joy walked in.

"Ah, there you are old girl," he began. "Did you know that..." Then he saw Feng in Margaret's grasp and stopped dead.

"Miss Andrews! What's going on? What did that man do?"

"Mr. Morley! Thank God, you're back. They are *killing* him!"

"Killing him? Whom? The prince?"

"Yes! Let's *go!*"

Joy looked around blankly, completely confused.

Margaret screamed in his ear.

"Hurry! He's held by pirates. *They're torturing him."*

Suddenly alert, Joy moved away and looked at her carefully. The devastated face told the story. At first he was astonished. Then his surprise passed. Margaret's fondness for the prince had been evident for some time but he had been too preoccupied to notice. Once he might have been shocked or jealous, or even outraged. But in Macau he too had found his 'native' woman and learned how excruciatingly beautiful was the experience. No wonder she was destroyed with worry.

Joy motioned the others to leave before turning to her.

"As I live and breathe, Margaret," he told her with complete sincerity. "We shall get him back."

BOOK THREE

A BEND IN THE RIVER

24

Splashed across a moonless sky, a brilliant Milky Way poured a blue-and-white radiance on the silver sand of Lan Tao island.

Margaret and Vikram sat side-by-side facing the sea. Voices from a small boat, came faintly over the growl of breakers. Something – a night bird? – squealed in the trees behind them.

"They were going to *torture* you!" Margaret was saying. "I was scared to even think how we would find you. And, oh, where *did* you find that little man?"

"Feng? He found *me*. He has saved me once before."

"He's worth a hundred soldiers. The rescue was his idea."

Vikram's voice broke.

"I am in debt to all of you."

"Nonsense!" said Margaret. "Listen, there is so much to tell. So much has happened in the last hours."

Vikram held up both palms.

"Wait, Memsahib. I have bad news. The pirate chief is going to capture the Indian ships."

"Yes," said Margaret and Vikram sat back in surprise.

"You know?"

"Yes, and I will tell you how I know," she replied and changed the subject. "Did they hurt you very much?"

"Me? No. It was Tau-pei."

"The Chinese sailor from the English ship?"

"They tortured *him.*" Vikram swallowed. "And I could not help."

"He told them that the Indian ships carried opium?"

"He did not know, but must have guessed. How do *you* know?"

"Know what?" asked Margaret.

"That Wu is after the Indian ships?"

Margaret sat back and looked around.

"Let me tell you the full story. *Albatross* sailed yesterday to this island. We approached with cannon run out, but no pirate junks were visible in the harbor. Captain Winkley landed an armed whaleboat in the main pier and found only a few old people and children in the hamlet. They recognized Feng and were hostile, but were more afraid of the English soldiers. Feng discovered that Wu had sailed with his full force for the opium ships. He also found they had taken you around the island to Wu's private cove. Captain Winkley wanted to go after the pirates at once as his first duty. Mr. Morley, bless his heart, wanted him to look for you. It was a bad scene and they almost had a fight. I had my heart in my mouth. I'm scared of that captain." She paused and looked at him anxiously in the starlight. "Something's going to happen soon. Something terrible."

There was a noise from the boat and a figure jumped onto the sand and came toward them.

"Go now?" Feng pointed at a headland in the distance.

"Go now," agreed Margaret. To Vikram she said, "I'll tell you the rest on board. You go with Feng to the boat. I'll come in a moment."

Vikram got to his feet and the two men strolled away. Margaret looked at the scenery for a few more minutes. Then she rose, brushed sand from her dress, sure she looked a mess. Her hair was in knots and streamed out in the breeze. Sand prickled inside her petticoats. But she was ecstatically happy as she looked out at the vista.

The first light was showing in a steel-gray horizon stretching toward neighboring Hong Kong island, its mountaintop hidden in mist. Swarms of gulls and terns circled its cliffs preparing for the morning catch. An armada of rosy pelicans sailed sedately by, flapping and floating in unison. The sky changed to light pink matching the color of the birds. She thought of the night's escapade, laughed out loud, and stretched luxuriously. After all the heartbreak, it was good to be alive.

The rest of the story was quickly told.

In spite of Joy's insistence, Jerome had refused to take *Albatross* into dangerous reefs around the island and made preparations to pursue Wu and the Indian ships next morning at first light. As darkness fell, Feng, Tat Au-yong, and three triad members, made ready to go overland to Wu's hideout to effect a rescue. Joy wanted to join them, but grudgingly agreed his frail condition would be a liability. As the rescue whaleboat separated from the ship, Margaret slipped unseen over the side, shushing the Chinese men to silence. She would face a thousand demons than be left behind.

"They planned a surprise attack. There is a man in the hamlet who owed Feng a debt and was willing to lead the way. We took lanterns and began to walk on a deserted and overgrown path with the man as a guide. It took us hours. It was hot and very muggy. All the mosquitoes on the island found us and I had to cover every part of myself except my eyes. But still they got a few pints of my blood. We walked in complete silence. It was...*oh dear!*...it was dark and frightening. Finally, we got to the cove where many boats were tied up. Then we had to decide which one you were on. The fact that there was a lamp on only one boat indicated a prisoner must be on it. We could have been wrong, but it was a chance we had to take."

She paused suddenly.

"Where *is* your Chinese sailor? He was not on the boat."

"Tau-pei is dead, Memsahib. He was not very bright or strong-willed, and they tortured him savagely. Wu is a cruel man. He realized Tau-pei was weaker than I and went for him. Tau-pei guessed the 'special' cargo was on *Gulab* and *Satpura* and not on *Albatross* as they originally thought. When they prodded him with a glowing coal for more information, he suddenly dropped dead. Of sheer terror. I understood a guard tell another that I was being kept hostage. Once Wu had the opium, there is no knowing what he would do with me. Especially since I gave him a half-truth before."

Margaret touched his arm and continued her story.

"I looked away as Feng drew a knife and killed a sleeping guard before he could raise an alarm. The men quietly went aboard while I waited alone on the pier. It was over quickly. There were only other two guards and they are floating somewhere out there. I felt sick with all the violence. But what else have I seen since we came to China? Someone cut the ropes and we sailed away on their boat. You know the rest."

An hour later they trimmed sail, negotiated the promontory, and were dazzled by the spectacle of a rising sun brilliantly lighting up a fully-rigged English clipper straining at anchor.

"They're still here!" Margaret shouted exultantly.

They neared *Albatross* and saw her starboard rail crowded with heads. A cheer went up. A jolly boat appeared from around her bows and in ten minutes Joy Morley was among them.

"Prince Vikram! Praise the Lord you are safe."

Then he rounded on the radiant woman and shook his fist in her face.

"You hot-headed, unthinking madcap! What the devil made you pull this jape?"

Margaret smiled at him impishly.

"We got him back, didn't we?"

"And gave me the most harrowing night of my life. Do you know when we couldn't find you on board we sent a search party to the village? They told us you had gone off with the Chinese thugs. Were you crazy? The bloody captain and I actually came to blows over having to wait for you. Newbond and Fenwick kept us from killing each other. Miss Andrews, you shall never, never, do this again, as long as you live. What...what're you grinning at, you unholy Calamity Jane?"

"Oh, nothing. Nothing at all. Did you know, Joy dear, you look positively commanding when you're angry?"

Joy made a very ungentlemanly noise and turned away.

ॐ

Albatross sailed the moment they went aboard. Fenwick issued rapidfire orders. Feet pounded on the deck. There were three hours of sailing back to Macau. The uppermost thought on everyone's mind was would they beat the pirates to *Satpura* and *Gulab?*

For those without deck duties, it was the time to rest. Margaret, who suddenly realized she had not slept for two nights, went to lie down in the cabin that had been Sir Paul's.

Joy took Vikram to his own cabin. The steward brought steaming cups of tea accompanied by fresh lychees and brandy. With the door and the stern window wide open, the breeze cooled their confined space and granted them the opportunity to talk undisturbed. Joy listened to Vikram's account of the rescue. When he finished they sat in silence, lost in their own thoughts. Then they discussed the captain and his increasing instability. As they talked they heard the anchor come up and the sails fill with loud cracks as the ship began its familiar rolling motion. After a while they sat back quietly, content in each other's company, their minds free and wandering.

A shadow fell on the threshold.

Jerome came into the cabin, stooping low to avoid the lintel.

Vikram and Joy sat up hastily as the captain stood motionless and sternly studied the prince. When he spoke it was to Joy in an unusual gravelly voice, but his attention stayed riveted on Vikram.

"Morley. Leave us!"

Joy jumped to his feet in alarm.

"Hey! What's the game this time?"

"I wish to speak privately with this man, Morley. Leave us."

Joy did not like this at all.

"Can't it wait until we're back in Macau, Cap'n?"

Jerome swung around.

"God damn you, Morley!" he roared "Get the hell out of this cabin! That's an order."

Still Joy hesitated. He did not want to leave Vikram with the volatile captain. But as long as they were on his ship, he had to take Jerome's orders. And since time was of the essence for recovery of *Satpura* and *Gulab,* he could not start a mutiny at this delicate stage. Seeing his indecision, Vikram nodded, indicating he could handle his tormentor. Joy waited another moment and irresolutely left the cabin. He climbed up to the quarterdeck so that he could stand exactly above the cabin and hear the conversation.

Vikram studied Jerome carefully.

So this was Captain-sahib. The demon of his nightmares. The man who had stuck a pistol at his head and kicked him in the chest while he lay defenseless. He thought back to the things Margaret had told him about the spiteful naval officer.

"You!" said Jerome abruptly.

He too had been studying the Indian.

Vikram, shaken out of his reverie, raised his eyebrows at the mode of address.

"You! Yer a lily-livered lout!"

Vikram stood up and stared eye to eye with the angry captain.

"I am Prince Vikram Sena of Rajmahal. What is lily-liver lout?"

"Yer an insufferable busybody! I'd flog ye and cast ye off again if it ain't for yer heathen-lovin' friend."

Vikram said nothing. His natural Buddhist equanimity was in control of his actions. The captain, he mused, would make a creditable pirate chief. Meanwhile, Jerome worked himself into a frenzy.

"Damn your heart, you dirty nigger. Get off my ship!"

"Sahib?"

"Get off my ship this instant!"

Vikram stared at him. The muscle above Jerome's left eyebrow was twitching spasmodically. *Tic, tic, tic,* it went. He looked quite dangerous. Why, thought Vikram, was the man so violently, so irrationally angry?

"What is the matter, Captain-sahib? How can I get off your ship? We are in China."

"You bloody rascal! Hobnob with white women, will ye?"

"Sahib! Hobnob? What is hobnob? I do not understand."

Vikram was confused. The man must know something about him and Margaret. What did 'hobnob' mean? He wondered if it was a word that stood for that wonderful thing he and Margaret shared, their love for each other. Or was he angry because Margaret had come to his rescue and held up the ship?

Jerome interpreted Vikram's look of wonder as one of guilt. He took a step forward with his face contorted.

"Toy with women, will ye? You stinkin' snake! How dare ye?"

"I did not 'toy' with her, Captain-sahib."

"Oh, yes? And who are you to judge that?"

"The memsahib is a good person."

"What? Who the devil d'ye think you are to talk dandy of an English lady? Don't ye know yer place?"

"I am Prince Vikram Sena of Rajmahal."

"Ye'r prince bloody pagan nigger! That's what ye are. Get away from my sight before I throw you overboard, you insufferable puppy!"

Vikram's control finally slipped and his eyes blazed.

"You shall not speak to me this way!"

Captain Winkley went rigid with shock.

"What? What did y'say?"

"I am a Sena prince of India!" Vikram paused dramatically. "Our Buddhist King Ashoka ruled an empire before you English learned to read."

Jerome's head snapped up. Vikram waved his fist.

"My ancestors wrote poetry when yours lived in caves!"

Vikram was so furious he did not notice Jerome's eyes glaze and continued his tirade.

"We do not need you. Even China does not need you. You need *us.* Be humble! Or...or go back to the land whence you came."

"You scoundrel!" Jerome raged. "You fornicating pipsqueak!

We'll blow your King to kingdom come and you with it!"

Like Joy, Vikram realized belatedly that the captain was unhinged. But it was his love for Margaret and the inhuman way Jerome had treated him that made him do it. Normally he would not have needled a hate-maddened man.

"If you try," he said coldly, "you shall fail."

Jerome was now absolutely livid with fury. He salivated. The muscle at his temple twitched frantically.

Then it happened in a flash.

By magic the captain had a pistol in his hand and Vikram shrank back in horror. Jerome drew back the firing pin and pulled the trigger. There was a loud bang. On the quarterdeck just above, Joy heard it and froze. The report of the gun was followed by a cry of pain. Joy dived down the ladder and burst into the cabin. Through the smoke he saw Vikram, ashen-faced, half-sitting, half-lying on the bed and Jerome standing in the middle of the cabin. The pistol lay on the floor. Jerome's face was twisted in pain as he wrung a bleeding hand. For a moment no one spoke. Then Joy gasped in relief.

"Oh, thank God! A misfire!"

And then the captain went completely berserk.

He rushed at Vikram and had him by the neck with both hands before the prince could defend himself. The fingers tightened relentlessly into a viselike grip cutting off Vikram's air supply. Blood from Jerome's wounded hand stained his victim's tunic. Frantically Vikram scratched and beat at the captain's face and tried to push him away by the shoulders. But the grip was too strong. From behind, Joy grabbed the captain's arms and tried to pry his hands away, but he too could not. The grip became tighter and animal growls came from Jerome's slavering mouth. Vikram's struggles became faint and he felt consciousness slipping away. A red haze with bright yellow spots filled his vision. He heard Joy shouting but could not understand the words.

Suddenly Jerome's frame jerked violently and his grip weakened. Then his hands fell away. From a seemingly long distance Vikram felt the captain's weight start to fall on him. Then Jerome pitched forward, slid off Vikram, and collapsed on the deck.

Joy stepped back breathing heavily.

Barely conscious, Vikram lay on the bed and tried to draw air into his lacerated windpipe, each breath causing excruciating pain in his throat. His sweat-covered face felt ice-cold. His neck pained horribly. Joy worriedly looked at him. Then he bent and turned over Jerome's body. It was not a pretty sight. The eyes were open with dilated pupils turned up in a snarling bright-red face. Joy controlled his repugnance and felt for a pulse at his neck. There was none. Captain Jerome Winkley was dead.

Joy's legs gave way and he sat down heavily beside Vikram who continued to draw long hacking breaths. They remained thus for some minutes. At last color returned to Vikram's face. He sat up, gingerly felt his throat and looked at his hands that were smeared with blood. Then he looked at the inert form at their feet.

"What did you do?" Joy spoke at last.

Vikram shook his head indicating incomprehension.

"He's dead" said Joy.

"Dead!" Vikram croaked.

"How did you kill him?" Joy asked.

"I did not kill him, Sahib!" Vikram spoke with difficulty. "I thought *you* did. His grip on my throat was *so* tight. Even with his injured hand. I could not push him away."

"Then how did he die?"

"I do not know, Sahib. He was very angry. Until you told me I did not know he was dead. Perhaps his heart burst."

Joy nodded.

"Yes, that's possible. There have been signs. He was definitely deranged. And you, my friend, have more lives than a cat. You have escaped the pirates twice, survived a castoff into open ocean, a pistol shot from point-blank range, and a death grip on your windpipe!"

"He would have killed me in another minute."

They studied the corpse with its gruesome grimace and upturned eyes. Vikram stooped, closed the eyelids while intoning a prayer. Joy stared out of the window trying to understand the implications of Jerome's death. What would happen now? Another fatality. So soon after Sir Paul. The trail of death was lengthening in the shadow of opium. Sir Paul, Piper, Kelsey, Qin-ai, Tau-pei, Winkley. Where would it end? It would all be in vain if the opium was lost to pirates. Was turning the tide of silver really possible? Was it worth the cost in lives?

But Captain Winkley was dead and nothing could change that. Perhaps someone somewhere would shed a tear for his passing.

As their thoughts turned to the future, Joy and Vikram

simultaneously felt a sense of release from the grip of an ogre, from a truly malevolent being that had oppressed their thoughts and hopes. The earth was brighter.

But the blissful feeling lasted only until Macau harbor came into view and everyone on *Albatross* saw the Indian ships were gone.

လ

The echoes of the ancient dirge reverberated from dark corners of the Church of Sao Paolo as Chaplain Medora conducted a candlelit tribute to man's mortality. The church was filled with the ship's company and members of the British community attending the third funeral service for an Englishman in the space of six weeks.

Margaret sat in the front pew between Alice and Joy, her face covered by a borrowed black veil. Flickering candles on the altar etched the statues of Jesus and Mary in deep sadness. Disquiet and a growing restlessness filled Margaret as she listened to a requiem for the dead naval officer. The future was insecure; the present was ethereal.

> *The grass withers, the tale is ended,*
> *The bird is flown, the dew's ascended.*
> *The hour is short, the span is long,*
> *The swan's near death, man's life is done.*

25

Following Jerome's burial, a somber group assembled in the drawing room of *Britannia*. For almost fifteen minutes, no one said a word. A footfall at the entrance made them look up, and Vikram entered with an expressionless face. Joy indicated a seat. Vikram subsided and everyone returned to their thoughts.

Vikram looked around and then at the sad green eyes of Margaret. Instinctively he smiled and the effect was instantaneous. Margaret sat up, looked around as if waking from a deep sleep into a scene from a Greek tragedy.

Irving Macardle, First Mate Fenwick, and Midshipman Newbond sat on hard-backed chairs intently studying the carpet. Joy was sprawled on a divan, staring into space. Engineer Burton and Chaplain Medora stood at separate windows, hands clasped behind their backs. Mrs. Burton wept quietly in a corner. Alice Macardle sat on a chair against the wall and wrung her hands. Compradore Liu stood in the doorway and methodically shook his head. Vikram's face had regained its grave profile.

Margaret was amazed at how overwrought everyone was. The captain was gone. Didn't they have to chase a few pirates and get their ships and cargo back? She got to her feet and walked across to Joy and laid a hand on his shoulder. Joy came alive with a start and sat up on the divan. She nodded to him, walked past Liu, and out of the room. Joy followed.

"Councilor Morley!" she admonished. "They're getting away. What on earth are you *doing?*"

ॐ

"Will you return?"

In Howqua's front room, Joy protested vehemently.

"Lian, how can you say that? I *will* return. Don't you want me?"

"Yes, Joy *shi sheng*, I want you. But you are a great man and I am an unworthy slave."

Joy shook her by the shoulder.

"I am not a great man. And you are absolutely not a slave."

"I *am* a slave. I am *your* slave." She looked up at him with huge eyes. "If you do not return I shall still be your slave."

Joy gave up.

"There's oriental fatalism for you. Listen! I *am* coming back. I am coming back often. My mission now is to build English trade with China. So I *shall* return. D'you hear?"

"Yes, Joy *shi sheng.* I hear. I shall wait."

Despite the tumultuous events, Joy felt at home in Macau. He knew he could make a difference. He knew he could live in China as Sir Paul had. The tall palm tree had relieved his loneliness with his Chinese woman. Lian would be there for him. He had even allowed his thoughts to wander to making Lian his wife. She was part-English, part-Chinese. His now knew his life and work in the Orient where suffocating Elizabethan rules of society did not apply. Would his father make an issue about the purity of the Morley lineage? Time would tell. Jerome's death had upset everything. Joy's assignment was incomplete without the opium cargo recovered and sold. He would come back to Macau after they had taken care of the pirates. Lian would wait.

He gathered her in his arms, kissed her tenderly, then took a step back and swallowed as he looked her up and down. She was heart-stoppingly beautiful. He wanted to stay. But he had to go.

A half hour later when Joy walked into the drawing room of the Residence, Howqua was waiting with Macardle. Upon seeing Joy, Howqua clapped his hands and Menezes, Angry Feng and Tat Au-yong were shown in. They bowed to Howqua and everyone sat.

A silence ensued.

Joy took the opportunity to study Au-yong for the first time. The middle-aged, scholarly-looking Chinese gentleman had been described by Feng as his teacher and leader of the most powerful triad in Canton. Au-yong, undistinguished by any physical feature, wore the customary black vest, black trousers, and thong sandals. But if his reputation was as exalted as Feng said, Au-yong must be a remarkable organizer and fighter. Joy had been told he had played an important part in Vikram's rescue.

The capture of *Gulab* and *Satpura* had been witnessed by hundreds of watchers from the shore. Not a single shot was fired as ten war junks sailed into Macau Harbor and surrounded the ships. The Indian cargo carriers had no armaments beyond a few muskets and their crews were quickly subdued. Within minutes their sails were raised and the ships disappeared with their Chinese escort.

Since *Albatross* had not encountered *Gulab* and *Satpura* on the way from Lan Tao, Feng had said Wu must have set course west to his village in Annam, the place where Vikram had been taken. It was remote and defensible and out of the Hoppo's reach. Wu would make his stand there.

Now, after several minutes of calm, Feng announced that his teacher wanted to help the English recover their cargo.

"Why?" Joy asked Feng. But it was Au-yong who replied with an unexpected question through Menezes. "What is the relationship between the boat people and the Hoppo?"

About to protest, Joy stopped himself and reconsidered the question. His objective of setting up the opium delivery was getting delayed. Even if they recovered the opium, the Hoppo's Eight Regulations had closed doors for their distribution. Anyway, what was the connection between the triads, who looked out for the interests of boat people, and the Hoppo, who regulated foreign merchants? Finally, he said as much.

"Perhaps there is a common goal," Au-yong added.

Joy's interest quickened.

"Common goal among whom?" he asked. "What has Honorable Au-yong to do with the Emperor's representative?"

"He is the Emperor's representative."

Joy did not understand.

Feng and Au-yong looked at each other. Then Au-yong made a long speech, accompanied by a lot of hand, eye, and head motion.

"We, the Tanka, have lived for centuries in Guandong, Fukien, and Guanxi provinces. Buddhism was prevalent and peace was universal until Manchu rule began a hundred years ago. The Manchus subdued the impotent Han in the north, overthrew the Ming in Peking, came to the southern provinces. They drove the Tanka from their rightful land into dispersed boats and fishing villages. We have been farmers, never fishermen or gang-fighters or pirates. We have been made so by Manchu's alliance with the crafty Hakka and warlike Punti. It is my dream to unite the Tanka against the Manchu Emperor and win back our land. The Tay Son have shown in Annam that even great kings can be overthrown by ordinary people." He stopped and made his point. "With the help of the British we can achieve this."

As he listened, Joy was struck by the similarity between the missions of Tat Au-yong and Vikram Sena. Both were chieftains dispossessed by emperors and wanted foreign aid to recapture their domains by supporting trade.

An idea hit him.

Joy had been wrestling with a conundrum ever since Sir Paul had fired his imagination in Fort William. Perhaps the tide of silver could be turned with establishment of opium trade. But would that be *enough* for ascendancy of the British Empire? How could Britain *rule* India and China from faraway London?

Au-yong had just offered him a possible sequence.

Step one would be in-country trade as was happening now in both countries. Step two would be divide and conquer. Playing power groups against one another to cement English interests. This was also happening today in south China and in eastern India, but by default. The Company could make it a policy! He must write to his father as soon as possible.

But wait, wasn't he putting the cart before the horse? They had to take the first step first. They had to get the opium back and show that it could be marketed and delivered.

"Horse, sir?"

Joy looked at Menezes blankly and then realized they were all staring at him. Joy became furious with himself. He *had* to curb his habit of speaking his thoughts aloud in times of stress. Howqua said something and the linguist had difficulty hiding his smile.

"Honorable Howqua he say, 'Speaking without thinking is perilous, but speaking while thinking can be unsafe too.'"

Joy smiled at Howqua. "Guilty as charged, m'lord." Then he became serious. "Menezes, I like this man."

"Which man, sir?"

"Menezes, please tell Honorable Au-yong I accept his offer of assistance. Tell him that the Hoppo has proclaimed the opium trade is banned in China. But the English will pursue the opportunity around the Manchu ruling. In addition, the English are opposed to the pirates of Annam. Wu has caused much distress and stolen their cargo."

"For many reasons Honorable Au-yong is also in opposition to Wu Cha-tan," Menezes translated the triad chief's reply. "First, though Wu is strong, he thinks only of immediate gains. Second, Wu's origin is not farming, nor fishing, nor piracy, nor is he from mainland China. He is only a pearl diver from Hainan island. He is not interested in problems of the people. Honorable Au-yong is! Feng Sheng-chi has lived among the pirates and the triads and is a leader. He can earn the people's confidence and win them over if the English help him overcome Wu and defeat the pirates. He will do this in return for English opium distribution by his group, the Kuan-yin Tui."

There it was. Step two!

Joy did not hesitate.

"Menezes, tell Honorable Au-yong I accept with gratitude."

౧

Margaret managed to stamp both her feet while sitting on a drawing room sofa.

"I shall *not* be left behind!"

"But old girl," Joy knew it was futile, but he still tried to reason. "There will be a fight."

Margare

"Mr. Morley, pay attention. Think hard now. There *was* a fight. Actually, there were *two* fights, in case your arithmetic is off. I was in both. Where were you?"

"Be serious, Miss Andrews. Englishmen have died fighting Wu."

"I am deadly serious. I am not the wilting female you appear to be used to. I can help."

Joy looked at her dubiously. Then he grinned.

"Is it because he's going?"

Margaret turned a bright red.

"You nasty heartless bugger! Don't you dare joke about us."

"Margaret!" Joy was genuinely shocked. "Where *did* you learn to swear like that?"

"It is obvious your exalted Lordship hasn't met the costermongers of Stepney. But never mind that."

Joy looked at her sympathetically, remembering how she had nursed him back to life.

"You poor thing. I'm sorry. Been through a lot, haven't we?"

They fell silent, remembering an unhurried pace of life once upon a time. Then they wondered about the future. What was ahead?

"Uh...Margaret," said Joy at length, looking at the carpet.

"Yes?"

"Uh. There's, um, something I'd like to..." He caught Margaret's eyes and subsided with "...oh, nothing."

"Joy Morley!"

Joy's head snapped up. "What now?" he asked irritably.

"Is it actually possible you're dithering?"

Silence.

"Oh my God! He's blushing! What've you gone and done now? Tell me this instant."

"Actually, it's not important. It can wait. We've plenty to do to get ready and leave at first light. I'll tell you later." He made to get up.

Margaret jumped off the sofa and pushed him back.

"Oof! Watch out, you lunatic. Mind my head."

"You'll mind your head if you don't tell me. At once. Is it a girl?" She watched his expression with sparkling eyes. "Oh my God, it *is* a girl! My oh my! What a quick worker we have here. All this while we all thought he was a poor invalid busy making deals. Where, may I ask, have you been occupied behind my back?"

"Margaret, stop it. You haven't been idle yourself."

Margaret's vivacious laughter rang out as she grabbed his jacket and pulled him to his feet.

"Joy Morley, you're a fraud and a rogue. And we're two peas in a pod." She stopped and, with her brows arched, said, "Guess!"

"Dear God. *Now* what?"

"Joy, I've a marvelous idea for our last night in Macau."

"Oh no! Not another of your japes. Never. I'm leaving."

"No you are not leaving, because...because we shall celebrate."

"We shall *what?* Celebrate? Where d'you think we are? Soho? Leicester Square? Are you completely out of your mind? And tonight! We've tons of work."

"Oh Joy, don't be such a stuff-arse."

Margaret took his hands and looked at him her eyes shining.

"Go and get her, Joy. Let's find him and we'll go out together."

Joy began to share her excitement.

To needle her he said, "Find whom?"

"You know who I mean, you rat. What's she like?"

"People will see us."

"Let them. Isn't this Macau? The Land of Vice?"

They were the wildest, happiest, the most exhilarating hours of their lives.

In an inner room of White Cloud Mountain casino, they slowly lost their self-consciousness. And their astonishment. Their secrets were known but the sky did not fall. The *fan-tan* players gawked for a moment at the strangely mixed group, shook their heads at ways of barbarians, and returned to betting. Joy dispelled his inhibitions. Emulating Howqua, he clapped his hands for rounds of *shaohing chiu*. They shut the door to keep out the noise and the child-waiters who came to stare at the barbarian woman with the impossible red hair.

It was Margaret's evening.

She opened pent-up reserves of gaiety, suppressed since her mother's death, and showered them with an ebullience and delight that was infectious. The revelation that their situations were all similarly precarious bound them close and made them heady with joy. The wine from Chekiang made then dizzy. Tonight they felt brave enough to believe there could be, might be, a tomorrow.

The fact that Lian was Sir Paul's daughter bowled Margaret over. She asked the dainty Chinese girl innumerable questions. Lian answered in antiquated English and warmed to the first woman she had met from the land of her father. Margaret's animation and good-humored teasing of Joy made Lian laugh in a most un-Chinese way. Caught up in the camaraderie, Vikram looked at Margaret, his eyes alight with worshipful admiration. He was glad for Joy and hoped his friend would find a way to make his love his life. Then he began to think of their own impossible future but, before his mind could cloud over, Joy pressed another glass into his hand.

They had to know everything about each other, announced Margaret, reading Vikram's thoughts. Just in case there was no tomorrow. And so, in turn they each told the story of their lives while the others listened enthralled, applauded, or shed a tear.

The hours swept by unnoticed.

Joy was in the middle of a story about an errant rhinoceros that had wandered into White Town of Calcutta, when he felt a tap on his shoulder. He put down his umpteenth glass of *shaohing* and focused his swimming vision on a sturdy young man in naval uniform.

"Ah Newbond!" he said. "You're a fine fellow, Newbond. Sit

down right here, Newbond, and have a glass of ambrosia."

"Thankee kindly, sir. But Mr. Fenwick sends his regards and says yer lighter be leaving the pier in less'n two hours."

Tomorrow was here.

26

The eastern firmament was showing the faintest glow when Mickey Fenwick, new master of *Albatross,* gave the order to set sail under combined effect of flood tide and morning breeze.

From the afterdeck, Joy and Vikram watched the hilly peninsula of Macau that had brought such upheaval to their lives, drop away astern. Margaret was not with them. She had come aboard totally spent after the night's revelry, with a tinge of green in her visage, and gone at once to her cabin to lie down.

A sorrowful Lian had been left behind.

Joy found it hard to believe they were actually sailing without the intimidating presence of Captain Winkley.

Fenwick barked orders from the quarterdeck.

"South by southwest heading, Mr. Norbert if ye please. "Back to the wind! Set main braces! And signal our heading to *Rupert!*"

Albatross's head came about as her topsails took the full force of the gathering monsoon. A mile aft, *HMS Prince Rupert* followed in her wake. She was a small and maneuverable barkentine of the Royal Navy, assigned to Canton. When it became known that *Gulab* and *Satpura* may have been hijacked to Annam, Macardle offered *Prince Rupert* for the chase. At their first meeting, Joy had liked the looks of *Prince Rupert's* dapper and bearded captain, Michael Holbrook.

It was a grim and determined group, primed for retribution, that sailed southeast.

"Hands to yardarms!" ordered Fenwick.

Deckhands swarmed up the rigging.

"Set all mains'l!"

The enormous sheets of the fore, main, and mizzen masts fell simultaneously from their yards and filled with sounds like cannon firing. *Albatross* skipped forward to open water like a gull taking wing.

With a nod of approval Fenwick came over to the two friends. His lined and leathery countenance never failed to bring to Joy's mind's eye a bleak scene of icy nights and biting wind. A lifetime of experience and wisdom was stored in the unassuming and god-fearing seaman. Joy spontaneously shook his hand.

"Important voyage, Mr. Fenwick. Your first command too. My warmest wishes for your future."

"Thank you most kindly, sir."

"Did Feng pass muster?"

"Aye, he did that. Has his head screwed on aright, that man. Best pilot I've had for as long as I can remember." He smiled ruefully.

"And that's longer than I'd care to admit." He sobered and looked closely at Joy. "Sir, ye looks right bushed. The lady's in her cabin feeling poorly, besides. The next eight hours'll be uneventful. Perhaps ye should turn in a mite. All of ye need rest. The steward has beds made up and ready."

Joy agreed reluctantly. These were the first minutes of inactivity in a long time. He was dreadfully tired. Vikram must be all out too. He was worried about Margaret. She had not looked well on the lighter ferrying them to *Albatross* from the pier. Poor thing. What a tremendous strain had she borne during the last weeks and then spun a golden thread into their last hours on land. She must be all in, physically, mentally, and sea-sick too.

"Can Prince Sena share my cabin?"

"It's yer decision, Mr. Morley. Fine by me."

However, the prince declined and Joy went to his cabin. Vikram continued to stand at the starboard bow, his mind a chaotic blank, gazing at the thin green line of mainland and the changing patterns of sky and sea. The smack of sail and creak of timber came and went in rhythmic counterpoint to the ship's motion. He felt suspended between the past and future.

"Morning, yer Highness."

Vikram turned from the rail.

"Good morning, Captain-sahib," he replied warily, thinking of Jerome. "How are you?"

"I am well, thankee, yer Highness," replied Fenwick. "And how ye be feeling? Ye left this ship by Singapore in dramatic circumstance, did ye not? If yer Highness don't mind my mentioning it."

Vikram's eyes darkened.

"Winkley-sahib tried to end my days."

Fenwick nodded solemnly.

"I've served under more captains than flying-fish ye can put in a tar barrel, but Winkley? He was the strangest. And meanest. Cap'n Winkley was me master for, I reckon, one year to the day. Had it out for ye, dinna he?"

Vikram thoughtfully looked into the distance.

"According to the Buddha, Captain-sahib, peace and harmony are life's ideals. To achieve the eternal state of happiness, one must perform good deeds all through life. I am sure in his own way Winkley-sahib was striving for *nirvana*."

"I've been a devout Christian, yer Highness, and begging yer pardon, a rabid one in me youth. In travels around the globe, I've done seen more religions than captains even. Animists, voodooists, taoists, baptists, muslims, ancestor worshippers, and many not too sure and some in-between. But when the north wind cuts ye like an ice wedge and waves run higher'n them mains'ls, all hands pray to the same One for succor."

Vikram warmed to the grizzled old seaman. He understood and shared Fenwick's philosophy of life. In companionable silence they watched *Albatross's* bow rise and cut cleanly through tops of rollers and pitch down their shoulders.

"I like yer Chiny friend, yer Highness."

"I was lucky to find Feng Sheng-chi, Sahib."

"Ye've known them pirates yerself. D'ye think he be right?"

"I believe Feng. He is certain that Wu has taken the ships to the village where I was held."

"Ye remember the lay of land yon?"

Vikram marshaled his thoughts.

"The village is on a narrow river that flows into the sea at a place they call Ha Long Bay. To get from the bay to Macau, there is a passage between the Chinese mainland and a big island. That is the way I came to Canton."

"Aye. Hainan island it is. It lies ahead south-west of us. I've a-heard of the strait ye mentions, but ne'er sailed through it."

"The river that leads to the pirate village is narrow and has a few turns. Unlike the Pearl River, its banks are full of trees and bushes, and so it can be held at many points by determined men. Wu has scores, maybe hundreds of men and women in the village under his command. Did you know, Sahib, that pirate women are very able? They row and fight with their men."

"Hmmm, interesting. May I ask Mr. Feng to join us?"

"Of course, Sahib."

Angry Feng had stood by the helmsman since they raised anchor, providing route information and answering questions. He knew the entire south coastline between Da Nang and Amoy, and the seas between Hainan and Canton better than anyone. Responding to Fenwick's hail, he came down to their side.

"We be discussing options for approaching the pirate village, Mr. Feng," began Fenwick. "What be yer considered suggestion?"

Feng did not understand.

"You will have to speak slowly, Sahib, and use simple words. I too have difficulty with English." He turned to his Chinese friend. "Feng Sheng-chi, what manner we go along village belong Wu?"

Fenwick looked at Vikram admiringly. Then he furrowed his brows and concentrated on Feng's reply.

"Honorable Wu, him wait for us. We shoot bang-bang long-fellah gun and kill-dead, heya? We go takee no shoot?"

"He wants to know whether we go in with guns blazing," Vikram explained, "and kill them all. Or surprise them and take them captive. *Albatross*'s guns will cut through Wu's defenses, but he has hostages." He turned to Feng. "How we takee no shoot?

"Ship, he go a'ound Hainan Tao to Cat Ba Tao befo' he commee Ha Long Bay. Wu him no thinkee devil ship he attack f'om Annam side. Ship he go in Ha Long Bay along night. Ship, he go along Chiang-p'ing village along morning he come."

The long speech needed a repeat or two before they understood.

"Praise the Lord!" said Fenwick. "He's thought it out an' makes it seem easy, don't he? 'Cept we've no charts of the region. We've got to depend on him entirely. Also it's another country. This Annam. Don't know much about it. Pirate country, I suppose. Hmm, Mr. Feng, how will ye take us? Through the strait or around Hainan island?"

This had to be restated in *pigdin*.

"We go a'ong China coast," Feng replied, indicating the distant landmass. "Big *tao*, Shang-chuan, he come, we decide quick-quick."

"When big *tao* he come?"

Feng wetted his finger, tested the wind, looked at the sun and said, "Two hour."

When Shang-chuan island came into view they held a council of war. Joy, back after his rest, pointed out that, for a decision, they needed a military advisor. Fenwick and Holbrook had never dealt with pirates. Joy was a merchant. Vikram an administrator. Feng, experienced in hand-to-hand fighting, had no knowledge of warships and armaments. *We actually need Jerome! How ironic.*

Fenwick asked them to wait and went below. He returned with a serious-looking middle-aged man in naval uniform, the newly promoted First Mate Norbert. Joy knew that Norbert, until recently a midshipman, had replaced Second Mate Piper, who died beside Sir Paul, and then succeeded Fenwick when the latter assumed command of *Albatross*. Naval warfare led to quick promotions!

"Gentlemen, Mr. Norbert here has seen enemy action in the Mediterranean."

"The Mediterranean?" Joy was surprised. "We've been at peace with France and Spain for years. What action did you see, Norbert?"

"I served as gunner under Decatur, sir. His expedition against Hamidou in Malta."

"Really? That's wonderful. Rais Hamidou, the Barbary corsair?"

"The very one, sir."

"You have to tell me about it, Norbert, but not now. Your experience against pirates will serve us well. Now then, we have an important decision before us."

They explained the situation to Norbert and he soon made it

clear that surprise was their most promising alternative. Joy was emphatic there was no persuasive reason to rush into a frontal assault and jeopardize the lives of Captains Fernandes and Irani and their crew if they were still alive. There were some negative aspects of going around Hainan, Holbrook pointed out, the primary being its circumnavigation would add a day-and-a-half to the time required to get to the pirates' lair when every minute counted.

"Yes, but Captain..."

"Sahibs!" Vikram interrupted. "Please excuse me. The decision is quite simple. The pirates are used to Chinese ways. They will expect us to pursue them as Chinese authorities would. Feng has told me that the Hoppo's forces do not like the outer sea and stay close to the coast. And so, Wu will expect pursuit along the coast."

Joy smiled broadly at another demonstration of his friend's original thinking.

"So we go around Hainan?" Fenwick asked.

"Yes, Sahib. Surprise *and* outflank the enemy."

"Ah, that do make sense. Intuition of the warrior."

With that important point decided, they considered the plan for the attack party. *Albatross* carried two whaleboats, two cutters and a jolly. *Prince Rupert* had one jolly boat and a cutter. Together, they could carry a complement of seventy-five, a third of the ships' companies.

Then they went into a huddle about logistics and armaments.

ৎ

Margaret awoke several hours later, feeling feverish and nauseous, shivering with cold. She tried to sit up and fell back with a moan. A chilly spasm passed through her body. After a few moments she tried again and managed to swing her feet to the deck. The cabin swayed unsteadily. She pulled a sheet tightly around herself but still felt cold. She looked around. It was dark outside the open window. A lighted lantern swung from a hook above her. She gritted her teeth, trying to shake off the sick feeling, and decided to go out to the deck to see what was going on. Perhaps she should eat something? What time was it? She tried to get on her feet, reeled, and fell back on the cot. She rested awhile and tried once more. This time she made it to the door. She leaned against it for a moment and, breathing raggedly, then pulled it open. A small lamp flared in the corridor. Margaret made out the steward slumped on a stool against the opposite bulkhead. At that moment the ship bucked sharply against a contrary wave and Margaret lost her balance, screamed, and fell heavily.

The steward awoke with a start.

"She is over-tired." Surgeon Morefield told Joy a few minutes later. "Her immunity's low. Has she been eating well?"

Joy did not know. He and Vikram had been summoned by the steward. Together they got the unconscious woman to her cot and covered her with blankets. Luckily Margaret was not hurt. When the steward went to fetch the surgeon, Joy gently told Vikram it would not be seemly for him to be seen in the English lady's cabin.

"Sahib, I understand it is best for her. But tell me how she is."

Vikram withdrew before the surgeon arrived.

"The fever and chills worry me," Morefield said. "She may have a touch of malaria." He coughed. "With Sir Paul passing on, who'll look after her?"

"I shall," Joy said without hesitation. There was no other woman on board and he felt a strong brotherly attachment to the sick girl. "With your assistance of course, Mr. Morefield."

"Of course. Thank you, sir. Make sure she's covered and warm. She must drink a lot of fluids. Tepid soup and warm tea are helpful."

"Do you really think it's malaria, doctor? Come to think of it, she *was* exposed to the night air on Lan Tao island."

"Good God!" exclaimed the surgeon. "Those out-islands are notorious for disease-bearing mosquitoes. This is ominous." He mused for a bit then shook himself. "Well, let's not jump to conclusions. The next hours will tell us without fail."

The day wore on.

They sailed southeast on a constant wind, making twelve knots between Hainan island and the Paracel archipelago, through a corridor heavily traversed by small craft.

Margaret's condition worsened.

Her body was racked by chills and a continuous thirst. Her fever rose and she lapsed into a stupor from which she periodically surfaced, asking for water and for 'him.'

Malaria, as Joy knew too well, was a scourge of the tropics with no known remedy. Newly-arrived Europeans were especially susceptible to the disease caused by mosquito-infested swampy locales. On the positive side, victims that survived malaria built up a lifetime of immunity. But many, a third, did not survive. Joy and the surgeon took turns staying by Margaret's side, and once, while Joy stood guard, a distraught Vikram came in to stand beside her bed. The wan face and thin sheet-draped form drove a spear through him. *He* was the reason for her night-time adventure. Alone with the woman whom he loved, looking down at the once-robust figure melted into the cot, he felt a surge of self-loathing. Turning, he rushed blindly past Joy to the maindeck. He spent the rest of the voyage as he had on the way from India, brooding and solitary beside the foremast, praying, waiting.

At the eighteenth parallel, Fenwick brought the ships around to a westerly heading and a beautiful sunset. But the next morning, when they tried to turn north around Hainan, they were forced by a strong and adverse land breeze to continue on a westerly tack across the Gulf of Tonkin toward the Annamese mainland. When they were close to the town of Hai Phong, Fenwick hoped they would be able to beat north up the coast to their destination.

When they cleared Hainan, the full force of the southwesterly trades hit them broadside. The ship's motion changed to a jerky and unnerving roll-and-wallow as she took on a beam sea. Waves broke in a maelstrom against *Albatross's* starboard quarter hindering a northward turn. Wayward spray left everyone on deck drenched.

Cabin windows were closed to keep out seawater. Margaret, now strapped to her cot, was sunk in fevered torpor, unable to eat, and able to drink only with difficulty. All on board knew the brave woman was fighting for her life. Morefield said the climax would come in the next two days. The only ray of hope was she was intrinsically robust and therefore had a fighting chance of making it through. She was now in God's hands.

"*Om mani padme hum!*"

From outside Margaret's cabin, from the very spot she had sheltered with Vikram after her rescue, the rhythmic cadence of an ancient Buddhist *mantra* invoking enlightenment and compassion, kept vigil as endlessly as the waves of the sea.

॰॰

"*Land ho!*"

Joy, craning his neck, trying to focus on the crows-nest, staggered, as the masthead, seventy feet above him, swung in an enormous arc across the leaden sky while *Albatross* rolled over a particularly high wave. He could not even begin to imagine what the lookout at that impossible height must be experiencing.

It was the following morning. Joy had come out to tell Vikram that, while there was no change in Margaret's condition, she was sleeping peacefully. They were numbed by their own sleeplessness and the miasma of wind and water. The lookout's cry gave them something to divert their minds. Soon the waves subsided and to everyone's relief, the rolling steadied. An indistinct line came into view on the horizon.

They were in Annam.

A little later, still several miles offshore, they made out a vista of flat land dominated by a high mountain that reached down almost to the coast. Joy tried to discern whether there were rocks or sandy beaches or rice fields along the coastline.

A shout from above made everyone jump.

"Hao! Hao! Shan!" yelled Feng from the quarterdeck, pointing agitatedly at the mountain. "Truong Le! Truong Le Shan!"

Joy called up to him.

"You know that hill?"

"Shi! Shi! Truong Le Shan. *"*

"Prominent marker I think," Joy told Fenwick. "Lucky for us."

"Aye, sir." He raised his voice. "Mr. Feng, how far be the island we have to find? What be its name? Cat Lamb?"

"No Cat Lam, sar! *Tao,* his name Cat Ba. We go along Cat Ba."

"Oh, all right, me hearty! Cat Ba it is."

Fenwick hid a grin. It was the first humor anyone had attempted in a long time. Feng came down and pointed to the north of Truong Le, standing on his toes to indicate a very long distance.

"Thanh Hoa big town he come. Savvy Thanh Hoa, sar?"

"Uh no," replied Fenwick.

"Fight! Big fight along Thanh Hoa," said Feng excitedly. "Many people they die. Tay Son fight in Thanh Hoa. Wu Cha-tan, him fight along Tay Son."

Everyone looked at him in alarm.

"Methinks we should give Thanh Hoa a miss," said Fenwick.

Joy nodded and the captain bellowed to his first mate.

"Take in sail, Mr. Norbert. Smartly there. Heading ninety degrees to starboard, if ye please." He turned to Feng. "But where be Cat Ba? I need to know the sailing distance."

Joy applied *pigdin*.

"How many day takee Chinese junk him go along Cat Ba?"

Feng understood and answered without hesitation.

"One day, sar."

Fenwick was taken aback by the uncompromising reply. He made to extract more information, but Joy stopped him.

"Let's go with his estimate, Cap'n. He can point out landmarks as we get closer. What's our speed relative to a junk's?"

"Three times in a favoring wind, I'd reckon. It's hard to say."

"That means we are very close. Matter of hours. Shouldn't we get the guns prepared?"

"Yes, sir. And I'll pass the word to *Rupert.*"

Joy went to check on Margaret while hands hauled on halyards. All canvas, except fore and mizzen topsails, was furled. The quartermaster put the helm over to starboard and the booms came swinging around. *Albatross* heeled over making everyone grab wildly at anything solid. Then she righted herself. Her prow rose majestically into a welcome bow sea and she sailed slowly and, after the mad rolling they had endured, ever so sedately along the coast of Annam.

27

"*Sail ho!*"

Albatross and *Prince Rupert* were traversing the brown effluent of a broad estuary that Feng identified as the Red River. They had sailed for two hours with shortened sail, anxiously looking for Cat Ba island when the masthead made the electrifying call.

The lookout continued in an excited babble.

"Deck there, Chiny sails on port bow. Many sails. Big sails. Three...no four, sir! Heading north."

Within minutes the junks came into view of the deck. Ponderous square-rigged vessels bearing typical patchwork sails that hung from bamboo yards.

"No Wu Cha-tan, sar," called out Feng and everyone's heart rate slowed. "T'ader f'om Siam."

As he watched the cargo-laden junks an idea came to Joy. Hurriedly he called his strategy committee together at the for'ard bow:

Fenwick, Norbert, Vikram, Feng.

"Gentlemen, listen. If *Albatross* is spotted by the pirates near their den before we're ready, they'll retreat and hide. Or even attack. If, however, our landing party went in one of those junks, the pirates will not suspect and we will have an edge. By Jupiter! The junks might even attract the pirates' greed and draw them out. *Albatross* could lie in wait for them just over the horizon. What d'you think?"

No one could find a flaw with the idea. They would offer the Siamese traders payment for temporary use of their ships as decoy.

Decision taken, Fenwick went into action.

"Signal the *Rupert*. Raise sail. Helm thirty degrees to port. Run down them junks!"

Albatross's speed increased. The distance separating *Albatross* and the junks diminished rapidly. Joy, watching through his telescope, thought they resembled a herd of sea-horses against the setting sun. The fear of premature discovery had bothered him throughout the voyage. Providentially now, they had an ability to get within striking distance undiscovered. It could mean the difference between success and failure. He fervently hoped the junks would welcome their proposal.

Then a strange thing happened.

Looking through his glass, Joy saw a puff of smoke emanate from the side of the closest junk. Seconds later he heard the report.

"They're firing! *On us!*"

Before Norbert's cry left his lips, Fenwick roared out orders.

"Action stations! Clear and run out guns on the port bow!"

The ship exploded into activity. Norbert rushed to the bows shouting instructions. Seamen poured up the companionway. Articles on deck were cleared away without ceremony. Four cannon on *Albatross's* port side were run out in minutes and gunner-boys scurried from the magazine, stockpiling powder, shot and flint beside the guns. A fire was lit to heat the oil cauldron to prime the cannon.

But why?

Joy was stunned by the suddenness and absurdity of it all. Why on earth would an insignificant Siamese boat fire on a target as impregnable as an East Indiaman? As he watched, a bang came from a second junk leaving no doubt about the hostile intent of the Siamese.

"Yang-ch'uan!"

There was another agitated shout from Feng.

"What's that?" Joy demanded. "Speak up, man."

"Yang-ch'uan. Long ship belong Wu Cha-tan."

"Really? Those are Wu's ships?" Joy could not believe it.

"Blow me down!" exploded Fenwick, his Lancastrian brogue pronounced. "It canna be. Set to surprise 'em we've done gone and stumbled on the benighted lot. A pretty pickle, I say."

"And they carry cannon!" Norbert added.

Joy was aghast. This could not be happening. In an effort to disguise themselves they had actually been discovered. It was the first time Angry Feng had misread the enemy.

"Five, ten gun belong *yang-ch'uan,"* Feng said.

"Aye, Feng be right," concurred Fenwick. "Junks in these parts been seen with brass guns lately. Eight-pound shot at best. But rest yerselves, gentlemen. We can blow 'em out of the water afore they have us in range."

"But if that's true, why did they draw attention to themselves?"

"Same reason as the prince gave us afore. They be treating us same as Chinese officials. And *their* artillery be poorer than them pirates' own."

"The fat's really in the fire. Mr. Fenwick! Let's catch them quick. Before they run to lair with news."

"Aye, aye, sir. I'll to it. *Mr. Norbert!*"

Before Joy's still disbelieving eyes, *Albatross* engaged the pirates in action. She slowed and changed her heading to stay out of range while her gunners set their sights.

"Guns at ready, Mr. Norbert, sir," called up Midshipman Newbond, head of the gun crew. "Permission to fire?"

"Permission granted."

"Fire One!"

The first cannon thundered, shaking the ship. Then another. Within minutes the deck was covered in smoke. The fourth misfired with a horrid thud and oaths of its crew. The ritualistic loading began.

"Load One!"

Ball and powder were inserted into cannon number one.

"Rod One!"

A gunner jammed a ramrod to tightly pack the powder.

"Return!"

"Cap One!"

The gun-crew capped the charge.

"Aim!"

The master-gunner set the sights.

"Fire One!"

A swabbed wooden pole was introduced into a cauldron of hot oil and withdrawn. A gunner-boy set it alight and the pole was inserted into the firing hole of the cannon. At once the gun detonated and recoiled on its rails.

"Fire Two!"

The second round of fire raised spouts around the junks without harming them. The master-gunners adjusted their sights while crews reloaded. Another salvo came from the junks.

A third cannon fired from *Albatross*. An exultant shout indicated a direct hit.

It was clear that at this rate *Albatross* would decimate the pirate convoy. When the sun tilted behind the Annamese mountains, she had sunk three of the junks. Finally gauging the overwhelming firepower of its adversary, the last junk turned to flee up the coast. Within minutes it realized direct flight was hopeless and reset sails to attempt a weaving run for shore with sea breeze behind. It took precious minutes before *Albatross,* realizing the changed intent of her quarry, brought her helm around to port and gave pursuit with guns blazing. But they had an unforeseen enemy. Darkness. Two miles offshore, in six leagues of water, *Albatross* came about and fired a last despairing shot while the junk disappeared into the murky backdrop of trees. Fenwick would not risk running aground on a sandbank or reef in hostile waters.

ༀ

Joy sat beside Margaret through the night. She was weaker and hallucinating. The surgeon was seriously worried. Was it the beginning of the end? Vikram was completely overcome and becoming fatalistic.

To keep himself lucid, Joy analyzed their chances of success in the impending action. If the escaped junk got home first, Wu would be forewarned and empty the village of opium. Joy desperately hoped their landing party would get to the village first and, if not, at least arrive in time to win back the precious cargo. Fenwick and Norbert shared his concern and decided, in uncharted coastal waters and against better judgment, to sail *Albatross* in moonlight, depending completely on Feng's familiarity with the coast.

The night wore on and the stars wheeled across the sky. The watch changed with the ship's bells. There was no mishap. The diminutive Chinese ex-privateer performed magnificently and when the sun rose, it lit a superb landscape of forested hills, sandy beaches, leafy mangroves and cascading waterfalls.

"Cat Ba Tao, he come!" announced Feng triumphantly.

Fenwick clapped him on the back.

With the island to starboard, *Albatross* sailed northeast under full canvas for several hours when, with the late morning sun shining brightly on a calm blue sea, she entered Ha Long Bay. Perhaps entry into the heavenly setting had a divine effect, because Margaret's condition improved. Her fever receded. She awoke to the first moments of lucidity since the onslaught of malaria. Joy brought Vikram and left them alone. When he came out Vikram's eyes were wet. The two men looked at each other with relief, the deep bond of shared ordeals needing no words. Vikram, who had not let his mind or body rest since Macau, felt himself collapsing in fatigue, and at Joy's insistence he went to his friend's cabin and was asleep before his head hit the pillow.

Joy went out on deck.

He had been enchanted by the splendor of the Cat Ba archipelago and had spotted birds, whales, dolphins, turtles, otter aplenty. But the first sight of Ha Long Bay was an epiphany. He put his glass aside and looked in respectful silence at the unending vista of tranquil water, sculptured tree-covered islands and graceful sails of sampans. The entire scene was capped by a mist-shrouded hilltop. He raised the spyglass and made out a pagoda at the summit of the hill. Feng told him the pagoda was called Yen Tu Shan. It was built by an Annamese emperor after he had defeated Kublai Khan's fleet in the bay. Joy could not believe his ears. Kublai Khan? Here? In *this* southern bay? The Great Khan whom Marco Polo met in Shangdu near Peking in the thirteenth century? He stared at Feng in total disbelief. Feng did not know about Marco Polo but vehemently asserted that after the pillage of Hanoi, Kublai Khan's Mongols and the Annamese had fought a sea battle in this very bay, and that King Tranh had won!

One for the history books, thought Joy, making up his mind he would visit the pagoda on the hill above the bay before he died. He raked the bay with the glass but saw no sign of the Indian ships.

28

"*By the mark five!*"

While Angry Feng guided the ships steadily across Ha Long Bay, a leadsman in chains called out depth soundings. *Prince Rupert,* with her smaller draft and with Feng aboard, led the way with lookouts posted on fore and main mastheads. They left the populated part of the bay and sailed to the wilder, rockier section and advanced toward a densely forested and seemingly deserted point on the coastline.

"*And a deep six!*"

At six leagues, with just the hint of a break in the tree-shrouded seashore, Fenwick signaled to the *Rupert* for conference and gave the order for *Albatross* to drop anchor. They were two hundred yards offshore and could have gone closer but Fenwick thought this would be imprudent until they checked the inlet more thoroughly. He would need room to come about if they were attacked. The stillness of the bay was shattered by the anchor chain roaring through the blocks and a swarm of birds took wing calling hysterically.

A furious Michael Holbrook came aboard and stomped across the deck to where the others waited. Feng followed in his wake.

"What's the game?" Holbrook began without preamble. "The light's going in a moment."

"Steady, Captain," Joy said mildly. "We're in this together."

"We're in six clear leagues of water. Let's go and rout them out."

"Go where?" asked Fenwick.

"Well, if ye had a wee bit more..." Holbrook glared but controlled his temper. "If you were as close to shore as us, you'd have seen the opening in the shrubbery. It's the mouth of the river we're seeking."

"*Shi, shi,* river," Feng said. "Bach Dang River. Chiang-p'ing belong river. Go quick-quick now."

Holbrook looked at Feng with an approving smile.

"I like this pilot, Fenwick. Give him to me and *Rupert'll* take care of your little business by suppertime."

"The pirates may be forewarned and fly, Mr. Holbrook. Ye might be rushing into a trap."

"Balderdash!" Holbrook's moustache bristled. *"Rupert's* always held her own against locals. Show some spine, man. If I'd the guns and ammunition of *Albatross,* I'd hold sway over...over Peking."

Fenwick's nostrils flared at the insult. His fists clenched and he was about to say something when he was forestalled.

"Sahibs?"

Everyone was on edge and wanted to speak angrily but they gave way to Vikram.

"I have entered this river mouth as a prisoner and have left as a fugitive. The pirate village is two miles inland, no more than an hour's slow sailing. The river widens behind the inlet. Wu's big war-junks sail into it. Feng Sheng-chi has told me much about Wu. He is shrewd and determined. If he is warned, he will not fly. He will fight. His every success strengthens his image and dominance of the seas. There are many avenues for him to escape if so chooses. We must be careful."

Holbrook moved away from the prince in disgust.

"I'm a-going in."

"Captain Holbrook!"

Holbrook turned, startled by the peremptory tone of Joy's voice.

"Captain Holbrook. I share your eagerness to bring the pirates to book, but I will not tolerate unilateral action."

Holbrook's face became red with anger and he puffed up like a fiery rooster.

"*You* will not, huh? Since when does a junior merchant order a naval captain about?"

"Sir, I wish to remind you that your Governor, Sir Paul Miller's death has devolved responsibility for the King's venture on me. This has been explicitly acknowledged by the Select Committee of Canton, *whom you serve!* We have embarked on this expedition with approval of the Committee and you have been assigned to *support* the expedition. Sir Paul's directive before his death was that the opium venture has priority over every – *every,* Captain Holbrook – every other task of the English East India Company."

While he had Holbrook's attention Joy did not want to deflect the aggressive energy of the man from the mission. So he ended with an olive branch.

"It behooves us to work together."

"To Beelzebub with you merchants," Holbrook fumed. "Let's get on before we fill the night with blabbing. What do you propose?"

Instead of replying, Joy said "Mr. Norbert?"

"Sir?"

"What is your view?"

"I support Captain Holbrook's view, sir. *Prince Rupert* has shallower draft and can attempt an entry into the river."

"And *Albatross?*"

"*Albatross* should stay in support. She should sail as far as she can behind *Rupert,* but only as long as she has leeway to turn about. Decatur took heavy casualties in his boat raids on Hamidou's strongholds because the pirates knew their terrain and could ambush an exposed landing party. He was once boxed into a lagoon, having overlooked setting a rearguard."

"The coast here is deserted," said Fenwick, his gentle nature still smarting under Holbrook's comments. "Mr. Feng? Where could a rear attack come from? Can boat along Wu hide there an' there?"

"*Shi, shi.* Many place him hide here and here."

They looked at the rocky coastline with concern. Some of the men trained glasses on it but only birds and rocks met their scrutiny.

"Well," concluded Joy. "That's that I suppose. Norbert has covered all the eventualities."

"How much time do we have?" asked Fenwick.

"Three hours to sunset, sir," Norbert replied. "By then it'll be dark in the river unless there are fields. Are there fields, Mr. Feng?"

Feng shook his head.

"Three hours or less," said Fenwick. "Belay until morning?"

"We shall *not* belay until morning, thank you," burst out Holbrook. He added with elaborate politeness, "With your kind permission, Mr. Morley, we shall engage the enemy *now.*"

Joy acknowledged the inevitable and let the sarcasm pass.

"We shall indeed, Captain. Norbert, Feng and I shall go aboard *Prince Rupert* with you."

"Why?" asked Holbrook at once.

To contain your bloody rashness, Joy wanted to say. Instead he said, "Our combined experience will be valuable to your success."

"And I, Sahib? I know the way better than all except Feng."

Joy thought for a minute before answering.

"With Feng on *Rupert,* Captain Fenwick may need help with directions in the event of a rear attack. You must stay on *Albatross.*"

A long look passed between the two men and Vikram nodded. Joy's unspoken message was clear. The opium venture was vital. Yet one of them had to remain with the woman who was just turning a battle with death.

Holbrook spun on his heel.

"'Nuff said. Let's go."

Norbert and Fenwick held a last-minute conversation. Vikram moved to Joy's side and touched his shoulder.

"Good luck, my friend. May your aim be true. May you return

safely for the one who waits."

Joy remembered Lian and found a lump in his throat. He quickly walked away to the sterncastle to get his muskets.

∾

Margaret awoke while the boats were being lowered. Joy checked on her for the last time before giving her over to the surgeon's care. Her eyes were open and she looked at him depthlessly from a gray pinched face. He smoothed her matted hair and smiled.

"You'll be on your feet soon, old girl. Just you wait."

Margaret's eyes brightened. Looking at the courage and beauty in her smile Joy thought to himself, God, she's astonishing. If only the prince hadn't got to her first.

Margaret spoke softly.

"Thank you, Joy dear. I'm sorry to be a burden."

Joy could not find the words to reply and patted her arm.

"Do you want to see him?" he finally asked.

In answer, the two emerald pools darkened and Joy stumbled out to find his friend.

Fifteen minutes later, as they were about to cast off, the whaleboat rocked violently as someone jumped from the rigging. Joy moved aside expecting Norbert. To his amazement he found Vikram beside him.

"Oh! What happened? Is Margaret all right?"

"Sahib!" Vikram spoke in a hoarse whisper.

"Didn't you hear me say good-bye?"

"I have to tell you before you go."

"What?"

Vikram spoke strangely, finding difficulty with the words.

"She said...she wants..." and then in a rush "she wants to be...be...with me, Sahib. Always."

Joy was blank for a moment, then he stared at Vikram, thrilled.

The boat rocked and Norbert boarded.

Joy could not find words for the happiness that coursed through him. Joy extended his hand to his friend as Vikram jumped back for the netting, but the boat had separated and Joy changed the greeting to a wave and then to a salute.

29

With shipboard cannon trained for'ard and to the sides, and with muskets primed and ready, *Prince Rupert* warily covered the last two hundred yards to the inlet. *Albatross* raised anchor and followed slowly. Leadsmen measured depths in subdued tones. Fenwick still did not like it. As a career seaman with a love of open water, he had a horror of running aground. But the lead showed six leagues and steady, so on they continued. Approaching the mouth of the river, they found it opened to an exceptional width and the bottom deepened. As Feng had said, the banks were dense with jumbled trees and bushes, cutting off much of the light from a slanting sun. There were no signs of human presence.

Standing at the bow of *Rupert,* with tension building, Joy began to have doubts. Vikram had said the pirate village was two miles inland. What guarantee had they their quarry was there? What if the

2

whole adventure was a wild goose chase? Perhaps the Indian ships were on the far side of Lan Tao island or at some unknown lair of the cunning Wu. The south China coastline was vast and the opium could be concealed anywhere. Had they come this far on the wild theory of a Chinese anarchist? Perhaps even now their cargo was making its way to the Chinese interior and a Hainan pearl diver was laughing himself silly at the ease of duping barbarians.

"Village him come quick-quick," said Feng by his side.

"Already?" Norbert was incredulous. "Come how quick-quick, for God's sake? We've come less'n a mile!"

"River he makee three fo' turn, then village come."

Norbert looked at the sky. They had an hour of daylight perhaps a bit more. Should they put off action until the morrow as his master had suggested? He began to fret.

Rupert had just begun to round the next bend when, from her quarterdeck, Joy made out something solid through the trees. They cleared the turn while he strained through his glass and saw what looked like a wooden house fifty yards ahead before the river took another turn. They came closer and the house disappeared behind a high grove of coastal bamboo. They cleared the grove and the object resolved itself.

"It's a ship!" he exclaimed. "It's...it's one of...yes, it *is Gulab!* It *is* here. We made it!"

Minutes later they saw *Satpura's* masts beyond *Gulab.* The two Indian ships, seemingly undamaged and deserted, were tied to branches on the riverside.

"Ahoy there!"

Holbrook's full-throated hail broke the silence before Joy could stop him. It was unnaturally loud in their confined space. There was no reply. The glade formed by overhanging trees returned to a complete hush. Joy spoke to Holbrook in an annoyed undertone.

"We're supposed to effect surprise, Cap'n. They heard that hail in Canton. Wu's sure to have scouts posted near those ships."

"Stow the bellyaching, Morley. Those're the ships we're after. Let's get the cargo and have done. Helm to port and approach ships!"

Behind *Rupert,* watching intently from the prow of *Albatross,* Fenwick heard Holbrook's hail and shouted a hoarse warning.

"Careful, matey. It could be a trap."

His warning was hardly out when, like a bolt from the blue, it came! Wu launched his attack.

Heads popped up along the side of *Gulab* and a volley of musket fire shattered the stillness. Something sounding like an angry hornet buzzed over Joy's head and he instinctively ducked under protection of the gunwale. Norbert, beside him, was not so lucky. With a wild yell he fell backwards on the deck. Further away, there were shouts and screams from the exposed sailors as bullets flew about them. More Chinese muskets showered deadly hail and screams changed to groans. Suddenly there was the terrifying roar of a fieldpiece opening up and *Rupert's* deckhouse exploded into fragments. Another cannon mounted on *Gulab* fired at point blank range. With a splintering crash, part of the *Rupert's* afterdeck gave way.

"We're caught! Like rats in a trap."

Aboard the besieged *Rupert,* Joy screamed in frustration and viewed the carnage from shelter of the gunwale. Norbert lay on his back, his hands thrown up, blood staining his uniform. He would receive no more promotions. Feng was crouched on one side of Joy. Holbrook cowered on the other. The maindeck was strewn with dead and wounded and those who had thrown themselves flat. Whoops of jubilation and another fusillade of shots came from *Gulab* and, horror of horrors, from the other side, the other bank of the river!

Where is Albatross, Joy thought. They were being annihilated in a pincer operation by an enemy who they had believed would run at the sight of English armory. And what was Holbrook doing? An all-consuming rage took hold of him. He knelt and hit out at the cringing captain. Then he took him by his jacket-front and shook him violently.

"Rally your men, Captain!"

There was a whistling sound in the air from behind and a moment later brush and mud flew into the air beyond *Gulab* as the first of *Albatross's* cannon opened up with a deep boom. Joy rejoiced. *Bless Newbond!* The quick-reflexed midshipman had again responded, this time giving *Rupert* a lease on life. For a few minutes there was confusion all around. Then Holbrook took charge and his surviving gun-crew and soldiers limped to their stations. The pirates continued to fire from *Gulab* and from the opposite bank. Finally, the first answering musket volleys from *Prince Rupert* rang out and her gunnery officer began the firing drill. *Load, ram, cap, aim, fire* filled the air.

There were howls among the massed pirates on *Gulab* as the second round from *Albatross* and a nine-pounder from *Rupert* simultaneously showered her deck with explosive shrapnel. In return, a new round from the pirate cannon blew a hole in *Rupert's* side, making her rear like a wounded horse.

A fierce life-and-death battle raged as English and Chinese musketeers fired on each other from behind protective rails. Then a ball from *Albatross* made a direct hit at the base of *Gulab's* mainmast and broke her back. Her decking collapsed and the pirates fell into her hold or jumped overboard with despairing cries.

But *Prince Rupert* could not rejoice as she fended off the threat of pirates firing from the opposite bank of the river. The waterway was two hundred yards wide at this point and the impact of gunfire from the far bank was mostly ineffective. But a fieldpiece, ferried across the river, opened up and scored a lucky hit on *Rupert's* mizzen mast bringing down the fifty-foot log of Norwegian spruce with a resounding crash. The crew scattered to avoid being crushed as the mast fell across the deck and slid into the water between *Rupert* and the dying *Gulab* in a tangled mass of rigging. Yet another eight-pounder fired from the river bank but managed to hit the unfortunate Indian ship.

This cannot go on!

Joy wished desperately he was in charge of the operation. What were Fenwick and *Albatross* doing? Couldn't she rake the riverbank with cannonade? But *Albatross* was silent which was very strange. Joy tried to look astern but she was invisible behind trees and bamboo stalks. He ducked and cursed as another cannonball from the far bank hit *Rupert's* jib boom and sheared it off. The next could be her end.

"Kill that gun, men!" bellowed *Rupert's* master-gunner. Her starboard gun-crew went into action and the forest on the river bank began to take a pounding.

Where was *Albatross?* It was fifteen minutes since she had fired the shot that destroyed *Gulab.* Joy walked across to Holbrook standing by the stump of the mizzen mast.

"Captain, why is *Albatross* silent?"

Holbrook looked at him blankly. He had quite forgotten the other ship in the heat of battle. His lip curled.

"Fenwick! Man's probably turned tail."

At that moment there was a loud report from *Albatross's* direction followed by another. But it was not cannon fire. Joy found himself shouting with a hatred he had never felt before.

"Captain Holbrook! *Albatross* saved your bloody bacon when you and your men were groveling like beaten dogs. Listen to me! Send a man to the masthead to sight her." When Holbrook looked at him rebelliously, he bellowed in the sharpest and loudest voice he could muster so that everyone could hear.

"Do it, Captain! That's a direct order."

A sailor began to climb the rigging of the mainmast. Halfway up he stopped. Joy, watching through a glass, saw his expression change. His mouth opened, but his words took a moment to carry down, the longest moment in his life, but when they did, they sent a chill down his spine.

"She's afire!"

30

When her cannon shot broke the decking of *Gulab,* every eye on *Albatross* had been focused on the raging battle ahead. This included her helmsman, the new second mate, Adamson, who should have been watching the course of the river.

Abruptly there was a grinding tearing sound and *Albatross* came to a dead stop throwing everyone to the decking.

"Hell's bells!"

On the foredeck Captain Fenwick picked himself up, surveyed their predicament and cursed mightily. *Albatross* had run aground at a most crucial moment. He ran to the front of the ship and joined the crowd that gathered there. He craned his neck over the jib boom and saw their keel had run into a submerged sandbar. He turned and hurried up to the quarterdeck.

"You godforsaken dimwit, you!"

DIPAK BASU

Fenwick bellowed in frustration at an Adamson holding an ineffectual wheel. The short dumpy officer shook with fear. It was perhaps the first time the god-fearing captain had sworn in public. In the background there was a crescendo of firing from *Prince Rupert*. Fenwick advanced on Adamson and was about to strike the man when he felt a restraining hand on his arm and a quiet voice spoke.

"Not useful, Captain-sahib."

Fenwick froze and regained his senses. He grunted and faced the mob clustered on the foredeck.

"Move, you lot. To your stations."

The crowd lessened.

"Mr. Adamson!"

"Sir?" Adamson croaked.

"Get her back afloat. At once."

The second mate looked at him vacantly.

"H-how, sir?"

Fenwick looked around wildly and was about to give an order when the first firebrand landed on his deck.

෨

After steadying Fenwick, Vikram had gone inside the sterncastle to make sure Margaret was all right after the violent jolt. He found that she was sleeping soundly in spite of the tumult and was greatly relieved to see beads of perspiration on her forehead and lip. The fever was coming down! Taking a clean wet cloth from the bedside, he gently wiped her face.

Meanwhile, *Albatross's* company was clustered around the masts, or climbed the rigging and stood on yardarms in response to orders to unfurl sails to move the ship. Everyone was looking forward at the offending mud bank ahead. No one, not even the masthead, noticed the danger looming from behind. And so Vikram, from the sterncastle window was the first to see the approaching sampans. As he rushed to warn the captain, pirates began loosening off that ancient weapon, fire arrows, from the sampans. By the time a general alarm was raised, arrow after arrow was landing on deck or hitting the massive targets of the unfurled sails. Within minutes, the canvas was smoldering and flames were being whipped up by the channel breeze.

As *Albatross's* soldiers and sailors aligned their muskets and fired at the men in sampans, one, then another, exploded with a high cracking sound. These were the detonations heard by Joy on *Rupert*. The sampans began to burn fiercely, but, even with their sails on fire, the flaming craft came rapidly toward *Albatross* in the strong current.

"Sweet Jesus!" cried Fenwick. "Boom 'em off, men!"

Midshipman Newbond yelled at his men and ran aft to commission the idle stern cannon. At point blank range, the first shot blew up one of the burning sampans in a pyrotechnic display. But the second was already under the stern and invisible to gunners.

With attention now focused aft on the burning boat that threatened to set fire to the ship, the spit of land on which *Albatross* had foundered, became filled with a multitude of pirates who had run up unnoticed. A rope, then another, was thrown to the jib that overhung the ship's unguarded prow and men began to climb the swaying ropes. Another rope was launched and took hold, and within moments there were Chinese pirates on *Albatross's* deck for the second time in as many months.

The clipper was in complete disarray, beset by musket fire from the bank, firebrands from the river, a sampan burning under her stern, and pirates boarding from the prow. Simultaneously, her smoldering mainsail burst into flame.

᪣

"She's afire!" screamed the sailor on *Rupert's* masthead, his high-pitched voice raising goose pimples. "Her sail, it's a-burning. So's her stern. An' sweet Lord..." his voice climbed another octave while everyone stared up at him, frozen, "...she's aground. Oh me Lord! There's fighting on her deck!"

Everyone listened aghast and immobile.

The tableau was broken by Joy.

"Rescue!" he yelled.

Others took up the cry.

"Holbrook!" screamed Joy. "To her aid, let's go, let's go, let's go!"

The captain was about to shout orders when another heart-stopping cry came from above.

"Deck there! Fireboats at one o'clock!"

One by one, three fireboats came around the bend in the river ahead. They were the same type of sampans that had attacked

Albatross, but these were filled with inflammable material and burning fiercely. Their semi-circular sails were burning, but they caught enough wind and current to move downriver to *Rupert.*

"Shoot 'em," Holbrook's voice broke. *"Boom 'em off!"*

In mortal anxiety, Joy could not but marvel at the enemy strategy. Because of sharp bends in the river, the two hapless English ships were in positions where the wind blew towards them from the launching points of the fireboats. He could not believe what he was seeing. How could they be under such mortal attack, simultaneously on so many fronts? This was not a ragtag bunch of fishermen turned pirates, but a coordinated naval operation with a well thought strategy.

Aboard *Albatross,* the first Chinese attackers were decimated by the ship's crew. For fifteen terrible minutes there was a pitched battle on deck with pistol, cutlass, musket, knife. But the overwhelming numbers of Chinese had to prevail.

Captain Fenwick faced three attackers. The sail above him was burning fiercely. Orange flames made him look as if he were on fire himself. He brandished his blood-stained cutlass. "Come ye blighters!" he roared. "Glory be to Jesus Christ, son of God, Savior of the repentant!" He thrust and parried. "Taste English steel, ye heathens!" He thrust again and ran his cutlass through the chest of a pirate. The man screamed. Then a musket banged and a bullet lodged in the Fenwick's chest and the battle for *Albatross* raged on around him.

Prince Vikram in the sterncastle was at the opposite end of the ship from where the pirates had boarded, and was not exposed to the initial assault. Hearing the uproar, he ran toward the battle scene, grabbing a musket from two dead crewmen, and joined the wilting defense against pirates coming aboard by the dozen.

The fireboat under them had done its damage. Flames were pouring out of hatches. Sailors began to jump over the side onto the mud bank where they were assailed and killed. Some tried to escape by plunging into the river and were carried away by the current and drowned. Contrary to popular belief, most sailors could not swim.

At the ship's stern Vikram was fighting shoulder-to-shoulder with soldiers when his sandal-shod feet began to feel hot. He looked down and noticed that seams of the decking had expanded noticeably. Then in front of his eyes a long seam snapped, opened with a crack, and a tongue of flame shot upwards and set fire to the breeches of the man just above it. Vikram's thoughts rushed to Margaret whom he had left sleeping on her cot. He dropped his muskets, pushed men out of his way, ran back to the sterncastle and came to an abrupt halt.

Black smoke poured furiously out of the entrance. Here and there little spurts of fire were breaking out as they had done under the decking. Covering his face with his shirt, Vikram rushed into the black interior. Hot fumes met him like a solid wall and he staggered back, coughing and gagging. He tried again and this time the tail of his long shirt caught fire and the smoke blinded him.

Vikram was frantic.

She was inside the inferno and he *had* to save her. He was

about to try another rush into the flames when he was seized from by two sailors who yelled at him. Vikram struggled ineffectually. As he was being dragged back there was a splintering cracking sound and *Albatross's* mizzenmast creaked and swayed ominously. The sailors released Vikram and looked up in alarm. The mast began to topple and as it did, the enormous falling beam and massive burning sail caused a rush of wind through the sterncastle opening.

Vikram saw his chance.

When the wind blew the smoke outward he closed his eyes and dashed into the corridor and from memory located Margaret's cabin door, pulled it open and entered. In the murky light he saw her sitting dazedly on the bed. Smoke poured in from the open door behind him. Quickly, he scooped the feather-light form in his arms and turned to the door. But the corridor was an impenetrable conflagration. Vikram reeled back, coughing and almost dropping her. Another cloud of smoke poured in. Vikram turned and, without stopping to think, charged across the cabin with the girl in his arms, clambered onto a sea chest against the open stern window, gathered himself on the sill, paused for a second to adjust his grip on the inert woman, took a deep breath, closed his eyes, and jumped into space.

At that same instant, the fires of hell ignited.

31

The Battle of Bach Dang River of 1786 is immortalized as an epic in the many historical records of Indo-China. Scholars have compared its importance to the earlier engagement in the region between King Tranh of Annam and Kublai Khan of China. Debates will continue whether the river combat was a display of atrocious English naval strategy or a landmark for British dominance in the Far East.

On the day of the battle, the pirate leader, known as Bombshell Wu, was watching action against the two English ships from a point on the riverbank, only thirty yards from the grounded *Albatross*. His face was expressionless as ever, but his heart was bursting with pride. His generals had outdone themselves, engaging the enemy on every possible front. They had applied the tactic of unequal war with murderous effect: change the focus of engagement when the impact of surprise from a previous move falters. It was a classically perfect execution of the Lao Tze's *Art of War*. When a mast of the second barbarian ship fell, Wu knew that annihilation of the enemy was near. The imminent death blow would be the crowning moment of his career. A career of meticulously planned and surgically executed operations learned in the David-and-Goliath wars of Annam. The moment of everlasting glory was just a heartbeat away.

But it was not be.

The reason was that Wu had outdone even himself. His offensive was so severe that in the end its destructive power engulfed its creator. Folklore of generations would pay tribute to first martyr to the curse of opium brought to China by mendacious barbarians. The very fact that he had managed to completely destroy so tremendous an enemy as *Albatross* was Wu's ultimate undoing.

Wu had never known of a ship that cached massive quantities of ammunition in a single repository.

Even as Margaret and Vikram plummeted down the clifflike stern of *Albatross,* a series of thunderous eruptions shook the earth as the ship's magazine exploded. An immense power propelled everything on land, water and air, away from the ship. The fury of the shock wave emanating from shell and gunpowder detonating, demolished everyone and everything in direct line of the ship for a hundred yards. It tore to bits the embattled people aboard her and the pirates on the riverbank. *Gulab* disintegrated as if hit by a giant cannonball.

Wu saw the cataclysmic explosion for only a mesmerizing

second. Then a hot hand picked him up and tossed him against the trees and rocks behind, while concentric *tsunami* raced away from the shattered *Albatross* as if mammoth pebbles had been dropped into the Bach Dang River.

~

Prince Rupert had managed to boom off her fireboats. The fact that, in doing this, she had delayed in coming to *Albatross's* aid was, in actuality, her salvation. She was three hundred yards away and protected by the riverbend when *Albatross's* magazine ignited. Still the scorching breath of the blast flattened intervening trees and swept over *Rupert* like a livid hurricane. It knocked men off their feet, tore shirts from their bodies and sails from the yards. Seconds later a twenty-foot wall of water broke over her bow as though she was in an ocean gale.

The ship pitched and bucked for several minutes and then the shock waves were past and a deathly quiet replaced the bedlam.

It was a long time before *Rupert's* company realized the battle was over and recovered their senses enough to position what sails were left and move the ship to the scene of the catastrophe. As they approached, they heard the crackling flames. They rounded the bend and the dying *Albatross* came into view. The ship was torn in two and broken open like a walnut. Each half was partially submerged and exposed sections were burning ferociously. Flames lit the fast-gathering darkness. Now and then a bang marked a stack of grape found by a searching tongue of fire. The bank closest to *Albatross* was a swath of blackened tree trunks. Intermixed with and inseparable from the mayhem ashore, *Gulab,* torn to matchwood, was pulverized into the mud and the riverbank. The edges of the swath were ringed with smoldering shrubbery. On and around devastated *Albatross* there were no signs of life. *Prince Rupert* came closer. Men lined her bow rail, horrified and dumbfounded by the grisly scene of destruction. They came within twenty-five yards, and still found no survivors. On the sandbar where she had grounded, all that was not burning was charred beyond recognition.

A strange and haunting aroma hung heavy with the stench of burning wood and flesh.

Burning opium!

Around them, the river serenely flowed on, carrying away debris. Holbrook gave the order to look for survivors who may have been washed downstream by the current. They lowered boats and scoured the river and its embankments through the night while the burning ships lit the scene with an amber glow. In the shallows and in sheltered tongues of land, they found fourteen survivors from one hundred and thirty men of *Albatross's* company: six deckhands, one soldier, three gunner-boys, a cook's helper, Second Mate Adamson, and, caught by overhanging branches of a muddy strip, Prince Vikram Sena and Margaret Andrews, mangled, but alive.

Joy was in complete shock, numb, cold, trembling, incapable of thought or speech. During the rescue operations, he looked out blankly from *Rupert.* Later, he came out of his trance with homicidal intent. Holbrook and his rashness were the cause of it all. He was forcibly restrained in the act of pummeling the captain. Then he became suicidal. *He* had been the cause of it all and tried to strangle himself. In this he was contained too. At last he lapsed into a black depression which lasted for the rest of their time at Chiang-p'ing.

On the next morning, Feng guided a subdued *Rupert* into the shell-shocked village and took command of the remaining pirates and scores of devastated families. Over two hundred pirates, men and women, had perished in battle and in the inferno. From a malodorous shack they released thirty Indian sailors and their captains, remnants of the Indian ships' crews. Others had died of ill-treatment and exposure. *Satpura* and her cargo had survived intact, sheltered from the blast by her doomed sister ship.

Without fuss, Feng took responsibility for unloading the remaining opium.

Prince Rupert and *Satpura* separated in Ha Long Bay, the former going east, the latter west. The Indian ship was homebound with Vikram aboard. Over half-hearted protests, Margaret bid everyone farewell and went with her prince into an unknown destiny.

The miasma that engulfed Joy continued to hold him in its grip as they made the woebegone voyage to Macau. Three days later, when the first lighter from *Prince Rupert* docked at Praia Grande, the Macardles saw, slumped on a thwart, a glassy-eyed shadow of the man who had departed in energetic pursuit of corsairs. Brooking no objection, Howqua took charge of the overwrought Englishman and before long Joy sat stupefied in the familiar armchair in the merchant's house. Lian was at his side round the clock, feeding him, comforting him, while he mechanically acquiesced to her every instruction.

On the tenth day, Lian placed a piece of paper in his hand and shook him until he looked at it.

The Rt. Hon. William Joy Morley
His Majesty's East India Company, Macau

Esteemed Sir,

I beg to state that with difficulty I have secured passage for your kind self to England. HMS Astoria *departs Macau for Bristol at noon on the morrow.*

Urgent that you return at once to the residence to prepare for the voyage.

Your humble servant,

Irving Macardle.

Lian and Joy were married next morning.

As the sun rose to light the pages of Chaplain Medora's Bible. Alice Macardle wiped her eyes and a mixed group watched the ceremony. Among them were Au-yong, Feng, Howqua, uncomfortable in one other's presence. When Lian said "I do" Joy gazed at the exquisite face and luminous eyes. In them he saw images of loved and departed ones for whom they must carry on.

From the deck of *Astoria,* through a thin veil of rain, Joy viewed the hilly ruins of Malacca, thinking of the report he would make to the

Court of Directors of the East India Company. Lian stood erect by his side, shielded from the rain by a straw hat.

Day and night he had beaten his brains against the senselessness of it all.

Why? For God's sake, why?

He had achieved the objective of his mission to China.

Was it worth the pain?

Through Howqua he had proven that Indian opium was commercially viable.

Was it worth the cost?

Through Feng he had put in place a distribution system for the forbidden cargo.

Was it worth the loss?

When *Astoria* sailed, Joy had felt the loss of Sir Paul acutely, And of Qin-ai, Newbond, Fenwick, Norbert, and a host of others. Where was his future? Would he see Vikram and Margaret again? The questions tormented him in a continuous barrage even though he had given up trying to find answers. Once the expedition was launched on the ramparts of an Indian fort, it moved him forward like a juggernaut.

Joy turned and saw Lian looking at him inquiringly. *I really must stop this habit of vocalizing,* he thought as Lian placed a comforting hand on his arm.

The hillsides were bleak in the rain, mysterious and forbidding. Joy's thoughts returned to the Portuguese Jesuits who for centuries had come to Malacca and certain death. What convictions motivated them to make the ultimate sacrifice so far from home? Were his experiences resonant with the sufferings of these evangelists? Would a British Empire flower one day? Would he find happiness with Lian?

The warm rain grew heavy.

Joy tightened his grip on *Astoria's* gunwale as Malacca's cluster of tumbledown huts and its overgrown fort, relics of a forgotten era, faded astern.

THE END

HISTORICAL NOTE

England's opium trade with China is a defining episode in the history of both countries. It began with risky enterprise of fortune-hungry merchants of the English East India Company. It grew swiftly in the late 1700s to reach its zenith in 1836, when England's annual opium export to China totaled eighteen million dollars and surpassed the combined import of tea and silk from China into England.

Throughout these years, successive Manchu emperors refused to give up the fight against the scourge of opium. In the 1830s, Lin Tse-hsu, Chinese Governor of Canton, made a determined attempt to stamp out British smuggling. The actions of this incorruptible official proved to be a thorn in Queen Victoria's side and took the countries to war. England's superior firepower and the novel deployment of steam to power her ships ensured her victory. The Treaty of Nanking, signed in 1842 aboard *HMS Cornwallis,* did much to equalize relations between England and China, providing security of British personnel. The Treaty opened four ports in addition to Canton to foreign trade, abolished the *co-hong* monopoly system, and banned use of derogatory terms such as "barbarian" and "petition." The Treaty also ceded the barren island of Hong Kong to England for a hundred and fifty years.

But the Treaty of Nanking did not specifically address the opium trade. Further, it was ambiguously administered by Manchu authorities which led to growing English frustration. When the

Chinese government refused to renegotiate the Treaty after twelve years as England believed it was required to, the countries went to war once more. The Manchu government capitulated, beleaguered by an escalating Taiping rebellion, the capture of Canton, and English gunboats threatening the very gates of Peking. The Tientsin Treaty of 1858 imposed extraordinarily strict terms on China. A supplementary clause explicitly stated that opium shipped in by England was legal, and a price was set for its import. Distribution of the drug to China's interior became the responsibility of Chinese authorities.

Consequently, more than a century after the Imperial mandate of 1729 banning import opium into China, its prohibition was reversed and the tide of silver, from the British viewpoint, was stemmed at last.

It was not until Mao Tse-tung's communist government came to power in the 1950s that consumption and production of opium in China were eradicated using unrestrained repression and social reform. Ten million addicts were forced into compulsory treatment, dealers were executed, opium-producing regions planted with new crops. Cultivation of the drug later shifted south of the Chinese border into the **Golden Triangle** region of Cambodia, Myanmar and Laos. Then, in the 21st century, Afghanistan took on the dubious mantle of the world's leading opium producer.